Habit

THE BOYS OF WELLES BOOK THREE

by USA TODAY bestselling author
GINGER SCOTT

HABIT

The Boys of Welles Book 3

Ginger Scott

WELLES

For Autumn and Brenda.
Thank you from my whole entire heart.

Chapter 1

Morgan Bentley

I'm so glad you're ok!
OMG, we miss you! So glad you're ok!
What happened? Did you die?
Did Morgan Bentley survive?
Morgan is totally using this whole accident thing for attention.
Appalling.
Gross.
So disrespectful.
Poor Anika! Poor Lily! And Brooklyn! Morgan probably hates that
she didn't get the same attention they did.
Bitch!

I haven't made a single post since the accident last spring, yet the messages and comments on my social media platforms still pour in, the toxic outweighing the positive by a hundred to one. There were four of us in that car, four joyful faces that still smile back at me from the past.

My last post was a photo from that night, only hours before my friend Anika veered off the bridge and our car hurtled into the river. She was beautiful in this captured moment, though something clearly had her distracted and a little upset. That was Anika—the best of herself even if she wasn't feeling up to it. She was always beautiful—from the inside out—in a way I aspired to be.

She had a seizure. It wasn't her fault. And now she's gone.

Life can change in a blink.

I've read that sentiment in memes and on T-shirts and stickers hundreds of times. It didn't sit as truth until I lived it. Until I blinked.

The three of us who survived promised to stay strong for each other and remain together because that's what Anika would have wanted. Brooklyn was the closest with Anika, and seeing her struggle after almost losing her leg in the accident breaks me because I'm not Anika. I try—I've been trying. I can't seem to inspire her the way Anika would have, though. I can't seem to inspire anyone. Lily needs someone to push her, but I lack the finesse our friend had. I'm brash. I bully, even when I don't mean to. It's how I was raised. That's how love is shown in the Bentley house, or at least that's the excuse my mom makes when my dad barks at me rather than taking the time to listen.

It's easier to talk to Brooklyn than it is Lily, who was the newest to our friend group. Anika introduced us. And she's right that Lily fits us. We need her. And I think she needs us. I only wish she knew me before I was broken. This version of me isn't right. Things that were so important before are rather empty to me now. Yet it all used to give me so much joy. Shoes, clothes, new clubs and restaurants—the glitz.

Being first to try things. Being the one to determine what was worthy and what was not. Deciding for the masses.

Empty.

This path I've carved is totally narcissistic. I know it is. But social media is the times, and I'd be foolish not to capitalize on the opportunity. If there's one thing Daddy has taught me it's that making money is always good business . . . *when it's legal.* He always adds that last part in with a chuckle to show he's kidding. I'm not sure he is, though. I get the sense that my father's business has had a lot of experience on both sides of the law. I'd like to think he's never crossed a hard line, but I'm not stupid enough to believe he hasn't blurred them over the years.

I figured out during junior high that I had a window to become something—*someone.* That's when I started growing my brand. My family is a name in this city thanks to my father's business, which means I have access to places few people do. I'm an automatic invite for any club, party, or exclusive event happening in Boston—assuming our family isn't already hosting it.

It all started with a selfie I took on the T on my way to a Louis Vuitton gala out on the Cape. Looking back at that image now is laughable. I felt so grown up . . . *at twelve!* Maybe that was the appeal, a child playing grownup in the city. Other pre-teens flocked to it, and then it spread to high schoolers and college students. Before the year was up, I was followed by some of my favorite celebrities. All because I rode a train by myself to a party I didn't truly want to go to. I was supposed to go with my dad, but per the norm, he was too busy and thought it would be rude if I didn't show up since he "forced them to make an exception for me." *Ha!* Now I'm the preferred Bentley guest and my dad is the one they allow in attendance because having me there puts their event on the social map.

The invites still come. I'm surprised the demand for my presence has held up despite my months-long absence. I read the comments. While the haters have grown bolder—*louder* —the digital landscape still craves me. Being gone has somehow stirred mystery and anticipation. And here I am, simply without anything to say. No motive. Just . . . empty.

"Earth to Morgan." Brooklyn snaps in my face, interrupting my gaze. I've been flipping through other people's posts, trying to look normal.

"Sorry, I was spacing." I click my screen off and flatten my phone screen-side down on my thigh. "What did I miss?"

Besides everything for the last hundred days.

"Me and Lily are hungry. Are you ready for dinner?" Brooklyn grabs her crossbody bag from the hook she put up on the back of our door while Lily throws on a Welles sweatshirt. The normal thing to do would be to join them.

"Starving," I lie. My appetite since the accident has been on the level of picking at my food. I came through with nothing more than cuts and bruises, but I was also hollowed out.

I straighten out my skirt when I stand and give my lips a quick check in the mirror by our door before I walk out. I touch up the gloss before letting the door fall closed behind me, then step between my two roommates and link arms with them. This is the kind of thing Anika would do, and maybe it's a small part I can play.

It's only the first week of the new school year at Welles. I managed to get my section of our room put together completely, including my pin board and all the photos that go on it. I thought being surrounded by my things would help turn back the clock. Time seems to keep moving forward, though.

"You know, we *could* ditch the dining hall and hop into Brooklyn's SUV and drive into the city for a dinner at Santo's on the patio." I know they won't want to do that, but it's the type of suggestion I would have made last year, so I play the part. I don't really want to drive into the city either. But I'm not exactly looking forward to the Welles campus dining hall.

"Pretty sure my food plan doesn't cover Santo's," Lily says with a light laugh.

I squeeze her arm with mine and lean into her closer.

"My treat," I say with a wink. "But maybe next time."

I replay that small interaction for the rest of the walk to the dining hall. I hope I didn't make Lily feel out of place. She's not from a family like ours, one with stupid amounts of disposable income and little regard for how we spend. She's practical and frugal and talented with the way she competitively swims. I'd trade places with her in a heartbeat. Though I'm not so sure I want the broken heart I see written all over her face.

Theo Rothschild, Anika's brother, is the first person we see when we walk into the dining hall. He and his friends enter from the other side, and in a matter of seconds, Lily and Theo have a thousand wordless conversations with one simple glance, a look that leaves Lily looking at the floor and pale as a ghost. Anika made me promise not to tell, but she told me how much Lily likes Theo. It's clear she was right about it being more than a crush, too. Anika set them up the night our lives were all ruined, and now she's not here to fix it.

I'm rushing toward Theo before my brain has a chance to sort through the consequences of what I'm doing. If Anika isn't here, then maybe *I* can fix this one thing for Lily. Theo and I are close. Our families have been close for years. I know him, better than a lot of people. Theo is holding in so much anger over his sister's death, and he's putting it on Lily's shoulders. If I can somehow untangle that for them, get them to lean on each other rather than fight, maybe I'll feel better, too. What a selfish way to get to a kind gesture.

I'm steps away from Theo when my gaze shifts to his left and I'm hit with hazel eyes, brown wavy hair, and what looks to be about six-foot-two of broad chest, contoured biceps and full lips that slowly stretch into a smile as I stare at them.

"Theo, who's your friend," I say, sliding into Theo's side and hugging him with one arm. My instant distraction by a guy I *know* I have never seen before has me forgetting the reason I came over here in the first place. *Refocus, Morgan. It's not about you. It's about Lily, and . . . oh my God, this man smells so good.*

"Morgan Bentley, meet the new Welles QB," Theo says.

Of course, he's the quarterback. I mean, *look at him!* I bet Toby, who was our mediocre quarterback last year, is shitting himself at the sight of this guy. He's twice his size, and judging by the way his arms ripple with the slightest flex of his forearms, I'm guessing he can sling the ball about twice as far.

My hand shoots forward toward our new quarterback on reflex. At least my social self hasn't forgotten how to do some things. His mouth ticks up on one side and my heart pounds out about a dozen beats in a single second before his hand wraps around mine, swallowing it up. His grip is perfect—warm hand, no sweat, firm but gentle in just the right way. His nails are well groomed, which means he gives a shit about how he looks. The calluses on his palm tell me he works his ass off.

"James Fuentes, and I don't have the job quite yet," he

6

says in a low voice with just a hint of rasp. He glances from me toward Theo. He's being modest, probably because he doesn't want word to get back to Toby. *He's not just gorgeous, but he's nice and respectful.*

Theo leans into me with a soft chuckle and I tilt my head so he can whisper into my ear.

"His dad's the coach."

I flash a glance to Theo at the news. His eyes fall slightly, I'm guessing because he didn't think through what his commentary would mean to me. Brennan Wallace was the coach at Welles for several years, until I got him fired. According to the paper trail, he resigned on his own. According to the rumor factory that is Welles Academy, he was let go for having an affair with one of his students ... *me.* Nobody has uttered my name out loud, at least not in a circle that I would hear. But they don't have to say my name. It's in the little things, like the off-handed comments about my taboo tastes. But the truth is, Coach Wallace was the kindest man I've ever met, and he listened to me the way I always wished my father would. When I was in a truly dark place, his was the open door I needed to keep my head above water. We were close, but not the kind of close that gossipy, privileged youths salivate over. He was a friend—a father figure. And helping me got him fired.

I swallow down the lump in my throat and roll my shoulders, straightening my spine. The smile I force is the biggest test of my life. If James hasn't heard the rumors yet, he will soon. And being the coach's son makes anything with him ... *complicated.*

"James, nice to meet you. You boys come sit with us. Lily's holding the big table near the windows." *Lily. That's the reason I started this conversation. To help Lily. Not myself.*

I glance to my friend, who looks terrified. Lily's not as

7

rehearsed at masking her emotions as the rest of us. That's a trait learned from years spent at country clubs and dinner parties where the only purpose seems to be trying to one-up each other.

"We'd love to," Theo says, his jaw rigid. I wonder if he regrets giving in so fast or is doubling down, determined to make this meal miserable for Lily. I won't let that happen. I can do this one thing. I note his reaction, tucking it away into my mental file the way Anika would have. Theo's not as angry with Lily as he thinks he is. He's drawn to her. He needs her. They honestly need each other.

We all do.

I follow Theo into the cafeteria line, eying him as he aggressively fills his tray. He takes two apples, and I'm about to question his motive when an elbow nudges my other side.

"Give it to me straight. Is this stuff any good?" James points toward the pasta salad with a gaping hole scooped from the center and tongs resting along the top.

"Depends. Do you like your colon?" I twist my mouth and glance up. I expect to be struck by his eyes first, because that's the first thing I noticed when we met minutes ago. But my lame joke makes him laugh, and it turns out that as sexy as his sharp jawline, narrow nose, and chameleon eyes are, it's the combo of smile and breathy laugh that legit stops my heart and sends a rush of tingles down to my belly.

"So, I'm guessing it's a pass on anything with tongs?" He quirks a brow. Also fucking adorable. If every expression is going to be like this, I'm doomed.

"Pretty much," I answer, flashing a smile of my own.

My usual move is to get coy, to bat my lashes and lick my lips, drawing attention right where I want it. But something grips me from inside, a faint echo in my mind telling me not to go down that road. I hover for a few extra seconds, and it's not until James flits his eyes over my head that I realize I'm holding up the end of the line.

"Oh, sorry," I say, turning and squeezing my eyes shut while admonishing myself for acting like a pre-teen with a crush. This is not my normal mode of flirting. I'm thrown, and I'm not sure whether it's because he's so goddamn good looking or because I feel guilty indulging after giving myself the little "be a better person" pep talk before we came to dinner.

I renew my vow to help Lily and Theo when I get to the table in time to see Theo basically force his extra apple on Lily. He's such an idiot. I'm sure he's telling himself he's giving her that apple to tease her and be a dick, but really, he doesn't like that she's not eating. None of us do, and he's as worried as we are. But he's too busy fronting to accept it. He'd rather be mean than feel something good about someone else.

"Fine. Starve." Theo ends his apple incident with Lily by pouting as I take my seat across from him. I shoot him a glare and don't let up until he glances up and sees it. I get an eyeroll, which lights that fire I get sometimes. I mash my lips together into a pissed-off smile and will my mouth to remain shut.

Do not let the tiger out, Morgan. Don't do it.

My mouth opens on its own, and my eyes flutter against my strong will as I fight to keep my words inside.

"Hey, let's compare schedules." It's as if James senses I need someone to redirect things. My mouth snaps shut, and I sit up tall as he pulls his schedule from his pocket and flattens the paper on the table. We all lean forward to look it over. I read through it optimistically, hoping for a class with him. Not only do we not have any of the same classes, but from a quick assessment it seems we are on opposite ends of the campus at all times. I hide my disappointment by popping a bendy straw in my soda and chewing on the end as I sip my Sierra Mist. I'm pretty sure that's the universe's way of telling me this one's off limits.

And that's when I notice the flicker in his gaze as Lily defends his selection of pottery as his fine art class.

"I'll make you a hot chocolate mug," he says, giving her a smile that is bigger than the one I got in the food line. A different smile. The one he gave me was because I genuinely made him laugh. But this smile . . . it's because he's interested. In her. Not me.

I suck up a big gulp, letting the carbonation burn the back of my tongue and clean out my throat as it bubbles its way down. It chokes me for a breath, and I cough. Brooklyn pushes her water bottle toward me, but I shake my head and wave her off. If I wanted to take another drink, I'd just put my damn straw in my mouth. And yeah, water is probably smarter. And sure, that tickle is persistent, and I am going to cough again right . . . now. But I don't want her help.

I form a fist and press it to my lips, shutting my eyes and willing my throat to calm the fuck down. Does my body not get that I am intently listening to Lily and James make tutoring plans so they can spend time together.

Alone!

A low growl leaves my mouth behind my hand as I attempt to clear my throat without drawing more attention, but it only makes the choking sensation worse. Bless Theo for timing his moody boy fit to right this second. I cup my entire face and cough hard, the kind that makes my eyes water and my cheeks heat, just as Theo storms away from the table. He's clearly pissed that Lily and James are flirting and making plans, regardless of the aloof tough guy act he's putting on. If I were Anika, I'd march after him and give him sage advice that would somehow encourage him to come crawling back to Lily, ready to be honest and apologize. But I'm not Anika. And I'm choking.

Without warning, I'm on my feet, and the same warm hand that I shook a moment ago is splayed out across my sternum. Even if I weren't choke-coughing, I lost my breath at the sensation of my feet leaving the ground. James hauls me into his body from behind, and before I have a chance to swoon over his embrace, his other hand slaps at my back. Twice. Nope, three times. And that's when I realize he thinks I'm *choking* choking, as in something is stuck. And everyone is looking on while he handles me like a puppy who swallowed a piece of shoe.

Mortified, I manage to grab his wrist and slap the back of his hand with my own as a signal that I'm okay. He sets me back on my feet and spins me around, inspecting my eyes. They're teary, half because the dry-throat cough does that to me and half because he just tried to Heimlich me using every single technique the professionals say *not* to use.

"I'm good," I croak out.

Honestly, I still need to clear my throat, but I'll be damned if I'm ever coughing in his presence again.

A few people around us clap and James smiles and takes in the praise while his cheeks redden from the attention. I wonder how many people caught that on video and are already tagging my social accounts. Other people's posts about me trend more than my own at this point. I'm sure this one will be viral in an hour.

"You should have taken my water," Brooklyn says, leaning into me and handing me her bottle. It's half full, and my pride is empty, so I take it begrudgingly and twist the cap off before bringing it to my lips.

James and Lily are exchanging phone numbers, and

there's an actual smile on her face. My esophageal distress eases, but I stay in the background, looking on while they make plans to meet up. I don't need to have everything I want. Besides, I don't really want James all that much anyhow. He's cute. And new. I can let Lily have this one. Maybe he'll be the distraction she needs. Or perhaps he'll be the signal Theo needs to get his shit in order.

I feel things out on our walk back to our room, asking Lily what she thinks of James. She brushes me off with short answers, which triggers my needling nature to pry even harder. I sound like a crazy jealous girl, hyper-focused on a guy I met only minutes ago. I'd like to say I'm not, but the more I question her about what she thought of his eyes, of his tall, built body, of him being the new quarterback, of the class she offered to help him with and so on, the more confused I am about my own intentions. I quit working her over when I catch a sideways glance from Brooklyn, whose pulled-back brown hair and tightly drawn lips give off a certain librarian-about-to-bust-me vibe.

Back in the comfort of our room, music playing and jammies on, I sit back into my corner filled with pillows and silently take in our new shared home for the next nine months. A day will come when it feels normal. I believe that. I pledge to myself not to bring James up to Lily again unless it looks as though there really is a spark between them. The silent promise stings, and I bury that feeling too because the only reason I feel it is jealousy. It's one stupid boy. One I've known for about seventeen minutes, three of which were spent with him essentially burping me. Besides, these feelings are probably more about me mourning attention that once came so easily. A year ago, there is no way I would not be either planning my first date with James by now or stringing him along on my own terms.

Curious, I settle under my blanket and search my social accounts for any mention of tonight's choking incident. I recognized a few of the students filming on their phones, so I scout their pages first, bracing myself to see the likes and comments climbing on the video. Only, there are no mentions to track. None of the obvious hashtags or keywords bring up the video. A novice might think people are simply waiting to post it, but that's not how this game works for people like us. A video of someone like me getting an unnecessary Heimlich is social media gold, and being the first to post that kind of thing is rule number one. At least, it would have been. Before.

Fact is, my numbers are down by more than thirty percent. I dipped below a million on my best platform. There are fewer people looking. Fewer people caring. And I'd venture to guess half of those people who filmed me at dinner have already deleted it from their phones to save space.

I didn't really want the video to be seen. But I did expect it. Negative attention is still attention.

Angry at myself for caring, I click my screen off and toss my phone into the folds of my comforter and give my attention over to Brooklyn and Lily who are doing a deep dive into Theo's behavior. I guess there was an incident during the internship interviews today, something about him tripping Lily in front of the panel. Somehow, the two of them landed the same internship at the end of it all.

"Where did you get in?" It's the first time anyone has asked, and I think Lily is bringing it up now simply to get the focus off her and Theo.

I shrug and sink deeper into my covers.

"It's a small PR company. Is it bad that I don't even remember the name? It's on my form," I say, nodding toward my desk.

Everyone at Welles assumed I would intern with my father at Bentley Inc. I told my friends I didn't want to give my dad the satisfaction of working for him, but the truth? I was afraid he would reject me. Being passed over by your own father cuts deep, and I'm not strong enough to handle that right now, No matter how many times I have before in my life.

"Opal and Jayne," Brooklyn says, standing in front of my desk with my packet in her hands.

"That's right. I picked them because I liked their name," I admit.

Brooklyn laughs out, "Oh, my God," and rolls her eyes, tossing my papers back on my desk and retreating back to her bed.

I also like that they do a lot of small business grand openings, but having to post on social media again regularly, if even for somebody else, does make my heart burn. I'm hoping I don't fail at this job, or worse, get stuck writing media advisories for ribbon cuttings.

Brooklyn is sharing the details of her posting, which was a given from the time she started at Welles. Her father is a big name in politics, and she'll be working in the mayor's office downtown. The business is in her nature and her blood.

She's reciting her interview questions and practically putting Lily to sleep when I feel a vibration against my knee. I reach down for my phone, sliding it up but keeping the screen hidden so Brooklyn doesn't see my attention being divided. I expect a calendar reminder on my screen, but instead it's a new follow request for my secret personal Instagram profile, the one I keep private and hidden, and only post on rarely and for close friends and the cousins.

I note the profile name: JimmyNo1. I'm biting my lip as I accept and follow back, tapping the side of my device with nervous fingers while I wait for JimmyNo1 to accept in return.

"Are you listening to me?" Brooklyn cuts in.

"Totally. You were telling them about a difficult situation you faced recently and how you problem solved." My listening skills are adept. Almost superhero-like. I think it's from having to multi-task at such a young age, making posts while people wanted me to mingle.

"Right, so . . ." Brooklyn continues.

My hand buzzes and I sink lower into my pillow fort, blocking her view of my phone as I tap on JimmyNo1's profile icon and take in the many, many workout photos of the newest Welles quarterback.

My heart kicks, and that steady drum keeps me awake until well past midnight stalking every post he's ever made and hoping he's doing the same to mine.

Chapter 2

James Fuentes

Of course I know who Morgan Bentley is. I'm an eighteen-year-old male who has been on social media since I was eleven. I may have grown up on the south side, but Morgan Bentley was the hot girl on TikTok down there too.

I figured I would run into her at some point, but I didn't think it would be in a social situation. I thought maybe a class, or from across the gym, or at a game or whatever. My friends from my old school have been asking. That's the only thing they knew about Welles Academy—this is the school the hot TikTok chick goes to. It's also one of the toughest private schools on the east coast, and my public-school experience is going to show in the classroom pretty quick. I'm guessing there won't be a girl here willing to let me copy her test answers over her shoulder.

I'm going to have to work, and that's fine. I want that. My dad's right. If I want to rescue my grandfather's business, bringing it back from bankruptcy and turning it into something to be proud of, I need to focus. The people who took his business off the map knew the loopholes and had an edge. An Ivy League degree gives me equal footing and connections. Football is my way in.

Our apartment smells amazing as I step through the door. I went to dinner with the guys because I need them on my side. I need friends. But damn, my mom's cooking is the only thing that comes remotely close to my grandfather's. I draw in the scent, practically tasting the flavors without taking a bite. *Ahhhh, home.*

"Come. Try this," my mom says while stirring a pot of simmering goodness on the stove. I drop my bag on the couch and head into the kitchen, obeying her request. I open my mouth and wait for her to hold up the spoon. It's steaming a little, so I blow on the red sauce before tasting it. Once I do, my tastebuds instantly transport me around the world. A piece of Mexico, and maybe some Brazilian hints in the seasoning. It's hot, but not in that way that burns the tongue. It's like the effects of a good whiskey, warming me from the inside out.

"You like?" She quirks a brow.

I lick my lips, making sure I get every spare taste into my mouth, and let my smile grow. "That's phenomenal. You come up with that?"

She waggles her head modestly.

"It's a version of Papa's, with my own little kick."

I reach in front of her and dip a finger in, then suck the sauce off of it.

"It's really good," I say as she smacks my elbow for touching her creation.

"Your dad is in our room working on practice plans. Check in with him," she says, waving me away.

I attempt to take one more taste before I go, but she

shoves me away with a push of her hip. I hold up my hands and laugh.

"Fine, I'm going. But that better reheat." I point to the pot. She waves me off.

My mom is insanely talented. My papa, her dad, owned a small bodega-style shop on the street level of an older south-side building. It was popular with the locals, but never big enough to really break through that bubble and draw in serious customers. But Papa had a plan. Unfortunately, the building owners had their own. Down came the building and up went the fancy new condo high rise. Papa's five-year plan turned into a decade-long one, and that deadline passed two years ago.

I was six when he lost the store, and sometimes I wonder if it made such a huge mark on me because I was so young. If it had happened later, when I started at Public High for example, I might not have been so invested in a small busi-ness dream. But that store—and the stool I sat on in the back by the chalkboard he let me draw whatever I wanted on—was everything to me. It was this magical little hole in the wall where everyone in the neighborhood was nice and where my grandfather whistled while he cut strips of meat in the back. And it always smelled like my kitchen does right now.

My mom doesn't belong keeping the books for other people's business dreams. She belongs learning and creating from her roots. She's happiest with a spoon in her hand and steam streaming from her pots. It's what Papa would want. All I need out of the deal is a stool to sit on from time to time.

I knock on the open door as I step into my parents' bedroom and my dad merely glances up over the golden rims of his glasses, the glow of the laptop screen covering most of the lenses.

"Studying *us*? Or are you checking out competition?" I

ask, flopping into the leather chair in the corner of their room. My dad has turned their bed into a mini-office with notes strewn around along with his enormous whiteboard that he keeps both the team schedule on as well as his thoughts on each week's strengths and weaknesses.

"Both," he grunts, flitting his eyes up at me briefly.

"You're going to need to do something for an office. They give you one in the field house, you know. Mom might want to come to bed at some point."

My dad draws in a deep breath through his nose then pulls his glasses from his face and squeezes the bridge of his nose before flipping his laptop around for me to view.

"It's kind of hard to scout your son's personal competition in a place where anyone can walk up behind you and see what you're doing," he says.

My brow furrows and I take his laptop into my hands, resting it on my thighs and playing through a few of the videos he's pulled up. The one he just paused is from the final game last season. I can tell by where my dad has it paused that he's focusing on Toby's footwork. He's slow getting out of the pocket and as I let the clips play on, the more obvious his desire becomes to remain there, protected by his linemen. The next one is Toby's scout video. It's average, and I only think that to be nice. Deep down, I can't fathom a college recruiting coach at any level flagging him as a prospect. Of course, his dad owns several golf resorts along the coast, so I'm sure that will help get him some looks.

His dad.

Kirk Sullivan.

That's why my dad is researching Toby.

"It's gonna be a problem, isn't it?" I lean forward and slide the laptop along my dad's mattress next to where he sits.

20

He pushes it shut, still pinching the bridge of his nose as he nods.

"There's already a lot of grumbling. And I have a meeting with Mr. Sullivan tomorrow. Can't imagine he's not going to put some pressure on me." My dad's hand falls to his lap, and he lifts his chin, leveling me with that honest look he wears.

"What can I do?" I lean back into the seat and slump down.

"Keep throwing the ball like you did today. When we scrimmage, make him look foolish. Make it impossible for anyone in their right mind to argue against you starting over him. We've been here before. I don't put up with pressure; you know that."

My dad stacks his papers and pulls his mess together while I let the pit of my stomach drop through the bottom of the chair and glue me to the floor.

"I'm a senior now. It's not like we can pack up and find another prep school looking for a coach and willing to give his kid a tuition break." My pulse hammers in my gut. This is why I hate getting my hopes up. There is always a barrier, always another hill to climb. I don't mind climbing them, but damn, man. When am I going to plateau?

My dad shovels his work and the laptop into his leather bag and moves it to the top of his dresser before reaching out a hand to help me up. I take his grip and stand square with him. He puts his other hand on my shoulder, holding firm—solid—and our eyes lock.

"You want this?" Like he has to ask.

I've watched my parents work so hard to do things that matter to them. My dad loves coaching, but he's never been able to break through that ceiling that keeps him out of the conversation for high-profile high school jobs. He'd give anything to coach at the college level one day too, but he's got

Ginger Scott

to get out of the basement first. And mom—she's a decent accountant. But she should be doing her own books, for her family's legacy. As for me, I simply don't want to work for anyone other than myself. I know at first I will have to. But I want that time of my life to be as short as possible. I've watched too many dreams by people I love get stuck under the boots of bad bosses.

"I want this," I reply. We both nod, sealing the same agreement we make every time adversity rears its head.

I turn to leave my parents' room, but before I pass through the door and head down the hallway to my own room, my dad stops me.

"On that note, son, I like that you are making friends. And it's good to see you bonding with some of the guys on the team." He pauses and I quirk a brow, waiting for the *but* part of this statement.

"But maybe let's stay focused and keep those relationships tight, and to the team."

And there it is. My girlfriend last year was what some might classify as toxic. Neveah was a bit into drama—starting it, spreading it, prolonging it. She was hot, which was my small-minded side's weakness. She wanted more from me than I could give, though. More time. More commitment. More compromise. Our fights were epic, and constantly found their way into my father's business. Of course, so did her drama.

"I'm older now, Dad," I reassure him. "More mature."

"James, you're literally four months older than you were when we had to file a family restraining order against her. Please take me seriously."

My chest falls and my mouth forms a straight line.

"What if I already got a tutor for something and she's a girl?" Lily's cute, and I know my dad is going to take one look

22

at her and make a boatload of assumptions about my intentions. As beautiful as she is, though, that's honestly not why I connected with her. Her story is at the top of everyone's mind at Welles, the girl who saved her friends from drowning in the river. I admire her for sure. I also found her to be encouraging, and this school is going to be tough for me. I barely made the academic cut at Public. I have a gap to close here, and Lily is willing to help me. She seems smart, but also patient. I simply want to be her friend.

My dad holds my stare for a few seconds before letting out a punch of a breath.

"I'm going to trust that you will make smart decisions. And if this tutor will help you find success, of course. But you need to stay focused on books and not—"

"Breasts, yeah . . . I got it." I roll my eyes at my dad's favorite quip. He chuckles behind me as I walk away, and I can picture his finger pointing at me.

"You laugh, but it's about as basic as it gets."

"Good night," I hum, my voice tinged with sarcasm as I push my door closed behind me.

I kick off my shoes and faceplant into my bed, my comforter cool against my warm face. I tuck a pillow under my arms and work my phone from my pocket, propping it up between my hands in front of me. I scroll to Lily's contact information and finish typing in her name, boldly labeling her as Tutor in the title area in case my dad decides to grab my phone and go exploring before he meets her. I think he'll agree I made a good decision when he does. It took a lot of extra hours, mostly on my mom's part, to get me through algebra and history at my public school. I don't even understand half of the names of the classes at this place.

I open my Instagram and look back at the few photos I have remaining. I deleted anything of me and Neveah, both because I didn't want to lead her on and because it made me nervous to be tied to her. I have a few posts, mostly of me working out, and two with the guys from my old school doing dumb shit like putting firecrackers in an old shoe and taking hard-thrown water balloons to the bare chest.

Without thinking too hard, I search for Morgan, whom I have never officially followed on anything. Her pages are easy to find. They're usually promoted and in the top ten trending categories. At least, they were. I pause on the first photo on her account and expand the image to really take in her smile. That's where her money is. The girl could smile and sell a shit sandwich to a million people, I swear. I let the pic snap back to its regular size and note the others in the photo with her. Before today, I wouldn't have recognized any of them. But Lily and Brooklyn look nearly the same, and I'm pretty certain the girl to Morgan's left is Anika. She looks like Theo.

This post is four and a half months old. While I knew who Morgan was, I didn't obsess over her like a lot of people do. I didn't realize she'd gone dark on her account. I open a different app to search her and find the same thing—four-month-old posts sitting in the most recent positions. I don't think she was injured to the extent Brooklyn was in the accident, but people can hurt in other ways.

I flip back to that image of her and her friends and read through some of the comments. There's a lot of adoration, and a lot of prayer emojis and hearts. But the deeper I go, the more the ugly side of humanity creeps in. I inhale a sharp breath when I realize I've been holding it, my temples hot from the pounding pressure of my pulse. People are cruel and so quick to hate on someone they probably took their beauty tips from a year ago.

My thumb hovers over the follow link. I'm sure the guys from my old neighborhood will get a notification the minute I press this, which means their stream of messages about what hot TikTok girl is really like will soon come pouring in.

Morgan's profile is a strange fit with my collection of college football programs and workout profiles. But those reasons aren't enough to stop me from being a fan for the right reasons. She needs someone in here to post more positive comments. Following her like this is harmless, and it's nice.

I press follow before second-guessing, satisfied my dad is clueless when it comes to social media. I'm pretty sure he thinks all of these things on my phone are recruiting apps. I scroll through a few more of her posts, seeing some that are clearly for sponsored purposes, like the fruity-flavored seltzer water, but I stop on one of her lying upside-down and sticking her tongue out, being silly, a kitten pawing at her neck. This girl has a glimmer of whatever I saw in the cafeteria line tonight. She's stripped of all the glitz, and not just the makeup and designer clothing and posturing for the camera to make sure her lips are full and her ass is popping out. She's just a cute girl being silly, like the one who made fun of the cafeteria food with me.

My hand buzzes as my phone gets a notification, and I thumb it open to see her request to follow me back. My chest tightens, that pang of guilt digging at the soft spot between my ribs. Ignoring her request is what my dad would prefer. But again, I can't completely isolate myself socially and succeed at this place. And Morgan, as distracting as he may find her, is a great contact to have. She's a businesswoman in her own right, having forged a path separate from her family. But that family name is mighty persuasive. The Bentleys sometimes get mentioned on CNN, they're that big. Can't hurt to have one of them in my corner.

I accept her request and wait for the tightness to ease in

my chest. It doesn't. The vise only grows tighter. And the more I try to ease it by glancing through more of her pics in search of ones that are business-worthy and fine examples for me to show my dad to prove my case, the more I zero in on that smile—those full lips and smooth skin. And her in a bikini on a yacht. And . . . yeah.

I'm fucked.

Chapter 3

Morgan

It's strange to feel I know someone from spending hours staring at their photos and reading their captions on social media. It's naïve, actually; I know that better than most. So many times, I posted photos of myself smiling, with hearts and hashtags about feeling blessed and believing in positivity above all. Meanwhile, I was sinking.

James is typical of most guys on social media. He quotes random song lyrics and matches them to pics of him throwing a football or doing a shirtless pullup. I get enough from his content to know the person he wants people to believe he is. And damn if I don't like that guy a little bit. He'd be perfect for Lily, honestly. And if I possessed even the slightest of similarities to Anika, I would play cupid. I'm not ruling it out.

But because I'm not Anika, and I have one hell of a selfish streak, I am also not committing. Instead, I'm pulling out the sexiest dresses I own for a party James and Theo are throwing in some stupid basement part of the library.

Other than a few glances across the table during lunch this week, my interactions with James have consisted solely of more late-night social media stalking. It took everything I had in my soul to not deploy the special apps on my phone that can tell if someone is looking at my content. I haven't used them in months because frankly I haven't had any content to put through the data test. I used to really get into the weeds with this stuff, breaking down my followers and interactions to sell to sponsors. Now I simply want to spy on a boy.

What the hell happened to me?

I strip my tight black dress over my head and toss it to the floor, leaving the matching black bra and undies on along with my black leather boots. I wonder how desperate I would look if I walked into tonight's party wearing this? I smirk at myself and breathe out a quiet laugh.

Pulling the green tunic dress from my closet, I eye Lily behind me in the reflection of my mirror before slipping it over my head. Maybe she has the right idea. She's wearing her school uniform, which, let's face it, clothing doesn't get much more in sync with the fantasy than a school uniform. I look back at my closet, overstuffed with designer rags, half of which I don't even like. I pull my red dress out and hold it up to my chest to consider which Christmas color works better, red, or green.

"James didn't give you any details on whatever this place is we're going?" Even I cringe at how obvious my question is when it comes back to my own ears. Lily spent the day tutoring James, which is good. It's a great distraction for her. Instead of twisting around and meeting what I'm sure are exasperated tight mouths and rolling eyes from my room-mates, I focus on the red dress in my hand.

"We talked about Willa Cather," Lily says.

"Willa who?" I respond. English and lit classes have never been my strong suit. One more thing James and I have in common, I guess. Too bad I can't tutor him.

"That's the first reading assignment. And Morgan, you look amazing in what you have on now," Lily says.

I drop the red dress down to my side to see what she sees. I feel like I'm trying too hard. I look desperate, and this sick need to be the center of attention leaves a bad taste in my mouth. I wonder if I'm even truly attracted to James or if I simply want to be the hottest—the best. The winner. *The* girl. Everyone else is second.

"I don't like James. Like *that* I mean," Lily pipes up after a long minute of silence. My eyes flit to her in the mirror and my stomach sinks. I wonder how long she's been watching me fight with myself. I wonder if she knows the bad thoughts I've been fighting about her all because a guy noticed her more than me.

Attention whore.

I shake those feelings off as best I can to focus on the good. Lily's being kind. Before Anika was gone, she hit me with some hard truths. I tend to distrust people. My instincts are to assume people aren't genuine, especially when they're paying me compliments. Yet I fight so hard to collect them, like magic coins in a video game that add to my character's life. I need praise to survive.

"Do you think he'll like this outfit?" I can't help myself. The only self-deprecating thing I can manage is the guilty, crooked smile I level back at Lily. She must know I'm fishing. I know Brooklyn does. She's been down the low self-esteem road with me more than once.

My hook catches more than enough as both of my room-mates lather me with admiration, play fighting over which of them gets to sex me up at the end of the night. It almost feels good, the attention. But like most addicts, I've built up a toler-ance, and their forced adoration doesn't taste as good as it used to.

I turn my focus to getting Lily ready for the party instead, and I'm relieved when Brooklyn joins me. Despite my own shortcomings and personal mental shit, Lily deserves to have our—*my*—real friendship. I want to give it to her. There's a lot of baggage between her and Theo, and as much as she wants to hide in the shadows whenever he's around, there's a part of her that wants to haunt him. I recognize it because it's the parts of her and I that are alike.

By the time we leave our room and head down to the main courtyard to meet one of the guys who will guide us to this secret lair or whatever, Brooklyn and I have managed to turn Lily into a sex kitten, swapping out her school uniform blouse for my black wrap-around shirt. Brooklyn looks as polished as she always does, like a CEO about to seduce her assistant. And I went with the green, not because it makes me feel good, but because Lily picked it.

I'm trying.

"Ladies, this way," Cameron says, rolling his hand out like a maître de.

We follow his drunk, high ass over to the back side of the library where James is prying open a door that looks to have been buried under vines for years. They seem to have invited a few other people, which is both a relief and a disappointment. James and Cameron usher the dozen or so of us through the door into the dimly lit archive room for the library. I've never seen this place.

My chest tightens as soon as the door locks shut behind us. I haven't been to a party since the night of the accident. I can't cling to the girls all night, though, despite how tempting that idea is. My head doesn't play as many tricks on me when I'm with friends. Alone, I feel the running commentary. I can't shake this sense that the world is looking at me and wondering what is wrong.

What is wrong with me?

"Lily." Theo's voice breaks up my nerves, but I can tell it has only spiked Lily's. I lean into her and squeeze her arm.

"Look, an olive branch. Go talk to him." I give my friend a nudge toward the source of her heartache, and it makes her stumble a tad. I wince when she glances over her shoulder at me.

"Sorry," I mouth.

Brooklyn peels away next, accepting a drink from Cameron and laughing easily at one of his dumb jokes. Their friendship is simple. *Easy.* I envy that.

An instant chill crawls up my arms then down my spine. Somewhere over the last year or two, I've lost the confidence I once had being alone. I used to feel comfortable in my own skin, solid with my self-worth. My spiral started around the time I stepped into an elevator downtown my freshman year and found my father inside with his hand up some woman's skirt. Spoiler alert—she was not my mom.

It's not that I was oblivious to his infidelity. None of us were. *Are.* It's still happening on the regular. Over the last few years, I've come to realize that my father has never been discreet. He was so casual that day on the elevator, asking me what party I was going to or coming back from. His fifteen-year-old daughter walking around unaccompanied in hotels for penthouse parties hosted by celebrities was of no concern to him. In fact, it was the first time I ever felt as if he was bragging to someone about having a semi-famous daughter. He showed me off, in his own way. *To his mistress.*

"Welcome to *Theo's Lair.*" James's warm voice snakes around my shoulders and I turn into him, our bodies close. He's wearing a fitted white T-shirt and faded jeans that hang on his hips, his dark brown hair combed back minus the few stray strands that have disobeyed and fallen on his forehead.

He's holding two drinks, whiskey from the looks of them. He hands one to me and our fingers graze on the exchange. I flit my eyelashes and glance up in time to catch his gaze locked on the diamond stud in the center of my bra. My nipples harden, and for the first time tonight, I'm glad I picked the green dress.

"He does know this is basically just a massive storage space, right?" I sip from my glass and smile with my lips pressed to the rim. James chuckles, the sound rattling his chest.

"I honestly think he sees a hundred-year-old speakeasy when he looks around," James says, his eyes scanning the room then coming back to me, sparkling with amusement. I hold on to his gaze until my insides warm, and when they do, I let my lips pull into a tight smile and stare into his eyes a second more. I like pushing myself like that, over the edge to discomfort. Sometimes, being uncomfortable can feel good.

"Well, this building is old enough. I doubt it's ever seen alcohol before, though." I mentally picture our library staff partying hard down here, and the thought makes me breathe out a sharp laugh. Welles librarians take their work seriously, to the point that the women actually wear their hair in tight buns and have those beaded chains on their glasses to keep them around their necks. There's only one male librarian, and he's British and in his sixties. I don't doubt he could cut loose if given the chance, but I can't imagine the bun-wearing ladies are his jam. I'm pretty sure I've heard them yell at *him* to be quiet a time or two.

"Wanna see something cool?" James eyes to his right, toward a glassed-in office away from the few lights glowing down here.

I glance around for my friends, spotting Lily still sparring with Theo across the room and Brooklyn now playing some made-up paper ball trash can game with Cameron and two of the other football players.

"Yeah, okay," I answer, tipping my glass back and swallowing the rest of my drink. It burns its way down, stunting my nerves. I hand James the empty glass and pass him, heading toward the office door.

"All right, then," he says to my back. "I just got drank under the table by a—"

"Careful," I interrupt, turning to face him as I walk backward, and he follows. "Don't say something sexist."

His mouth snaps shut and curves. He nods, acknowledging his faux pas, then drains his own glass, depositing it on a bookcase shelf as he closes the distance between us. I turn around, smirking, and proud of myself for finding my old fire. At least a spark of it.

I step into the office and head toward the desk on the far end, my insides tingling at the sound of the door clicking shut behind us.

"I was going to say *total babe,* for what it's worth," James says.

I spin around and sit on the desktop as I punch out a hushed laugh at him.

"That's even worse!" Of course, I like that he thinks I'm a babe. I wish maybe his words were a touch more poetic, but babe will do.

I bite the tip of my tongue then pull my lips in to stifle the smile inching into my cheeks under his glare. His eyes are glossy, and maybe a little red. He's not drunk, but he's definitely feeling the buzz. I wonder how long he and Theo were in here waiting for the rest of us.

"Show me this amazing, cool thing you spoke of," I say, breaking the quiet as I hold my palm out and gesture around the room. "Please say it isn't motivational posters from the nineteen seventies."

I nod to one plastered to the wall behind him, and he twists to read it out loud.

"Don't wait for opportunity. Create it." He stares at it for a few long seconds and turns to face me, nodding. "That's actually *not* what I wanted to show you, but now I feel like anything else will pale in comparison. That prose. The message."

He forms a fist and taps the center of his chest with it while closing his eyes and feigning being moved.

"Maybe I'll swipe it for you, give it to you on your birthday," I joke.

His smile lingers, as does his gaze.

"I'd like that."

Warmth coats my insides again, and I immediately go to work deciding how I'm going to get that poster off that fucking wall without him noticing.

"Seriously, though. Let me show you," he says, slowly closing the gap between us.

My legs are crossed, my thigh muscles vibrating with the urge to unfurl and part, inviting him to step between my knees. The almost-touch is my favorite feeling. His eyes hold mine hostage, and I wonder if he's wishing for me to part them, too. He stops less than an inch away from my leg and bends to his side, pulling out a metal drawer that seems to be hiding more than just a few expensive-looking pens. A box of condoms sits next to a silver flask with the name ABE engraved across the center. Before I can react to that, he continues to slide the drawer open, revealing a small bag of extremely aged pot and a nudie magazine.

"Oh, my God!" I laugh out, cupping my mouth and hiding my wide-open lips.

James pulls the flask out and flips the cap, taking a swig. My eyes bulge out and my head turns to check over my shoulder and see who is watching this.

"That could be rancid!" I whisper-shout when my gaze lands on his again.

His shoulders shake with his quiet laugh and his lips pucker to hold in his smirk.

"You already knew it wasn't, didn't you?" I purse my lips and lower my eyelids.

James shrugs and takes another hit from the flask before passing it to me. I sniff a few inches from the cap, noticing it's basically odorless.

"Vodka?" I quirk a brow.

"Maybe?" James shakes his head slightly.

"Maybe. That's your comforting response. That what you want to drink out of a God-knows-how-long-it-has-been-in-here flask is possibly vodka." I squint and study him, but he doesn't budge.

"Pretty much," he says.

I stare at him for a few quiet seconds before he reaches to take the flask back and let me off the hook. But before he can take it from my hands, I bring it to my mouth and tilt, letting the scorching liquid coat my tongue. I cough and instantly shove the flask back at him before running my sleeve over my lips, probably smearing my lip color, assuming there is anything left after running it under what tasted like turpentine.

"Right?" He chuckles.

"That is moonshine, James. That is not *maybe* vodka. That's some straight-up home-brewed shit." I cough again, the kind of hack a cat makes to rid themselves of a furball. I can't help it.

James takes another swig then offers it to me again. I touch my fingertips to the metal side and push it away.

"No, thank you."

"Suit yourself," he says, his mouth curved with amusement. "If you prefer the finest selection of whiskey I swiped from the alumni stash, ask Theo."

"Ah, so you're the source for that stuff," I say.

James shrugs.

"Maybe."

He recaps the flask and tucks it back into its space in the drawer. Before he can close it, I reach in and swipe the nudie magazine and lay it flat on my lap.

"Let's see what's doing with these ladies, shall we?" I lift a brow as I glance up at him.

"Sure," he agrees, sliding the door closed with the side of his leg and resting half of his weight on the desktop next to me. I'm tucked next to his side, his palm on the desk behind me and his bicep skimming my back. I'm tempted to lean into him, but instead, I flip through the first few pages of HOT LADIES.

"Original title," I utter.

"Hey, nothing wrong with to-the-point marketing. Their readers knew exactly what they were going to get," he says.

I snort out a short laugh.

"Readers," I joke.

I can feel James's breath against my neck as he peers at the magazine in my lap. My skin beads in reaction, and it takes me a moment to retrain my focus on the girl dressed as a sailor in the centerfold.

"What do you think? Your type?" I lift the magazine and turn it sideways to give us both the full picture. The magazine is from the nineties, so there's a little grunge vibe to the model's look. She's not completely naked, either, though her nipples are on full display through the ripped-out pockets of her shirt.

"I mean, she definitely has something," James says. I shift my head a tad and glance at him in my periphery, expecting his gaze to be on Tammy and her exceptional outfit, but his eyes are on my face.

"She does, huh?" I chew at the inside of my cheek, my skin buzzing with excited energy.

His eyes scan down my profile, lingering on the place where my bra peaks out from the draped neckline of my dress. His eyes flit to mine again, a suspicious smirk tugging at his lips. Twisting next to me, he brings his right hand toward my body. I brace myself, every nerve-ending in my body firing with electricity that he might kiss me. My tongue passes over my top lip to quell my eagerness and my eyelids grow heavy.

"May I?" His index finger outstretched and pointing toward my me. My brow pinches, because if he's going to feel me up, this is literally the strangest approach I have ever seen. It's even more awkward than the Mosely twins, who both spent time with me in the Rothschilds' coat closet during their Halloween party when we were twelve.

"Uh, you . . . may?" I laugh through the words, baffled but still so aware of how close he is—his mouth, his hand, his body.

James reaches forward and slips his finger under the delicate chain around my neck, lifting the crystal pendant up and rolling it between his finger and thumb.

"My grandmother gave it to me when I turned sixteen," I say, my throat a little dry. I don't clear it, though. I don't want to sound nervous because I'm not. I have him exactly where I want him. This is all going according to plan.

"It's unique," he says, the tip of his tongue caught

between the front of his teeth before our eyes meet again. He smiles through it but doesn't shy away from our stare. If he thinks I'm going to back down, he's mistaken. Doubling down, I blink at him slowly then glance down to the crystal in his hand.

"I like that it matches," I hint, knowing that his eyes have not missed the crystal stud in the center of my bra, the round curves of the black satin cups fanning out over the cowled neck of my green dress.

A soft laugh leaves his lips as his smirk grows higher on one side, his eyes dipping lower to the matching piece I mentioned. This time, he stares long and hard at the stud centered between my breasts, and I watch his eyes and mouth the entire time.

"It does indeed," he finally says, a tinge of huskiness to his hushed voice.

He lets the pendant glide away from his hold and rest against my skin again, but his knuckle grazes against the sharp cut edge, tracing along the teardrop shape. I take in a long slow breath, my chest lifting and back arching slightly, my breasts aching under his stare. James breathes out quickly at my slight movement and looks off to the side, leaning back on his left palm again and running his other hand through his hair.

Satisfied that I got to him, if even just a little, I lift the centerfold back up and tilt my head to one side so I can study it as if I'm standing in the Museum of Modern Art.

"I don't know. I think there's only one Tammy," I say. I close the magazine and slide off the desk, turning and handing the booklet to James, who is leaning back on both palms.

After a short pause, he reaches forward and takes the

magazine from me and leans to the side to deposit it back in the drawer. I begin to walk away before he's done.

"Where are you off to?" he asks.

I stop at the doorway and chew at my lip, that giddy feeling of having someone looking at me with desire temporarily easing the void in my chest. I look over my shoulder to find him leaning back on his palms again, his head angled to one side.

"Nothing else to see in that drawer. But thank you for showing it to me." I blink slowly and let my seductive grin pinch the sides of my closed mouth.

"I'm going to go get something to drink from *this* century," I add before turning to face the glass door again, gripping the handle and dragging it open so as to not draw attention from anyone else.

"Hey," James hums at my back before I slip back into the archive room. I turn and press a palm against the glass wall, leaning my weight through the doorway so I can hear him.

"There's only one Morgan Bentley too. Just so you know." His smile lingers long after his words. He doesn't move an inch, but his eyes stay on me. My cheeks heat, and though it is rare, it does happen from time to time—I am blushing.

"Enjoy your moonshine," I finally utter, pulling the door closed behind me this time then turning to search out my roommates.

Nobody noticed where I went, and nobody seems to be missing James. The perks of surrounding oneself with those who are self-absorbed. My head swims from the mix of real whiskey and whatever the fuck was in that flask. But it's the elation of James's singular attention that has me truly buzzed. I don't take another drink for the rest of the night. And James doesn't leave that office.

Chapter 4

James

I definitely should not have drank from that flask. I think I'm still flammable. I was trying to be cool. Like the way Squints tricked that lifeguard, Wendy Peffercorn, into giving him mouth-to-mouth in the movie *Sandlot*. Only there was no mouth-to-mouth for me. And I don't even know what my goal was. To get her super drunk? That's not like me. I think she makes me nervous, and my dad has my head filled with all of these rules about sticking to business—*football* being that business for now.

And he's right.

Really? If I want to get my ass into an elite university—which is pretty much essential if I hope to be a restaurant entrepreneur while my mom is still young enough to handle running a kitchen—it's only the first step of many.

I'll need to make connections, which being a winning quarterback at a place like Welles and then again at a school like Dartmouth or Brown can make happen. People are quick to lean into winners. And they'll invest in winners with Ivy degrees.

"Slacker. Ass out of bed!" My dad's heavy hand pounds on my door.

"Coming," I shout. My own voice hurts more to hear than my dad's did. This is going to be really hard. Why my dad insists on six a.m. lifting baffles me. He swears it builds character and preps those of us who want to go on and play in college for what's to come. But isn't getting enough sleep supposed to be critical for our development?

"If you went to bed earlier, you would not feel the pain in the morning!" he shouts from his own room. *How does he read my mind?*

I pull myself up to sit, my head pounding with every inch I rise. Last night was a bad idea. At least, the drinking part was. The Morgan part, that was impulsive. And maybe it was a bad idea too, but after staring at her social media the night before I got a little star-struck seeing her in person, I guess. It's stupid. She's not a movie star or anything. She's a rich girl. A hot one. Who got popular on social media because she's a hot, rich girl. I need to move past that and focus, like my dad says.

"I'm heading to the field house. If you aren't the first athlete through those weight room doors, you'll start your morning running bleachers." My dad finishes his statement with a couple more pats on my door.

"Yes, sir," I respond, my hands instantly moving to my temples. I rub slow circles in an attempt to stem the throbbing that reverberates throughout my skull. I can do this. I've partied and practiced before. Hell, my friends in southside threw series parties that would have knocked most of the Welles guys on their asses in an hour. It's one workout. Then class. Then practice. Then . . .

My head falls forward and I catch my face in my palm, breathing out hard in an effort to psych myself up. One thing at a time. That's how today is going to go. Thing number one? Cold shower and getting dressed.

I gather my clothes and drag my ass into the bathroom. I'm tempted to turn the water to warm, but I know better. If I do that, I won't get out of this room for an hour.

It's strange living in an apartment while the rest of my teammates bunk up in dorm rooms. Life is vastly different here, and while it's nice having my own space, it also makes me feel like an outsider. I'm glad I met Theo, but I'm still not quite sure I can count him as a friend. Nothing feels solid yet —with anyone—but it's early. I can lead this team. The buy-in will come. I have to believe that.

The cold water does enough to slap my face awake, but nothing is going to stop the pounding in my head. I throw on my workout clothes and chew three ibuprofens while grabbing the mango and spinach smoothie my mom left for me in the fridge on my way out the door. The sun isn't up, and campus is empty. Despite the effect my hard steps have on my headache, I take them anyway, switching to a slow jog when I finish choking down my smoothie. What I need is water.

I fling open the field house doors and rush down the corridor toward the weight room, relieved to not hear the clanking of weights. I swing the door open and head toward the far corner to drop my gym bag and pull out my water bottle to refill at the station, but my dad's telling cough slows my steps until I'm at a dead stop.

My head falls back, and I blink at the ceiling before swiveling to glance to my right where my father is standing with Mr. Sullivan and his son, Toby. There's a fresh glint of sweat on Toby's forehead, his hair damp with it. It's five forty in the morning, and from the looks of it he's already gotten in a run.

Fuck!

"Yes, sir," I utter without pause. Spinning on my heels, I drop my bag by the entrance and suck down some water from the fountain instead of filling my bottle. I don't make eye contact with anyone in that room, instead pushing back through the doors and retracing my path back outside and toward the football field.

The Welles bleachers are built into a hillside in two tiers. It's bigger than most of the stands I'm used to, and I wonder if this place is full on game days. I feed off a crowd. I was a better quarterback at Public because of the fan base, and I hope I can find something similar here. I wonder if they will take to an outsider.

If you win them games, they will love you.

My dad's advice cuts through my thoughts, and I suck in a deep breath at the base of the stands, clearing my head of everything else. After a short stretch, I begin my slow jog up the stands, every step increasing the blood flow through my body—and my head. I take half of my steps with my eyes closed, regretting every second of last night's choices along the way. My dad didn't have to give me direction. I know his rules. Ten sets for the first infraction, fifteen for the next. There won't be a next for me, though. There's never been a first before, and I'm livid that I let this happen. I'm also pretty sure Toby Sullivan is my new number-one enemy. No way he showed up here early on accident. This was orchestrated. Part of a bigger plan. And I'm going to out-pass the shit out of him this week.

By my eighth trip up the bleachers, my head pounding has calmed. Unfortunately, nausea has taken its place. Spitting every few steps, my mouth waters with the worst acidic bile that keeps reminding me of my poor decisions. I literally will my body back down the bleachers for my final set before falling palms first into the grass and heaving vomit in front of me.

My stomach instantly feels better, but the rest of my body pays the price. The headache comes roaring back, and my chest burns. I spit at the ground while panting, eventually mustering the strength to stand. I don't know how I'm going to survive this, but I have to somehow pull off the performance of my life while feeling the self-inflicted effects of a life-threatening virus.

I'm pouring sweat, which is unusual for me, so I pull my shirt up, slipping my arms out and letting it hang around my neck while I cool down in wide circles with my hands folded on top of my head. I would do anything to get air into my lungs faster, but I'm pretty sure I'm pulling out all the stops with this. Once my pulse slows, I head toward the water station and flip the switch to turn on the pressure. I bend forward and douse my face, neck, and head, both wincing and rejoicing at the cold water.

I let out a growl to get myself amped, then march back into the field house. I twist my shirt around and slip my arms back through on my way into the weight room, which is now buzzing with music, the clanking of weights, and the voices of my teammates.

Grabbing my bag on my way in, I head toward the back corner to again fill my bottle with cold water. My body is both craving and refusing the idea of taking in more liquid, but I'm going to be super dehydrated if I don't start chugging. I'm pretty sure I'm done throwing up. I'm also fairly certain I look like hell.

"Someone's hungover," Theo utters at my back. I'd laugh in response but nothing about how I feel is funny right now.

"How are you fine?" I glance over my shoulder and note

his perfectly clear eyes, wide-awake expression, and the pink color in his cheeks. *Asshole.*

"I didn't drink much. I didn't see you all night, though. What, did you find a dark corner and drink alone like a bum?" He elbows my bicep.

"Something like that," I mutter before bringing my bottle to my mouth and chugging down several large gulps. My stomach turns as the water fills it, but I push through, fighting the urge to throw up again. I won't do that here. I refuse.

I run my sleeve over my mouth and flip my water bottle closed, setting it by my bag on the floor and meeting Theo and Cameron at the squat rack.

"We got our first sets in. You're up," Cameron says, patting the weight he's already loaded with one palm.

"Right. Let's do this," I say, settling into position while the guys flank my sides to spot me as I move the weight away from the bars so I can begin.

"Kind of a pussy amount there, isn't it, Fuentes?"

My jaw grows rigid at the sound of Toby's voice at my back.

"Go play with your blocks in the corner where your daddy can see you," Cameron spits back at him.

Toby's breathy laugh fades as he leaves behind me and I turn my head to the right and meet Cameron's stare.

"I got your back. I hate that guy," he says.

"Thanks," I grunt out, the weight growing heavier on my shoulders.

I return my focus to the whiteboard in front of me, my dad's scribbled writing filling the space with our workout plan for the day. I should have left with him this morning. I should have been ready before he was today. I failed, and I can't let that happen again.

"Six," Theo says to my left as I push my way toward my

first set of ten. The weight is easy for me, but every time I exert myself, my veins swell and my body wants to curl up and die. I swear my head is going to pop off my neck before this morning is done.

Somehow, I manage to get through the full workout without a single cheat. While being late by not being early is my dad's second edict, cutting corners when it comes to putting in the work is his first.

"Nobody gets ahead by half-assing," he always says.

He's right.

I gather my things and get ready to hit the showers, eying my dad and Mr. Sullivan talking by the doorway while the rest of the team exits. My dad's laughter isn't genuine. I've heard him put on the polite and political act before.

As soon as Mr. Sullivan leaves, I hoist my bag up to my shoulder and head toward the exit. I'm stopped, though, by my father's palm planted firmly on the center of my chest. My eyes flash to meet his, and if I wasn't sick already, I most definitely am now. There are plenty of things my dad can say with only his eyes, but his complete and utter disappointment is the expression that stings the most. I don't get hit with the squinted eyes and hard-lined mouth often, but when I do, I instantly revert to that feeling of being a fourth-grade troublemaker waiting for my dad to pick me up at the school front office. Back then, I got caught throwing wet paper towels up onto the ceiling of the boys' bathroom. Now, I fear I'm being scolded for throwing away my future.

"What the fuck are you doing?" He doesn't mince words. Probably for the best.

I swallow hard, my throat dry from throwing up an hour ago despite the gallon of water I've forced down.

My dad tucks his chin, almost as if he's unable to look me

in the eyes, and that act stings more than his words. His voice low, he grumbles out his frustration.

"You're drunk. Or you *were* drunk. And that man and his son were waiting for me to arrive this morning. They are making a statement, and those actions are going to feed into every argument I have no doubt they will make when it comes time for me to start someone."

"I'm the better quarterback," I spit back. My dad's gaze flashes up and the fire in his eyes scorches mine.

"That may very well be. But that's not enough in a place like this."

His jaw flexes as his brow lifts a tick to drill his point home. I hold his silent stare for a few long seconds finally swallowing down my pride.

"Yes, sir," I say with a nod.

His hand falls from my chest and I nod to him once before moving through the door and into the locker room. I shove my things into my locker and strip my clothes into a sweat-soaked pile that I shove into the space left at the bottom. I grab a towel from the equipment room counter and sling it over my shoulder before taking my angry body into the shower room.

I tug the frosted glass door open and breathe in the steam from the dozens of stalls all pouring out searing hot water. It feels good, but too long in here and I'll be passed out on the floor.

I head toward the back where a few open stalls remain, but before I get there, Toby steps around the wall of the next stall to walk right at me. Our eyes locked in this truly stupid game of chicken, my fists clenched at my sides with the growing temptation to punch him in the jaw. I don't even know this dude, other than the few practices we've had and the team meeting he had with my dad in our apartment. I got a good sense of his cockiness then, and I am sympathetic to his feeling threatened. I didn't come here to replace someone, but that is an unfortunate consequence.

Distance closing between us, we both shift our focus, no longer staring into each other's eyes. I brace myself for him to call me more names as we pass. If that's what he needs to do to feel better, I can let that fly. But he will never outwork me. There will be no repeats of today. Ever.

I hold my breath as our shoulders meet, mentally guarding myself for whatever insult is at the tip of his tongue. But when my feet are suddenly swept out from under me, I fly forward, feet scrambling to hold on to the slick tiled floor to no avail. My knees come down first—hard—followed by my palms, and eventually, my face. My nose stings from its quick introduction to the beehive pattern on the floor and my lip feels swollen from where my teeth bit into it.

"What the fuck!" I bark, twisting my naked body on the floor and looking up in time to catch Toby laughing at me over his shoulder while he walks away. I scramble to my feet, ready to rush him, but Cameron shoves a wadded-up towel into my chest, pushing me back a few steps.

"Don't react to him. Don't give him that," he cautions, and though his face is close to mine, I look right through him, my eyes lasers on the back of Toby's fucking head.

I breathe through gritted teeth until the door falls closed behind Toby, then blink my focus to Cameron's serious gaze. His brows inch up as he pushes the towel into me once more, likely in an attempt to shake me out of my rage. I slap his hand away and grab the towel, which I realize is the one I lost during my fall. Our eyes meet once more before I huff out a breath and spin toward the back of the shower room and duck into the final stall on the right.

I twist the faucet and plant my hands firmly on the tiled

wall, letting the spray sting my face. My mouth opens to take in the burn of the water, and I let it fill my cheeks several times before finally dropping my chin and letting the water blast the back of my neck.

My dad's right. No more fucking around. Zero distractions. It's football and class and nothing else.

Chapter 5

Morgan

G ames.

That's what James was playing at the party the other night. I recognized it. I've played them myself, and I indulged again. There's nothing wrong with being young and having a good time, flirting with the cute boy, and maybe feeling sexy about it. But that high doesn't last as long as it used to—the way it did before I learned intimately how cold and cruel and rare and precious life is. And how fast the wrong kind of attention can make you feel ugly and alone.

Anika and I both liked to play games. She was always willing to sneak into nearby college frat parties with me and indulge in the free beer and cute older guys. We were each other's wing woman, complete with test strips for our drinks and safe words to make sure we always got out of the parties together. Only once did I decide to stay on my own. I was seventeen and the guy was an eighteen-year-old college freshman. He and I ended up dating for almost a month before I broke it off because the social media comments on every photo of the two of us together started to chip away at me. I swear half of the people following my accounts are simply there to hate on things.

If only those people could comment on the morally gray things my father has done.

Anika was the only person who knew my full truth. She's the only person I trusted sharing about my late-night talks with Coach Wallace. She was glad I had someone to confide in other than her, someone who could do something if they had to. I ate dinner at his table many nights, the same table James and his family eat at now. It was me and Brennan Wallace's two girls, who he let me babysit sometimes when he had to travel with the team for away games. I loved those girls; they were like little sisters to me. He was like a father.

Coach Wallace listened. And I knew he would never tell anyone unless I told him it was okay. And he never has. Still, after everything that happened to him because of holding my secrets, I don't believe he's told a soul.

Somehow, though, my father knew I had been confiding in him. Perhaps it's his good business sense. Or maybe that's simply how Christopher Bentley quells his paranoia—by wiping out all possible triggers. Whatever the motivation, my dad detected I may have been spilling what he considers family business to an outsider, and he made sure he knocked over all the chess pieces.

I should have stopped playing games a long time ago. And I should have known better when I played them with James. Games never go anywhere. They finish with a winner and a loser. And it's pretty clear from where I sit, across the table from James, who has yet to say a word to me since the first party five days ago, that this time I am the loser.

"You're staring," Brooklyn whispers at my side.

I unclench my teeth from the straw of my smoothie and set my drink on the table.

"I know," I admit.

I won't pretend with Brooklyn. She knows me too well, even if she doesn't know everything.

"Lily and James are not a thing. She promises. *I* promise. We've all gone over this, the three of us, in detail." She's trying to quell my jealous streak, but it's too far gone.

"And James? Does he know they are not a thing?" I lift a brow as I meet her gaze.

Games.

"I don't know James," she says.

"That's a get-out-of-jail-free card kind of answer. You can't say that. It's meaningless," I retort. I grab my smoothie again and return to biting on the end of the straw. I don't want any more of it, but I need something to do with my mouth, so I don't say stuff I'll regret. "Why do I even care?" I mumble around the straw.

"Because he's nice and he's really pretty to look at," Brooklyn hums.

I sigh, then my lips close around the straw while I attempt to suck fruit juice through the mauled plastic.

Nice.

Nice guy.

Is that what this is about? Am I simply desperate to know what it's like to date someone kind? To get attention from a good guy? To not be treated like an object, a sponsorship tool, a bargaining chip for my father's company?

My phone buzzes against my thigh as everyone clears out from our lunch table, and I know it's my mom before I look.

"You are coming with us tonight. We all need a trip to the mall," Brooklyn says, hugging me in the middle of the lunch room.

"Fine," I huff. "But I get to tell Lily what to buy."

Brooklyn releases me from her embrace and smiles at me with her perfect red lips.

"Don't gloat. I'm going," I say, play-pushing her away.

She laughs, then skips off toward her class in her black heels that slap against the tiled floor like tap shoes. Part of me is looking forward to a trip to the mall with everyone. It sounds normal, and it's been months since I've done something that felt that way. We promised to help Lily pick out new clothes for her magazine internship, and I do like to be in charge of a makeover. Besides, I can pick up a new outfit for breakfast tomorrow morning with my mom. I'm sure that's what her message is about. I cradle my phone now that I'm finally alone and read while heading to my fourth hour class.

MOM: *We're booked at the bistro at 8 a.m. Please dress like a lady.*

My eyes flutter at both the thought of waking up that early on a Saturday and my mom's passive aggressive tone in text. She's never been a fan of my style. My designer tastes don't match hers, which consist of chunky yellow-gold jewelry and brightly colored pant suits. It doesn't help that there are nearly forty years between the two of us. I'm often reminded by both of my parents what a "surprise" I was. What they mean by that is *accident*. My mom got pregnant with me at thirty-nine, and when she had the C-section delivery, my father was in Silicon Valley inking a tech investment deal—and discovering the seven-year-old son he had from an affair years before. Braden's my half-brother, and he now has an executive title with the company. My father gave it to him the day he graduated from UCLA with straight Bs and a case of chlamydia from a hooker my dad bought for him for his recent birthday.

Executive Officer Braden Bentley is actually a nice guy,

which is why I don't hate him for being the chosen one. Besides, it's easier to hold on to the grudge with my father. Especially when the only thing he thinks I'm good for is breakfast dates with the sons of potential business mergers.

I type a response to my mom.

ME: *I'll iron my best pant suit.*

She knows I'm kidding, and I'm sure she's rolling her eyes and calling me any number of names under her breath. But the fact is, I'll be awake and ready for breakfast tomorrow, and I'll wear something nice that will impress whomever it is my dad is saddling her with to meet me. She never said it in her previous texts, but I know it won't be me and her dining alone. It never is. In our family, we don't do things because we're close and like each other. We do things because they're strategic. And I am my father's favorite chess piece.

* * *

I should be elated for Lily. She and Theo had a major breakthrough. Basically, they finally both quit pretending they weren't mad for each other. Seeing them kiss was like watching the end of a really great rom-com. And Lily looked great in the clothes we picked out. She left with Theo twenty minutes ago, and I could tell by the way they playfully touched one another as they exited the mall that they were excited to have some alone time.

This is the kind of stuff I live for—real-life romance working out. But something has me stuck. That jealous pang in my gut still cuts into my diaphragm with the same sharpness as before, which means this feeling? It has nothing to do with Lily and James. It's something more insidious. And I'm not quite certain what that is.

Brooklyn braved going into the sporting goods store with

Cameron and James, and I'm supposed to be finding that perfect outfit for breakfast with my mom and whomever I'll be entertaining for my dad tomorrow morning. I can't seem to find the energy to shop, though, which for me is definitely a symptom of something being wrong. I know accumulating material things brings about a temporary high, but I have always loved it anyway. The luster over new things is simply gone. Maybe it's not as exciting to shop when I'm not documenting it for the entire world to see on social media.

Or maybe my melancholy is directly tied to the two girls sitting across the mezzanine from me, their phones poised in such a way that it's obvious they are capturing video of me. I'm sure they're streaming that they've spotted me alone in a suburban mall. I also bet the comments are spectacularly insulting.

Awe, rich little loner.

This is what it's like to lose the spotlight.

I never liked her.

I'm so over Morgan Bentley.

Loser.

Bitch.

"You know, this is the second straw you have mangled today." The sound of James's voice injects a small dose of adrenaline in my chest.

A brief smile tugs at my lips as I let go of my grip on the straw in my lemonade. I set the Styrofoam cup down and twist in my chair, expecting to see all three of my friends loaded down with shopping bags and ready to head back to Welles. It's only James, though.

"You should see what these teeth can do to a pen cap," I joke.

His mouth twists.

"That's a gross habit, you know."

She's so gross.

I shrug and glance down at my now fidgeting hands.

"Yeah, you're right."

The food court is emptying out, the mall nearing closing time. The metal feet of a chair scrape across the floor as James pulls a seat from a different table and places it across from me. He leans forward, elbows on his knees and hands clasped, like a guidance counselor gearing up for a lecture.

"Why so glum? I thought shopping was sort of your thing?" He glances around us to the boutique storefronts.

"It was. Maybe it still is. I don't know." My mouth pulls in on one side, and on instinct I glance to the girls across the way, their phones still locked into position as they lean together and giggle. James follows my gaze then leans back, chuckling.

"You have fans," he says.

"I have haters. Trust me." I know the difference. Fans come over and ask to take photos or videos together. And nervous fans don't video for that long; they get their photo and send a text to their friends, then move on. These are digital creators who are going to get a lot of play off of my image. Or more accurately, *bashing* my image.

James grows quiet, and after several seconds I shift my gaze from my teenage critics back to him. He holds his thumbnail between his teeth, head tilted to one side as he studies me. A smirk plays at his lips.

"What?" My brow pulls in and my arms rush with goose bumps under his stare. This feeling is better than the other one—feeling sad and pathetic. But I'm still off my game and nervous.

"I don't know much about this social media shit other than the funny videos I pass around with my friends and

highlights from college football games and stuff, but it seems to me . . ."

He leans forward just then and grabs the base of my chair, pulling it toward him so our knees touch. A nervous laugh leaps from my chest, my yelp loud enough that it fills the food court area and draws a few more eyes our way.

"You get to control the narrative here," James finishes, lips drawn tight into a playful smile. "If they want to fill their feeds with videos of you, why not show them how great it is to be Morgan Bentley and not them?"

His eyes dazzle with his words, and the way he's looking at me hits me dead center in my chest. His hand moves toward my face, his fingers hooking a lock of hair and sweeping it behind my ear. His gaze slips past me to the girls who are now at my back, and while I'm drunk on his attention, I'm also very aware we have an audience. Only I don't care about them as much as I did a moment ago.

"Are they still looking?" I ask.

His smile grows deeper into his cheeks just before his tongue tastes the center of his lips. My focus is locked on his face, every nuance of his expression from the creases caused by his smile to the flutter of his dark lashes as his gaze tracks our audience.

"Oh, yeah." His words come out with a hint of arrogance and pride, and as his attention moves back to my face, his tongue takes another pass at his now parted lips. Without my permission, my tongue does the same, my lips numb from the fantasy of him grabbing my head and drawing me toward him for a kiss.

"How far do you think we should take this?" That's how my question comes out, but what I mean is how far are *you* willing to take this?

"You know what gets clicks and views more than I do.

What do people want to see?" His head leans to the right as his hands flirt with the frayed denim tears on my knees.

"Well, that . . ." I nod down to where his palms are now flat on my thighs. "Is probably something that has my haters gossiping."

"Gossip, huh?"

His hands inch higher, now gripping the tops of my thighs, his thumbs toying with the seams along the insides of my legs. Rather than pulling away, I relax, letting my knees part a few inches more. I'm not wearing underwear—I normally don't with low-riding pants—and the harsh material of my jeans pushes against my bare center. The lack of a barrier has my body overreacting to the slightest movement, and I'm dying to shift in my seat just a little to give myself some relief.

"People love a good story," I force out through a sigh. I'm doing my best to pretend I'm not completely spellbound by his touch. I'm putting on the act of being in complete control, as if I am the one driving this spectacle. Because in the before? I was always the one in charge. I knew when phone cameras were filming me, and I gave the exact show I wanted seen. This time, though? I'm an understudy. I'm getting schooled by my director. I'm completely clueless about what comes next.

James leans in closer, lifting one hand and running it through my hair again, but this time leaving his palm against my cheek and drawing me closer. A needy breath slips from my mouth, my lips growing fatter, my tongue humming with nervous energy and the want to be kissed. James's gaze blinks from my eyes to the world behind me as he urges me toward him until his mouth is nearly touching my ear. His weight on the palm still gripping my leg, I'm pinned to my seat, not that I would want to move from this spot if I had the chance.

"Hey, Morgan?" he breathes out.

"Yeah?" I whisper, my eyelids fluttering closed as literal electricity travels down my neck and spine into the pooling desire growing between my legs.

"Your haters are gone."

My eyes blink back awake, and my chest explodes with a panic-like feeling. It's strange, and the rush hits my skin down to my fingertips. Nobody is watching us. All of this was for nothing. I bet they left when I started to look happy. All they wanted was to fuel the conversation about what a miserable loser I am now. They missed the moment that someone was into me. They'll never know. Nobody will. And if nobody knows, was any of this real?

James presses his lips softly against my temple and I'm snapped back to the present, away from the intrusive thoughts tearing this moment down.

"They left a long time ago," he says softly against my cheek, our mouths inches apart, our gazes a mere head shift from locking. "I did that for me. And because I wanted to."

James leans back, our eyes meeting midway, the faint smile on his lips lingering in question. I think he wants to know if that was okay. If I wanted that, too. It's pretty clear I did, but again, I'm not used to guys who give a shit about what I want and don't want. I'm used to people who take.

"All right, kids! Who's ready?" Brooklyn's voice breaks through like thunder, and I wobble to my feet. My friend's eyes dash between where I was sitting and James, clearly noting the tight quarters we were keeping.

"Took you long enough," I say, faking frustration. In reality, I would be perfectly happy to sit here for hours in what I now realize is a completely empty food court. I would be okay with James simply running his fingertips along my bare kneecaps while whispering his literature homework into my ear.

"Sorry, someone wasn't satisfied smelling like a dozen cologne samples and apparently needed to spray his other wrist with about a dozen more." Brooklyn rolls her eyes toward Cameron who stretches his arm out toward me. I don't need to get closer to smell the musty scents emanating from his body.

"Dude, you're Ubering home. Either that or you ride on the roof racks." I wave my hand in front of my face to clear the rich odor from my path.

"Is that a thing? You have roof racks on that thing? Because I'm in," Cameron says. He's always been a little off and into daredevil shit. Part of me wants Brooklyn to give in to him and let him do it. His body is an allergy nightmare right now.

"I'm not getting a ticket because you're a dumbass," she says, shoving him away from her as he pretends to sulk.

"We'll put him up front and let him hang out the window," James says, suddenly at my side. The four of us head through the exit and into the parking lot, the crisp air nearly erasing every remnant of heat left from James's earlier touch. But before the last vestiges of physical proof leaves my body, his palm grazes the curve of my back, his touch growing firmer as we near Brooklyn's SUV, and he doesn't pull away until he ushers me into the back seat. He gives me one more dose of attention—a reminder that his attention feels nice, and that it's not about anyone but me.

Chapter 6

James

I don't think my dad has ever been waiting for me to come home from anywhere, not once in my entire eighteen years of life. Not even when I was ten and coming inside after playing football with the boys under the yellow glow of the streetlights until the neighbors shouted at us for making too much noise.

Trust was always there.

And I did my fair share of testing his trust. There were keg parties by the docks with the guys, and of course the time we decided to paint our chests with our school's crimson and navy colors and streak across our rival's soccer field during the girls' soccer season wearing nothing but our boxers. Even the nights I was out until the sun came up with my ex, Neveah, whom my father reminded me on the daily he did not care for, he still trusted me to be out on my own and make smart decisions. He said he believed mistakes were good for growth, reasons to learn, and the way I would be shaped into a man.

All of that makes his presence in the Welles student

parking lot at nine at night even stranger. It's clear by the way his arms are crossed and he's leaning against the tailgate of his truck that he's waiting for me. As we pass, he pushes away from his vehicle and takes methodical strides towards Brooklyn's parking space.

"Oooooh, you're about to be grounded, daddy's boy!" Cameron twists in his seat to tease me around the head rest. I smack the leather back and make him flinch.

"Hey, relax, man. I was kidding," he says, his hands up by his head, fingers flared. I can feel the heat of everyone's stares on me in the car, and Morgan's body recoiled a little in my periphery. I look like a hothead.

"Sorry. It's just that . . . something must be wrong. This is weird for him," I say, my hand on the door handle. I exit before Brooklyn is fully parked and swing the door closed behind me, wanting to get to my dad before he gets too close to the rest of us. My pulse speeds up with my irrational thoughts that something's wrong with Mom.

"Good evening," my dad says as we close in on one another, his eyes over my shoulder toward my friends.

"Coach," Cameron responds.

"Hi, Mr. Fuentes," Brooklyn adds.

I turn in time to see Morgan smile shyly and offer a little wave in hello.

The five of us linger in the parking lot for a few seconds until my dad drops his hands into his pant pockets and he shuffles his feet in a clear indication that he'd like to talk to his son alone.

"I'll see you guys tomorrow. Cam—" I reach a fist toward Cameron, and he pounds the front of it with his own. "Game ready, buddy," I throw in.

"Yuh!" he grunts, slapping his chest like Tarzan.

"Keep that fire, Cameron. I like it!" my dad says, pointing to him with approval.

I mimic my dad's posture, dropping my own hands into the front pockets of my jeans, pushing my fists down as I lock my elbows and scrunch my shoulders in an effort to kick off this heavy feeling suddenly weighing on them. Morgan is the last to turn around as my friends walk away, offering a small scrunch of a wave down by her hips where her pinky fingers are now looped in her pockets. She mouths *bye* and I do the same, my insides swirling with the aftereffects of earlier.

"Please say you all were not out breaking school code and drinking again," my dad says, his focus still on my friends as they walk away. I turn to face him and wait until our eyes are square because I want him to look into my clear eyes and apologize for assuming the worst.

"We went to the mall." My voice is flat.

He doesn't give an inch, instead meeting my stare with his own.

"Good. Because you have eyes on you, and if you pull anything like you did earlier this week, I won't be able to help you." His tone is flatter than mine. It's enough to kill the few remaining butterflies in my chest from my evening with Morgan.

"I'm guessing that's why you're stalking me in the parking lot?" I lift a brow.

My dad spins on his heels and nudges his head for me to follow as he heads back toward his pickup truck. His hands are still in his pockets, his body stiff, and muscles in that ready flex, as though he's anticipating a fight. I've seen him like this at practice, usually when our team was on a losing streak, and he was trying to keep his temper in check.

As he pulls the driver's side door open I take the hint and move to the passenger side. We both climb in and close the doors. My dad fires up the engine, backing us out while I buckle up and he does the same.

"Where are we going?" I ask.

"Away from here. Your mom needs eggs."

He scans our surroundings and checks his mirrors as he pulls onto the main road. I'm pretty sure there are two dozen eggs in the refrigerator at the apartment. This trip suddenly puts me more on edge.

"You'll be splitting time with Toby tomorrow," he finally lets out.

My jaw locks at the news and I blink my gaze from his profile to the empty roadway ahead.

"Is this *your* decision?" I know it's not, and his silence is the only confirmation I need.

"This place isn't like Public, son. There are games going on here that I don't understand, and frankly, your mom and I don't have the money or clout to compete in them. But Saturday—Saturday there will be a lot of important people in attendance. And if you can show the glaring difference between this team with you taking those snaps versus Toby, I think we'll be all right."

"You think," I repeat, a hint of skepticism showing in my voice. I laugh silently and turn to look out the passenger window.

Un-fucking-believable.

"He'll lose the game for us. You know that, right? He's terrible. He's a joke, Dad!" I turn back to face him as he pulls up to the stop light and he shifts in the driver's seat, leaning into the center console and hitting me with a serious, hard expression.

"I won't let that happen. Just do your job, and I'll do mine."

The red glare on his skin changes to green and he breaks

our stare, sitting upright again and pulling into the intersection.

Trust. That's still what it comes down to. I need to trust
him as much as I expect him to trust me. My dad's twice the
coach anyone has ever let him be. He's never had the pieces
to be truly great. He doesn't have those pieces here, but I
believe in him, and I've seen the things he can do when
working with very little.

I don't know how he plans to give Toby plays that he can't
fuck up but still show his weaknesses, but I need to believe he
will. And I need to deliver on my end. I have to shine.

We pull into the grocery store parking lot and my dad
slows near the entrance.

"Your mom needs eggs," he says, leaning forward and
glancing beyond me out my window. I follow his gaze into the
store where I spot Headmaster Powell loading up a cart with
liquor. Whiskey, to be more exact. The same kind I swiped
from the alumni dining room a few days ago to supply our
little underground campus party.

"Yes, sir," I respond, my words quick and tainted with a
little shame. I leave the truck and let my dad park and wait
for me to buy eggs we don't need.

I know what this trip was really about. And I showed up
just in time for him to let me catch the headmaster in action.
While the head of Welles may not know why his whiskey
inventory is down a few bottles, someone does. And that
person is sitting in the truck cab right now.

Chapter 7

Morgan

My mom will be thrilled when she sees me. I'm wearing the black pinstripe pants with the fitted jacket she bought me for her New Year's soiree last year. I didn't wear it then—on protest—and it's not my style at all. But I figured I may as well walk into this breakfast with her on my side, and pant suits are the way to that woman's heart.

The bistro isn't far from Welles. Two stops away on the T. This early on a Saturday morning, the train is typically empty. But there's a college game in the city, so I get stuck standing for the few miles I hop on. That wouldn't be so bad, but I wore the heels my mom picked out for this outfit as well. I'm a size nine, which for whatever reason, my mother finds unladylike. I can't do anything about the size of my feet, but my mom insists on buying me eights as if somehow shoving my feet into a smaller size will make them shrink.

Blisters. That's the only outcome of her stubborn, passive-aggressive ways. Every time. Blisters.

I'm early to the bistro, but I expect my mom to be here. A

quick glance around the restaurant patio, though, clues me in that I'm the first to arrive. I'm not sure who is joining us, or how many will be in our party, so I eye the four-top near the window and by the heater. I'm about to ask for it when a man stands from a table on the other side of the window and waves emphatically.

"Miss Bentley?" A tall, slender woman with a hint of an Irish accent draws my attention to the hostess table to my right. I don't recognize her. She must be new since my last visit.

"Yes, that's me," I say.

"Your party is here, ma'am. Mr. Flannery is waiting for you."

I look back to the man, who is now standing by the chair across the table from his seat, holding it out for me, I presume. Two chairs. Not three. Not four. *Two.*

"I see him. Thank you," I say, biting my tongue and not questioning the hostess about who made this reservation, and whether there's any chance a Mrs. Ambrose Bentley will be joining us. My mom won't be. She was simply playing the part of Father's secretary.

Tucking my clutch under my arm, I lift my chin and march toward my apparent date for the morning. He's young, but still much older than I am. I'd put him at twenty-three, maybe.

"Hi," he practically shouts as I step up to our table. He shakes his head nervously, squeezing his eyes shut as he presses a tight fist to his forehead. "I meant, it's nice to meet you, Morgan."

He cracks an eyelid open and offers a sheepish grin before reaching his hand toward me.

"No worries," I excuse him. I tilt my head a hitch as we shake hands. "It's nice to meet you . . ."

I have no clue who he is, but I'm guessing by the way he's blinking and smiling that he thinks I do. It gets awkward after a few seconds when I don't say his name, and he chuckles.

"Wow, this is not a blind date, is it?" We're still shaking hands as it dawns on him, and as my eyes flit to his grip, he lets go and instantly shoves both hands deep into the pockets of his dress pants as he lifts his shoulders to his ears with a wince.

"It is not, but . . . I think we should enjoy breakfast. And it *will* be going on my father's tab, so please feel free to order literally anything." I pull my seat out before my date—whose name I still don't know—can reach my chair, and he's left with one hand stretched toward my chair by the time I'm sitting.

"I'm failing left and right, aren't I?" he says, loosening his tie and taking his own seat across from me.

"You were set up to fail, so don't take it hard. Though, I *still* don't know your name. Unless I should stick with Mr. Flannery?" I scan the menu, then glance up as he chuckles.

"You're right. Sorry. I'm Paul."

"Well, nice to meet you, Paul," I offer, keeping it pleasant. My father has put me in worse situations. The last out-of-town guests he asked me to entertain pulled back the curtain on a lot of longstanding issues between my father and me—namely, how he sees me as an instrument to getting what he wants.

And when I needed a father to defend my honor, all I got was a man chalking things up to "locker room behavior."

"May I take your drink orders?" Our waiter is a fresh face too. This is a favorite spot of my mom and I, to the point that I have a decent handle on the staff, knowing most by name. I haven't been here since last spring, though, and apparently I've missed some of the service turnover.

Let's see if this new guy has gotten the memo about me. I lean forward to get his name to up my charm.

"Jensen, I'd love a strawberry mimosa. In fact, make it two. Mr. Flannery is my guest, and he simply *has* to start his day with one of those." I level the poor kid, who's maybe only a couple of years older than me—probably the same age as Paul—with my most persuasive smile. I wore my pale pink lip color today, and for whatever reason, my confidence inches up ever so slightly when I wear this color.

"Oh, uh . . ." poor Jensen stutters.

"And we'll be charging this to my father," I add, knowing that's not *really* what has our waiter stuck. I'm not twenty-one, but Jensen isn't quite sure whether he should card me. Partly because I'm me, and most people around our age know I've been drinking my way through Boston's social scene for two-plus years. But also because my father owns the land beneath our feet and the walls around everything in this joint.

"We can go with tea or something else," Paul pipes in.

Aw, Paul. Not good with conflict.

"Oh, I don't know, I really had my heart set on the mimosa," I add.

Paul's cheeks are red, the flush from social anxiety only rivaled by poor Jensen's neck. I'm about to let them off the hook when dear old dad makes an appearance.

"You. You're new," my father bellows over my shoulder. I startle in my seat, but nobody notices. Probably because Paul is now stumbling to get on his feet in an effort to either run away or earn my father's respect, and Jensen . . . he's frozen solid.

"I started in May, um, sir?" Jensen's voice cracks with his words. I close my eyes and touch my index finger to the bridge of my nose in anticipation. Christopher Bentley has a great disdain for weak personalities.

"Why would you say that like a question? Who hired you?" My dad moves closer to our poor waiter before spinning on his feet to scan the restaurant, apparently searching for someone to come running in to haul Jensen away.

"I'm Abby's nephew, sir." Jensen clears his throat after his answer. He's practically leaning forward on his toes, as if he's dangling on a cliff's edge waiting for my father to simply push him off. But his answer must hold weight because instead of growing more irritable, my father tilts his head a tick, pulls his glasses down his nose and squints.

"Huh. You look nothing like her," my father says through a gravelly laugh. "Bring another chair over here."

My dad motions to the open dining area with few patrons, and Jensen rushes to a four top and quickly carries over a chair. As is his way, my father manages to make a major production of taking his seat and scooting closer to our table. There's the swinging of his jacket around the tall wooden back followed by the screech of the wooden legs along the polished concrete floor as my father hopscotches the chair forward under his weight. When he finally unfurls one of the rolled-up cloth napkins—*my* napkin, to be precise —he cranes his neck to see if our young, terrified waiter is still within earshot.

Jensen is standing two feet away.

My father snaps.

"Three mimosas. Go on." He waves and again, Jensen obeys. All I can do is laugh lightly and shake my head.

"You are a study in behavioral psychology, I swear. Why people continually perform for you when you treat them like golden retrievers, I will never know." I reach across the table and take Paul's napkin, knowing he's the weakest of the three at this table, and when Jensen returns with our drinks, Paul asks him for another place setting.

My dad fills the quiet with small talk about why he bought this property, and how the land rights were tricky, something about reverting to the original owner whom he sued on breach of contract between his father and the now deceased patriarch of the family he fully took advantage of.

What a proud legacy.

"I'm sorry, I'm confused. Why are you here?" Paul has finally hit the bullshit limit. I've seen it plenty of times. I've hit it myself. The only reason I'm hanging around is they truly do have an incredible mimosa. I lean back and sip at my drink, waiting for this all to play out. Paul will walk away shocked. I won't. I never do.

"Ah, your dad, Mickey Flannery. He's . . . sixty-percent owner of Molten Unlimited?" My dad knows this percentage to the decimal. He's toying with Paul.

"I don't know. I guess? Maybe?" Paul's stammered response is his tell. My dad swivels his head slowly until our eyes meet, and we both quirk a brow. Paul's not so innocent, and he knows that decimal, too.

All of this means that I, once again, am that fucking chess piece.

A faint, knowing smile hits my mouth. I hide my reaction against the lip of my glass, and when Paul's gaze clicks to mine, eyes wide and searching for help, I simply look away.

"You know, something's off with mine. Sit tight, Paul. All will be clear in minutes." My dad takes his mimosa in his hand as he steps away from our table. I follow him toward the bar with my gaze. He hadn't yet tasted his drink. He's making a move.

"What is this? Are you in on this?" Paul leans toward me,

his fist heavy on the soft white linens that drape over our table.

I take one more sip of my drink then lean forward, crossing my ankles under my chair and cursing these miserable shoes. I slide my glass forward and play with the stem, scratching the frosted glass with my long French-tipped nails. I look up through my long lashes and let the rage and disgust from years of being used just like this fuel my response.

"So, tell me, Paul. Are you one of my followers? I mean, you do know who I am. You did all along, which, to your credit, you never pretended you didn't." My tongue presses firmly inside my cheek while I await his response.

"Yeah. Of course I recognize you. We've been at the same parties. You're online all the time, and I've probably seen your videos and stuff. So what?" His sudden hostility is telling. My mouth twists into a subtle sneer. Paul isn't a nice guy deep down. I sense it.

"And my dad . . . I'm guessing he maybe mentioned that I was interested . . . in you. Meeting you, or getting to know you?"

Paul's tongue lodges in his teeth and his chest flinches with the sudden exhale that accompanies his realization.

"He mentioned you at the club when we were talking recently, yeah," Paul says.

I let my focus drop to the table and I chuckle under my breath.

"Son of a bitch," I utter under my breath.

"I'm sorry?" Paul cuts in.

I laugh a little bolder, then glance up to meet Paul's confused, pinched expression. He's fallen too many moves behind. So have I, but I'm still ahead of Paul.

I dab my napkin on my lips, then fold it next to my glass

on the table. It's hard to abandon two-thirds of a strawberry mimosa, but my stomach is suddenly sour.

"You've been played, Paul. Or rather, your father's been played. You are more like a pawn." The hairs on the back of my neck stand up, my instincts never failing. I spot the paparazzi across the street as I turn and glance out the window. At least Paul had the sense to get a seat inside. It won't matter much, but at least the glass will blur his shots a little.

Fucking zoom lenses.

I turn my back to Paul completely and head toward the bar on my way out of the bistro, my dad's back to everything he orchestrated. His jacket's still on the chair, which he conveniently pulled out of the frame when he left our table.

"If I'm a pawn, then who are you?" Paul says, catching my ear only a few steps away.

I pause and smirk to myself before glancing over my shoulder.

"I'm the queen. And the only reason I'm here is to protect the king." I speak loud enough for my father to hear my response.

I don't bother to stick around for my dad's check mate. I'll see it soon enough. Within hours, likely. It will read something like this: *Son of Molten heir caught sipping mimosas with social media star Morgan Bentley.*

The details aren't necessary for the buzz. Those will come from the followers who will pile on with comment after comment to fill in the rest of the story, the one they will make up based on the fabricated visual my father instigated for them. I'm used to being the high school girl out with older guys. But Paul is in for it. He's about to be the college grad trolling high school girls and plying them with alcohol. He's going to be an obsessed fan, the kind of guy who probably stalks young girls on social media. And his credibility is going to take a missile-sized blow.

I'm not sure what his father did to piss off mine, but it was enough to make him pull out his classic bag of tricks. From getting my mom to lure me to lining up his favorite loyal photographers for the proof, my dad really threw me all-in—right to the fucking wolves. I hope that decimal point was worth it, because I am never talking to my father again.

Chapter 8

James

I always thought Public High's field was shit. But it turns out when you've been pounding the same dirt and grass for a hundred years, the terrain gets a little rough. I was hoping my feet would get used to the Welles turf with practice, but somehow today—game day—it feels like this ground played host to a tractor rally the night before.

Maybe it's the lights. Rather, the *lack* of lights. Who plays football on a Saturday morning besides Pop Warner players?

I've been pacing in the locker room all morning. I got here early. A good hour before anyone, including Toby. Especially Toby.

Fuck Toby!

The locker room is overwhelmed with the sound of guys who are not taking this shit seriously, and it's pissing me off. I need them on my side out there, though, so I keep my mouth shut. My dad drags what looks like a fifty-year-old chalkboard into the center of the locker room and I take a knee on the floor, both to give our linemen room on the open benches and to set a leadership tone. Toby makes it hard to rise above the bullshit when he takes a knee next to me, his pads pushing into mine and knocking me off balance. I smash my molars together and catch my balance with a fist to the floor.

"Ooops," Toby mumbles at my left.

My mouth tightens into the kind of smile meant to hold in all the not nice things I've got to say.

"No problem," I grit out.

Glancing up, my eyes connect with my dad's serious glare for a brief second, just long enough for me to get the point —*keep my emotions in check.* I draw in a long breath and let my focus get fuzzy while I do my best to mentally block out the noise.

This should be an easy win. Augustine isn't known for their size, and the coach isn't experienced. He's only in his third year with the school, and from what my dad could tell from film, it seemed he relied a lot on a weak quarterback with zero running game. My only hope is I get enough time to show my versatility to everyone who matters. Never in a million years did I think I would need to prove my talent to a bunch of CEO's and hedge fund darlings. I wanted to come here because life at Public *maybe* meant a roster spot at a junior college or a crappy Division II school. And after that, I'd probably be working on the docks or at some sales job that put me behind a desk and on the phone for ten hours a day.

I want more than that for myself. I want to see Papa's legacy live on through my mother's talent and dreams. But damn, do I miss the guys at Public right now. I bet my dad does, too.

"They're slow to the hole, so that's where we need your power, Theo. *Theo?*" My dad snaps his fingers as his eyes widen, and I glance over my shoulder to catch Theo's rock-hard gaze on the back of one of our teammate's heads. I'm sure he has some issue with the guy—I think his name is Raskin? Theo has issues with a lot of people, which I won't fault him for. The dude has been through hell—a lot of people here have been through hell. I never met Anika, but I'm learning she was a sort of nucleus for peace. I remind myself to keep my focus on the game—on *my* game—and leading this team.

"Yes, sir. I'll be on it," Theo answers.

"All right then. Let's go get our first win. Break it down!" My dad pushes the ancient chalkboard out of the way, the wheels creaking as it struggles to glide over the rough floor.

"Bring it in!" I shout, getting to my feet.

Toby claps loudly at my side and my stomach tightens.

"Let's do this, guys!" he shouts, his deep voice ringing out, and more of the team responds.

I mentally work to calm the boil in my stomach that's growing up my chest. I recognize this burn. It's the pain of insecurity. I growl along with the rest of the team, but before I can count out for us to shout 'win,' Toby steps in and does the job.

He is not a threat. I am the quarterback for this team. I can get this done. Show them and they will follow.

We cluster as we jog through the cramped locker room hallway, breaking through the back exit of the field house where the Welles drumline waits to announce us taking the field. The snap of drumsticks against snares cuts through the air like hard rain, and the boom of bass drums being pounded rattles my chest. This is one thing that rings similar to Public. We always had a good crowd at games, even if we were mediocre compared to some of the other schools in our division. Our cheer and drumline were always there for us to run through and amp ourselves up. I let my mind morph the scene in front of me so it feels like home, convincing myself it's the same people I played in front of for years. It's just enough to ground me. I forget about Toby being next to me, and I let go of the silent competition happening between us. The only battle ahead is the one that's two hundred yards down this grassy hill, where a surprising number of people fill the stands.

Toby and I both lead the team through stretching. We clap everyone in for pre-game prayer, which thankfully neither of us has a right to give. That job is done by the school chaplain. I think if it weren't, there's a good chance Toby and I would be battling for who gets to say the most amens.

When my dad calls me in to run the first set of downs, I catch Toby's narrowed eyes staring me down behind his face mask, but I stop my invasive thoughts there, before I fall down the rabbit hole of wondering where Toby's father is and whose ear he's bending about my dad playing favorites.

Do your job, James.

I know the plays by heart. It's the same offense we ran at Public last year—fast, aggressive, and pass heavy. That's to lean into my strengths, and all I have to do to prove myself is execute.

I call the first two plays in the huddle so we don't waste time between downs. If I do this right, we'll march down this field ten yards at a time.

I take the first snap and fall back a few steps until I spot Cameron on the Augustine thirty-five-yard line. I drop a perfect side-armed pass into his hands. He fights for an extra six yards and my chest opens up with relief.

All right. We're doing this.

Then the fucking whistle chirping hits my ears. I scan to my right in time to see the head referee bending over to pick up his flag.

You have to be kidding me! Fucking holding?

I grab the sides of my helmet and turn away from my team to growl on my own. I don't know who failed at their job, but thanks to the holding call, we're now moving ten yards the wrong way. Basically, a net loss of twenty-six yards.

I glance to my right to catch my dad on the sidelines, and he rolls his fingers together in a quick sign to run it again and run it fast. I get our team to the line of scrimmage and start my count before the Augustine line knows what to do. I bank on catching them off-guard, this time faking the same pass and rushing for the down myself. I slide when I've made up most of the penalty and then some, but before I get to my feet, I see that fucking flag fly to my right again.

"Come on!" I shout, unable to mask my massive frustration.

This time, I see what's going on. Theo's going through something. I saw it brewing in the locker room, and the fact he brought his personal shit out on the field pisses me off. Back-to-back holding calls is unacceptable, and I let him know how I feel as we huddle for a new plan now that we need to go thirty yards.

My legs are primed to run, and while the best chance to gain yardage is to throw deep to Cameron, at this point I want to keep the ball in my own damn hands and run the full length of the field to take care of this on my own. I barely make it past the snap, though, before the flag comes out and Theo's called for offsides.

"Oh, fuck that!" he shouts, waving his hand at the ref. I close my eyes and choke down the angry bile rushing up my throat, knowing what's coming next.

"That's it! You're outta here!"

Thank God Cameron is there to march his ass off the field before we completely ruin any favor with this referee crew. I lock eyes with my dad for a breath, his mouth a hard line and eyebrows low, heavy with rage. My father has little patience for hot tempers. That's not to say he can't get worked up. He just has the emotional intelligence to know when it's safe to let it out and when it's not.

I do my best to regroup, but without Theo on the field, Cameron gets doubled-up and the only other passing option I have—Devin Williams—is nursing a bad hamstring. He probably shouldn't be on the field, but we don't exactly have the biggest roster, and Devin's as competitive as I am. I wish he was at a hundred percent. I could use his speed right now.

We're able to get close to the original line of scrimmage after three downs and are forced to punt, giving Augustine decent field position. I come off the field and push my helmet up so it balances on my forehead. My dad barks his version of a pep talk at me as I walk by—"Our defense will get that ball back for you!"—but his words are meaningless. The only thing I see is Toby throwing the ball to stay warm on the other side of the bench. I hate that I have to share the field with him today.

My mini session of self-doubt and irritation is broken up as Theo rushes into that Raskin guy he had issues with in the locker room, smashing the side of his face with a helmet then sending him tumbling backward into the Gatorade table. Orange liquid spills into the grass and tiny white cups roll across the track, some catching in the breeze and traveling all the way to the snack bar at the end of the stands.

The crowd is a strange type of silent, occasional *Ohs* mouthed in unison as two of my teammates beat the shit out of each other. I rush over with Cameron and my dad, along with a few of the other guys, and we manage to pull Theo and Raskin apart.

My dad has Theo by the waist, his forearm flexed and digging into his gut as my teammate struggles to break free.

When his arms and legs finally stop flailing, my dad lets go of his bear hug but spins Theo around so he is forced to look my father in the eyes. My dad orders him to the locker room, and as the seconds pass, Theo's body relaxes more and more. He's more willing to obey.

"He was talking shit about my sister," Theo croaks out. His shoulders heave, his breathing still echoing his emotions.

"I understand, Theo, and I'll deal with him. But this is not acceptable. This can't happen on my field, you hear me?" my dad says.

Theo nods and my father unfurls his fist where it clings to his jersey. Before my friend can amp himself up again, I step in to lead in a different way. I throw an arm over his shoulders and urge him to walk with me—away from everyone.

"He was talking shit about Anika . . . and Lily," Theo says, his voice raw. The hurt shows in his words. This was personal, and while I might not let things interrupt my work on the field, I can't exactly begrudge Theo for letting in the noise. His circumstances are different . . . elevated. *Tragic*.

"I know," I say, continuing our march forward.

"I fucking lost it," Theo finally relents.

"You did," I say, breathing out a short laugh. Lost it is an understatement. He went full MMA fighter on Raskin.

When we reach the top of the hill, I pause and let him finish cooling down. We're not so different. I let my emotions get the best of me in private, and sometimes I say things I regret. I can't even imagine how it felt for him to hear someone speak badly about his sister, and the fact Raskin did immediately puts him in my off-limits category. I don't need negative shit like that in my life, and if I have any say about it, his time on the field will be cut dramatically—assuming neither of them are kicked out of school after this.

Theo's breathing finally slows and he scans the stands, probably looking for Lily or his family. His eyes finally make it back to me and he flattens his palm on top of his head, weaving his fingers through his hair and gripping, tugging.

"Fuck!" he shouts. His body rocks with this new wave of pain. This is regret.

I place a hand on his shoulder and dip my chin so our eyes meet, coaxing him to hold on to my gaze.

"Hey, it's going to be okay. Everybody knows he had it comin'. It's going to be all right, dude. Just breathe." I try to keep him calm and present. I know grief, too. Maybe my journey wasn't as public or horrific, but it still hurt.

It still hurts.

His lips vibrate as his emotions shift again. Rage and regret have the ability to quickly turn into helplessness, and I think that's where Theo is headed. I would never point it out because I sense he would rather I didn't, but Theo's eyes are glossy and red. Whether he wants to or not, he's going to cry.

"Go dress out. Shower, or maybe go for a walk. Put some distance between this and you, for now. I promise, I've got your back." I move my hand to the back of his head, nearly cradling him as our eyes meet once more. He finally nods in agreement, and I pat him on the shoulder before turning to jog back to the field.

While I was playing therapist on top of the hill, we managed to get the ball back and Toby is currently getting his shot at showing what he can do. I wouldn't worry about his three-yards-at-a-time running game and shit passes if it weren't for the fact I literally almost led us back into the wrong end zone when I was in. I do my best to live by my own words, though, and I shout encouragement and move along the sidelines as our offense slowly chugs along, still heading the right direction, even if it's slowly.

I wince when Toby throws an interception, but clap loudly to pump up our defense, telling our guys to pick him up. I pat his back when he comes in and tell him it's all right as he heads for the water station. But when I'm finally on my own, I slip my helmet on and grin, ear to fucking ear. There is no way I'm not scoring the next time I touch that ball.

Despite the slow start to the game, the remaining minutes fly by, and while I manage to complete twenty-one passes with two in the end zone, Toby doesn't totally suck. He handles the running game and takes the ball in himself for our last touchdown. It's nothing impressive, and he basically gets pushed in with the help of our offensive line. But it's the last score of the game, and it's the one that sticks in memories.

I should be celebrating. I am on the outside, for now. The locker room is full and everyone in here is on the high of our big win. My dad's speech echoed my feelings. Nobody would know but me, but I sensed those things he was communicating behind his words. It was in his tone. The way he was guarded and told everyone not to get lazy and that we simply did what should have been done—we were the better team going in.

What he said to me without speaking, though, was that we should have won by more. *I* should have scored more. And if I can't get my so-called group of friends to snap out of acting like dicks out there, I'm going to lose this starting gig. That can't happen.

My father makes eyes at me as he passes through the locker room from his office, giving knuckles to a few of the guys on his way out. He lifts a brow at the last second, and I feel his message like a punch to the gut.

You gotta do better, son. Gotta do better. That's the message I get. I have zero doubts I'm wrong about it.

I spend extra time in the shower to avoid Toby and the guys who are clearly rallying on his behalf. None of this is about winning for them. It isn't about what's best for the team. This is about status and ego, and their guy is the one they want wearing the QB1 title because he's one of them.

Me? I'm an outsider. I've gone and made friends with people at this school who all stand out because of their own baggage. Most of it isn't their fault, though I'm not sure why Cameron feels the need to be high all the time. Theo's grieving, and he has so much to work through, and Lily and Brooklyn are processing a lot, too.

And then there's Morgan. I probably shouldn't have spent as much time looking for her in the stand as I did, but she's like this celestial phenomenon pulling me in. And even though there's a risk to getting too close, I can't fucking help it. I spotted her when Lily left her sitting alone so she could go after Theo. Brooklyn joined her after halftime, and every time I did anything remotely worthwhile on the field, my attention zoomed right to her for approval. For praise. For affection.

The locker room is empty by the time I drag my ass out of the shower. I take my time getting dressed at my locker, throwing my towel into the bin with angry zest, the same fire I put behind the fling I give to my locker door as I shut it. I shove the metal door so hard it fails to latch and flies back at me, catching my forearm.

"Ahhhhh!" I pound the door again with my fist, using my arm as a hammer, and my aggressive closing breaks off the pin that keeps my locker closed. I laugh quietly at how pathetic this entire scene is. I came here with one job, and it's a job I'm good at. Throwing a ball might be the only thing I'm good at. But talent doesn't matter here because the only thing my dad has to offer this place is his acceptance of the coaching title. They could fire him in a blink. Hell, they got rid of the last guy.

I slump down on the bench and drop my bag at my feet before running my palm over my face. I have to find my calm. I'm no good like this. Papa would be ashamed. He said ego was the devil's work, and I think he was right. And as if the devil himself were watching me now, something draws my gaze a few lockers to the right and up, to the name and number plates that flank every locker owned by someone. It's Toby's locker, and even though I know nobody gave him the right to put that plate up there, it still mocks me.

SULLIVAN

#17

QB1

I breathe out a small laugh and shake my head. It's a tin plate made in the school's shop class. Everyone has one. Mine says FUENTES #5. So what that he had someone make his special. It's sad that he needs that to feel good about himself. What's sadder, though, is that I want to rip it from his locker and destroy it.

My stomach twists with envy, and I mentally imagine cutting off the QB1 part and gluing it to my plate. When Toby confronts me, I'll step up in his face, towering over him by at least five inches. I'll make him feel small, and dress him down with shame. I'll let my worst instincts come out to play.

I've gotta get out of this room.

I'm about to get to my feet when the locker room door creaks open. I freeze, my fist tingling with the urge to fight. A large part of me wants it to be Toby walking in, and an even lower version of myself wants it to be his dad.

"Hello?" It's a female's voice. My hand flexes as I rid my arm of the desire to go to battle.

"It's just me. I'm almost done," I call out, figuring it's one of the ladies who collects the laundry after games.

"James?"

I freeze hearing my name. There's a raspiness to the voice, but I recognize the way Morgan's pitch goes up at the end of my name. She must have been screaming at the game. For me. She was screaming for me.

"Yeah, it's me. Come on in," I say, lowering myself back down to sit on the bench.

The sound of the door clicking shut is followed by the shuffle of sneakers against the concrete floor. I lean back and grip the bench between my legs as my eyes refuse to blink, afraid they'll miss the moment Morgan clears the corner and comes into view.

"Good game," she says the second her eyes meet mine.

I laugh silently to myself and tuck my chin.

"It was definitely interesting," I respond, shifting my gaze from my thighs to the glitter W painted on her cheek.

"You're very spirited," I say, gesturing toward her face.

Her mouth twists with the cutest smirk—part playful and maybe a little embarrassed. She pushes away from the wall she was half hiding behind and steps toward me. I sit up tall and move my palms to my thighs.

"I wasn't sure what your number was; otherwise, I'd have painted that on this cheek," she says, tapping the other side of her face.

"Maybe next time, assuming I'm not benched for Toby Sullivan," I huff out in a jaded laugh. I sneer for a brief second, ashamed of letting my bruised ego show in front of her.

"Toby Sullivan is an idiot. In the classroom, and on the

field. Even *I* know he's shit at football," she says, still making her way closer to me. When I realize she doesn't intend to stop, I rub my hands along my thighs and chew at the inside of my cheek while my dick swells underneath my joggers, which I wish were a bit thicker.

I nod as she approaches and push my tongue behind my teeth as my smile gives me away.

"He is fucking shit at football," I say, as if that's what I care about right now. I scratch at my chin as my gaze dips down to where the flare of her Welles skirt tickles her upper thighs. She's wearing those dark navy socks that stop just above her knee with her white canvas shoes, and her Welles sweatshirt is definitely not the kind they sell at the school bookstore. It's cut in half, high enough to expose her belly button and the silver ring piercing it.

"How does the country club feel about that little piece of hardware," I say, glancing up briefly before zeroing back in on her tummy. She's close enough to touch, and my fingers itch to reach forward and grab her hips.

"They don't see it. There's a lot of things I keep hidden from other people," she says, stepping between my knees and removing any of the doubts I had a few seconds ago.

Her hands land on my shoulders and I give in, moving mine to her hips. She smells like cotton candy, and specks of blue and orange glitter cover her body. I bite my lip as I stare at that damn belly button ring, my mouth watering with the strongest fucking desire to lick it. I scan up to the cut edge of her sweatshirt and swallow hard knowing if I were to lift it even the slightest bit I'd find what I think might be the most perfect tits ever made. Morgan steps in closer and my cock flexes when she reaches down and lifts my chin. There is no way she doesn't see the effect she is having on me, but I don't give a shit. She is literally the only thing on my mind right now, and I can't even remember why I was pissed off about winning a football game five minutes ago.

Her hair is pulled up high on her head, the ponytail curled into caramel waves, and her eyes are this bright green that are nearly impossible to look away from. She bites her candy pink lip and offers me a coy smile, which gives me the courage to run my hands down her skirt to the bare skin of her thighs. She shifts her weight and takes in a quick breath as my palms trail up her legs and follow the curves of her ass until the tips of my fingers reach the small lace triangle of her thong.

Fuck, do I want to see that.

"So, what kinds of things do you hide . . . under there?" I glance to her skirt then back up to her eyes and her smile grows a tiny bit. I'm so hard I might bust through the seam of my pants.

"Why don't you look for yourself?" Morgan drags her knee then inner thigh over my leg until my hand is forced to slip away and make room for her to rest her foot on the bench next to me.

I glance up, my eyes heavy with the desire to rake over her most intimate parts just before I taste them. I can't believe this is fucking happening. Morgan's hands slide up my neck until she's stroking my jaw with her cool thumbs. She bends down enough to bring our mouths together and I suck in her bottom lip so hard it nearly snaps as it leaves my mouth.

"You taste fucking amazing," I say, giving in and pressing my lips to her bare stomach before glancing up and smirking. Both of my hands inch their way around her hips again, my thumbs flirting with the thread on her skin. So delicate. So easy to tear away.

Our moment comes to an abrupt halt with the sound of the locker room door creaking open then slamming closed.

The heavy clomp of shoes grows closer in a breath. My hands fall to my sides as I twist to straddle the bench, putting my back to Morgan who has moved to flatten her back against the locker. There's nowhere for her to go, and thank God I didn't rip her clothes off, making what someone is about to see blatantly obvious.

"Oh, hey."

Fucking hell, it's Toby.

My head bobs up and I swing my legs around, acting as if I just finished tying my laces.

"Hey, Toby. Man, great game today," I say, acting as if there is nothing wrong with Morgan waiting for me inside the men's locker room, only feet away from me, her skin flushed.

I hold out a fist, grateful that my dick deflated the moment panic set in. Toby leans toward me and pounds it but shifts his focus to Morgan for a beat, a knowing smirk playing at his smug mouth.

"Thanks. You, too. You, uh . . . need help getting dressed or something?" His smile slips into something more sinister as his eyes shift between Morgan and me, and I push down the urge to punch him in the center of his face.

"That's what I said! He was taking forever," Morgan says, crossing her ankles and folding her arms over her midriff as she feigns irritation. "He lost a bet, and he owes me a very expensive lunch."

Toby chews at the inside of his mouth, his superior expression lingering as he studies her, then me.

"Yep. I promised her three touchdowns, but I only got two," I say, a superior tinge to my tone. If we're going to make shit up to throw Toby off what was really going on, I may as well point out that I scored more than he did.

"Ah, well . . . maybe you should get her to count mine in

your favor too. I closed the deal for you," Toby responds. Prick played me right back.

"Nope. I said him and him alone. Next time, maybe," Morgan says, pushing away from the lockers and wrapping one of her curls around her finger. "I'll meet you outside."

I nod and utter, "Okay."

Morgan makes her escape, but my chest still burns with nervous poison, maybe even more now that Toby and I are alone. No way he bought any of that bullshit.

While Toby heads to his locker and pops it open, I gather my bag, glad it was already packed and that my locker was closed. I get to my feet and am about to tell him to enjoy his Saturday when he cuts me off before I utter a word.

"You should be careful there, Fuentes. With that?" He glances toward the exit, where Morgan just left.

"Yeah, okay," I say, unable to stop the roll of my eyes. I salute him and keep the Saturday well wishes to myself. But before I round the corner to head down the hallway to freedom, he dishes out one last piece of advice.

"Wouldn't want the headmaster to know you had a girl in here . . . alone. And I gotta say, if he knew it was *that* girl . . . *oof!* Let's just say Morgan Bentley is not an easy case to prove your innocence." He shrugs, then pushes his locker closed before slipping on his platinum watch that is definitely worth more than my pitiful college savings account.

I press my molars together and tighten my jaw, forcing my best version of a smile with what's left. My hand flexes around the straps of my bag, gripping with the force of a life-or-death tug-of-war. I should leave without speaking. I should turn around and simply go; nothing good will come of me being in this space with him for any longer.

"I hear she's a really good fuck, though, so . . . don't blame you there."

And that's it—I break. In a blink, I throw my own rules out the window, forget my dad's advice, and risk my entire future. I drop my bag to the ground and hurtle at Toby, flatting my palms to his chest until his back is pressed against the metal locker doors. I grip his shoulders hard and toy with the idea of wrapping one of my hands around his pencil-thin, pimple-scarred neck. I'm grounded enough to hold myself back from crossing that line, but I hurl back and throw a fist into the locker next to his head, denting it and busting my knuckles open. I leave it there, letting the blood pool on my fingers and stain the locker door.

Toby's fear flashes across his eyes as they widen, and his jaw tightens with his held breath. But just when I think I've scared him enough to stop playing this dangerous game, his body rumbles under my hold with quiet but menacing laughter. I push into him again before backing off, and he coughs at the feel of losing air from his lungs. But that fucking laugh keeps going. I hold his stare as I walk backward and pick up my bag, turning around the second it's in my grip and leaving before I make things worse.

Thankfully, Morgan isn't waiting for me outside. I want to make sure she's all right, and I'd love to take her to dinner for real—to laugh with her and kiss her again and touch her. But I have to go home and get my head right, then find a way to repair the damage I've done. My fantasy got soured in seconds, by a rich kid with zero talent but enough money to erase my hopes and dreams on a whim.

Chapter 9

Morgan

For about an hour, I thought James would show up at our dorm room and make good on my fake bet scenario. The more time that passed, the less weight I gave to indulging the fairytale and the more I let practical possibilities take over.

He'll check on me to make sure I'm okay and not in any trouble.

He'll thank me for helping get us out of that situation.

He'll text me and tell me it's probably not a good idea to visit him in the locker room again.

Any text. A message. Some sort of sign that we both still exist on the same planet.

The hour turned into four, then it was nighttime and I was spending it in my room alone while both of my roommates were out.

All hopes of sleeping in—maybe sleeping away an entire Sunday—are dashed with the fifteenth phone call from my mom. My voicemail is full, so she's taken to simply calling on repeat every ten minutes. I haven't blocked one of my parents since I was sixteen. It seems childish, but so does calling your daughter on repeat to force-feed her your bullshit apology.

I avoided looking at the fallout all day yesterday, but I'd rather see it for myself before someone around here whispers about it behind my back. I open one of the gossip apps first, my mentions in the thousands. My stomach sinks.

The first image I open is clearly the money shot. Paul Flannery was leaning in, our drinks in clear view, and he was making that face—that sad puppy face that guys get when they're around pretty girls. It's not what the story truly was, but it's the story I knew they would tell. And here it is, in viral digital view.

Is Molten Unlimited CEO's son Paul Flannery stepping out with social media darling Morgan Bentley? Eight years younger and a newly minted 18-year-old, the famous Bentley has been quiet on social media since losing a friend in a tragic car crash last spring. Does this mean she's resurfacing? Is this a budding romance? Or is this a power marriage brokered by her father—mega-mogul Christopher Bentley—and the beloved Boston Flannery family?

I flip through several posts to see more of the same. Some lean into the salacious, and the look is never good for Paul. He looks like a creeper who was waiting for me to come of age. I'm sure his PR people are already at work. That is, unless he struck that deal with my father, in which case my dad will have the stories and photos virtually zapped from extinction thanks to his sketch media connections. Every new story I click through makes my stomach get tighter until it's basically one enormous knot.

A year ago, I wouldn't be worried about the negative comments of being part of a paparazzi blast, but things are different this year. I haven't posted for myself in months, and this is only going to drive people to my personal accounts where they'll see people postulating about me.

Curiosity, and probably vanity, drive me right into my own accounts, but before I let myself fall too deep into the cesspool of new followers and trolls, I type in James Fuentes and instead lose myself in him. He posted before the game yesterday, and he has a dozen likes on the image of him flexing his right bicep in what looks like the locker room mirror. His expression is almost stoic, definitely serious. He takes his game seriously, which makes me wonder why he would waste his talent at a place like this. Welles isn't known for star athletes, unless they count chess and debate as sports.

Rather than wallow in my own pity party, where I have to deal with my phone buzzing with my mom's incessant co-dependency, I decide to take a rare and novel approach. I turn my phone off and toss it in my purse.

After a quick change into workout clothes, I grab my keys, ID card and nothing else and head to the field house gym. It's eight in the morning, which means the rest of campus is likely enjoying dreamland. *Lucky assholes.*

I expect to find an empty gym, but the clank of weights being snapped in place stops me with one foot inside the weight room door. I step in completely to see James positioning himself under the squat rack bar. His wrists are taped, and I wonder if it's so they don't snap under the weight.

I ease the door shut behind me so I can watch without him knowing. There's something beautiful about the way he's here alone putting in the work. And *real* work. Not easy weight amounts for the sake of bragging about reps. Nobody is here to document it, either. If my father weren't such a massive narcissist, I would love to introduce him to James. He'd love his work ethic. My dad might be heartless, but the man is always working—always scrapping for the next dollar, the next company to own, the next dominion to conquer.

It's clear by his soaked gray T-shirt that James has been in here for a while. His shoulders and back muscles flex under the cotton fabric as he lifts the bar from the rack and situates it on his shoulders, then sinks into a squat with a heavy exhale. His thighs bulge and fill out his shorts as he pushes up, lifting the bar like some superhero.

As he works through his set, I tread into the room and take a seat on a bench across the room. I pull my leg up and hug my knee, resting my chin on top to steady my breath and remain silent. The last thing I want to do is startle him, but I can't tear my eyes away. The thought that Toby is even in the same league as him is comical. If he wanted to, I think James could literally fold Toby in half.

After ten reps, James shuffles forward until the weight bar aligns with the pegs on the rack and he rests it there, ducking his head as he backs away, then spins around. I clap as he spots me and his head snaps up.

"Shit!" He jumps back and grabs the front of his soaked shirt, bunching the material over his heart. He laughs nervously as I get to my feet and move closer to him.

"I didn't want to interrupt. Seemed like a super bad idea to say hi while you were mid . . . *that.*" I motion to the weight that I quickly add up to somewhere in the four-hundred-pound range. I can barely lift the bar.

"Yeah, my spine thanks you for that," he says through a breathy laugh.

I sit on the bench next to his as he grabs a towel from his workout bag and runs it over his face. He hangs it over the bar before taking a seat across from me and stretching out his legs toward me. His quads and calves are still pumped from his lift, and I'm not even the slightest bit shy about staring at them.

"Hey, I'm sorry I ghosted you," he says, and I blink a few times before bringing my gaze up to his face. His head is tilted a hint and his lips form a tight, guilty smile. I'm a little thrown by his frankness. His apology is earnest; I can read it on his face. I'm not used to guys talking to me that way.

"It was a weird day. Don't sweat it," I say, my stomach twisting because I did sweat it. Still, who am I to him really? We barely know each other. There's some attraction, *clearly*, but other than the basic observational things, what do I know about him? Or him about me?

"I still should have messaged or something. I don't want you to think I'm the kind of guy who . . . ya know." His mouth twists on one side and he shirks his shoulders with what I think might be an embarrassed shrug.

"After I came on to you like a cougar at a BTS concert?" I respond.

My self-deprecating joke pulls a hard laugh from his chest, and he shakes his head. I can't help but warm a little at the memory. My skin still tingles where his hands smothered me, and there's a part of me that wants to pick up where we left off.

"I wouldn't exactly describe what happened like that. And I'm pretty sure I invited you into the locker room." He bites his bottom lip and leans his head to the other side. His eyes soften with the sweetest guilty haze.

And now I'm a little turned on *and* smitten.

"I promise. It's okay. *I'm* okay." I think I truly am, too, now that we've talked, and he's made that face.

"So, I know why *I'm* here at eight on a Sunday morning. But what wakes Morgan Bentley out of her beauty sleep to hang out in a place like this?" He stands as he questions me, moving around the bar to take the weights off. I step up to join him. I let him handle carrying them away, though, because no way I'm grunting my way across the floor while hugging a forty-five-pound plate.

"I, uh . . ." My mind runs through the many things going on in my life that keep me from feeling at peace, and the only way to finish my answer is with laughter and open palms. "Is it bad that I don't even know where to begin?"

He gives me a crooked smile.

"A little," he admits.

It is bad. And it's all getting so heavy.

We finish clearing weights from one end of the bar and James pauses before pulling the clip from the other side, instead hanging his arm over the bar and pinning me with his perfect hazel stare.

"Does this have something to do with mimosa-gate?" He squints one eye as if embarrassed to have to bring up something so ridiculous. Why is he even talking to me? Other girls at Welles don't have these types of problems.

"Mimosa-gate, huh? That's a good one. You should call the tabloids," I laugh out. I turn my attention to the pin and pull it from the bar, taking off the ten-pound weight, then leaving the heavier ones for him.

"I didn't mean anything by it," he says.

I wave him off.

"No, I know. And yeah, that's part of what's keeping me up. You know there's more to the story than a picture, right?" I plop back down on my bench and fold my legs up, holding on to my ankles.

"I do. Probably more than most." He gives me a tight smile before turning around to rerack one of the weights. His response intrigues me, and part of me wants to press him for

102

details. But I get the sense he would have said more if he felt ready.

"What's the story, then?" he asks as he moves back to the bar to remove another weight.

I breathe out a sigh and let my shoulders sag as my head falls back.

"I'm guessing it's a long one?" he chuckles.

"Let's see . . . it's about eighteen years and forty-seven days long." I grimace at my own words because it's true. My life's story is a twisted, miserable mess in many ways.

"Well, I've got about ten hours today. Why don't you get started?" he says over his shoulder as he takes away the final weight. When he's done, he walks back to his bench and steps over it to sit facing me. He clasps his hands together and leans forward, ready to listen.

"Wow." I lick my lips and raise my brow, not used to having *this* kind of attention. It feels intimate and frightening. My pulse echoes in my ear; I pucker my lips to draw in a slow breath in an effort to relax. James lifts a brow.

"I don't open up a lot," I say, glancing down to realize I'm rubbing my hands around my ankles. I leg go and shove my hands under my legs to lock them in place.

"Would it help if I interviewed you?"

A hard laugh leaves my chest and I cup my mouth, embarrassed at how it echoes around the empty gym.

"Come on, it'll be fun," James insists, rubbing his hands together and prepping his first question.

"Okay, yeah. Sure. Shoot," I say, doing my best to hide my racing pulse and near panic attack.

James scrunches his face in thought, acting the part of hard-hitting journalist as he holds his thumb against his pursed lips.

"Tell me about the mimosa," he utters.

My nerves ease when he moves to sit on the floor, leaning his back against the bench as he stretches his legs out and crosses the ankles. Somehow his relaxed state shifts mine.

"Ah, strawberry mimosas. Yeah, those are . . ." I make the chef's kiss motion and James hums out a quiet laugh.

"Where is this place? And how, may I ask, do they let you order mimosas?" He's starting me off with softballs, and I'm grateful. This is the easy stuff to share.

"It's called Met's Bistro, and it's only ten minutes from Welles. It's in this really cute cluster of historic buildings in Appleton, on the way into the city. My mom always loved the place, and my dad bought the building—well, the entire block of buildings, actually—for my mom as a gift."

"Wow, that's some gift!" James's features stiffen as his eyes widen. I suppose that does sound insane to anyone other than our family's circle of equally eccentric people.

"Yeah, I suppose it is. It was more of a bribe, really. Or hush money? Or maybe a *mea culpa*?"

James stares at me with a drawn-in brow.

"My dad cheated on my mom. That was his apology," I explain.

"Ah," James says, nodding as if he understands, and this fucked-up behavior makes sense. "So, that was, like, his version of flowers."

I punch out a laugh and cup my chin with my palm as I prop my elbow on my knee.

"Yeah, I guess so. Flowers, multi-million-dollar real-estate deal. Same thing," I joke.

"Totally," James says, letting a slight eyeroll slip through.

It gets quiet between us for a few seconds, and we take turns meeting each other's gaze then flitting it away. There's a sweet comfort settling in, and suddenly I feel less guarded, less ashamed.

"My dad and I, we . . . we're not like you and your dad," I begin.

"I mean, I would imagine, yeah," James says. "Like, we're both dudes."

We both laugh.

"Yes, there's that. But . . . that's not what I mean," I say.

Rather than probing me, James simply pulls one leg in and rests his folded arms on top as he angles his head to the side slightly, eyes soft and mouth closed in a faint smile—every bit of him ready to listen.

"My dad didn't want to be a father. I'm not sure he really wanted to be married, but it was the thing to do. He liked the look of a family man, I guess. And my mom came from money, which seemed like a good match. He was thirty when they got married; my mom was much younger. *Much* younger. She was a bauble he could parade around to parties and business events for attention. When I was born, *I* became the thing he got to show off and use to get his foot in any closed door. Being a family man made him look grounded, which he is anything but."

"How so?" James asks.

I rock where I sit, hugging my legs as I sigh.

"My dad's the epitome of a psychopath. He knows how to pretend to have emotions, but really? He's cold and unfeeling. He likes success, for himself. He speaks the language of dollars and commodities, and his worth is summed up by the things he's amassed in life. Family and things like that are dressing," I say, feeling the sting of that truth in my gut. I have to look away from James because the droop in his eyes is too much to take.

"Family's everything," he says, and my only instinct is to laugh once.

"I wouldn't know," I say, rolling my head along my folded arms until our eyes meet.

"So, how does that tie in with the mimosas?" he asks.

As easy as it's been to open up about my father, crossing this bridge feels hard. It cuts right to my broken heart.

"I always wanted to be noticed by my dad. When I was younger, like eight or nine? I wasn't the baby he could show off, or the cute toddler he would parade out for a quick visit before sending me off with my nanny.".

I shift and move to the floor so I'm on his level, and maybe in an effort to make myself smaller, as if it will make this secret safer to share. The gym is empty, but the space is still big. My words feel risky, like saying them will make him look at me differently. My palms sweat, so I rub them along my calves while I chew at my lips. He's being patient—quiet. He must sense that I'm struggling. When I glance up to meet his kind eyes, I can't help but mirror the faint smile he's wearing. I take in a slow, deep breath.

"When I started getting noticed on social media, like *really* noticed—"

"You mean famous," James cuts in.

I laugh and look down at my hands that I'm kneading in my lap. It's such a silly thing to be famous for. And I'm not *really* famous. I wouldn't consider myself on the level of actors and musicians. I take a decent selfie and know how to work a brand into giving me free shit.

"I kinda thought my dad would be impressed, I guess. From a business perspective?" I give him a sideways glance and he nods.

"You're brilliant at it . . . using those tools for influence? Brilliant." His admiration doesn't feel like hot air.

My mouth pulls in tight on one side for a reluctant half-smile.

"Thanks," I say. "My dad thought so too, only . . . I became a tool as well."

"How so?" he asks.

God, James is so gentle.

"I was fifteen the first time my dad left me alone with a group of much older men."

James shifts, and I let him come to terms with that statement before I share more. I'm sure he's thinking the worst thoughts, which, thankfully, the *worst* never has happened. But that doesn't make anything that has okay. And saying these things out loud is an enormous and terrifying step for me.

"It was at one of the new nightclubs downtown. It was part of a hotel deal my father partnered with, and the guys were investors. They wanted to meet me. By then, I'd been on MTV a few times and showed up in *People*. I was known beyond the digital app-obsessed generation, I guess. I was . . ."

"You were a pretty, young girl," James fills in.

My mouth snaps shut and my chest caves in at the truth of it all. His jawline flexes and he rubs his palms along his thighs, almost as if he's holding back some anger on my behalf.

I shake my head and blink nervously, dismissively.

"It was a long time ago," I say.

"Morgan," he hums my name.

The sound of his voice—his tone—cuts into my heart, and my eyes sting at the cold truth of my relationship with my father. I look to my side and run the sleeve of my sweatshirt over my watering eyes. I won't cry over this. It's done.

"It was mostly just taking photos with them," I begin explaining. I can't look James in the eyes because if I do I will stop wanting to share. I don't want him to see me the way my father does, and a twisted part of me has always felt that sharing how I feel will spread the disease, as if acknowledging the disfunction of my family diminishes me in everyone's eyes.

"Everyone had a cell phone and they all wanted to snap a photo of me with them as a memento. I'm sure I'm still carried around in their sim cards or clouds, this photo of a girl who looks older than her age draping herself against some man her father's age. I didn't get it. Or maybe I did but simply didn't care."

"Your dad was noticing you. You felt seen," James says.

"Yeah," I say, nearly smiling as I speak. He gets it. I still look away as I continue, but my shame fades a little.

"And the mimosa guy?" James leads. I think he's put the pieces together.

"He's the son of a guy my dad needs to bend a little. Not every photo of someone with me is used to make them feel good about themselves."

James pulls his mouth into a tight line and nods.

"To be fair, he hasn't used me for one of his ploys in a while. The last time before this did not go so well. Rich men can get a little . . . handsy."

"You mean be classless assholes," James adds.

I waggle my head.

"You're not wrong," I say.

I leave my description of the yacht party out of our conversation. James doesn't need the details, and honestly, just bringing it to the forefront of my mind makes my body shiver. The memory of my father's longtime lawyer trying to slip his hand down the back of my dress makes my skin crawl. I can still hear the sound of beads spilling on the ground when I jerked away from him, and his hand ripped the pearl string that held the back of my low-cut dress together. Probably ten thousand dollars' worth of pearls were lost to the floor of my father's boat, likely swept into the Atlantic Ocean when all was said and done. By the time I got off the boat, I had no intention of attempting to retrieve them. I had worn the dress on loan from an up-and-coming designer. I had my mom buy it outright . . . and then I burned it.

"So, what happens to mimosa man?" James asks.

"I'm sure mimosa man will be fine," I retort, a little defensive because truth be told, Paul Flannery isn't exactly innocent. He leapt at the chance to have breakfast with me, knowing *exactly* who I was.

"You're right," James relents.

His eyes settle on my face and rather than look away, I decide to stare back into them. His lips rest on the verge of opening to speak, but I sense he's not sure what to say. What is there to say? *I'm sorry.* What does he have to be sorry about?

"Your dad sounds like a fool," he finally says, and somehow, it's the right thing.

I let myself chuckle at the thought and smile faintly.

"I'm sorry to insult him, I know he's *your* dad and all, but really, calling it as I see it. The man's a fool," he reiterates.

The strangest feeling settles inside my chest, almost like a calmness but more tinged with a dose of confidence. Instead of reminding me that my looks are why I get attention and making me feel guilty for disliking it the way my mother always does, he focuses on my father. On his behavior.

"I think I really like talking to you, James."

We lock eyes for a few long seconds, and while his touch had me wound up for hours last night, his words have done something entirely more permanent to me now. I think he's changed me a little. I think I'm better.

"Good. I like listening to you," he finally says.

The longer we stare at one another, the harder it is to

keep our smiles tempered, and eventually the blush hits my cheeks with enough force to cause me to laugh and bury my face in my hands.

"Here, let me help you up," he says, getting to his own feet then reaching a hand down to me. Our hands lock, his grip tight on mine as he pulls me to my feet, and he doesn't let go for an extra second or two. The lingering touch is long enough to leave a mark, and long enough to still be happening when his father steps into the gym to join us.

James drops my hand when his dad walks in, and he backs up a few steps, rubbing his neck like a kid caught looking for his Christmas gifts. His dad glances between the two of us, and I tuck my hands under my arms, hugging myself. Imagine if he walked into the locker room and saw us last night.

"Dad, hi. Have you met Morgan?" James's gaze bounces between me and his dad, and rather than feel offended that he was so fast to rid himself of our physical connection, I'm more amused at his nervous, bashful side.

"I have not. Morgan, nice to meet you. Dave Fuentes," his dad says, shifting his stack of papers and clipboard under one arm before reaching to shake my hand with the other. I grip his hand tight, the way my father taught me.

"Nice to meet you, officially. Big fan," I say, glancing at James in my periphery in time to catch him laugh under his breath.

His dad tilts his head to the side, still shaking my hand as he pushes his tongue in his cheek. He's staring at me with a hint of a smile as if he's trying to work out what I'm all about.

"This is my sixth year at Welles," I explain. "I don't think we have ever won our home opener. So, yeah . . . big fan of your work."

James's dad's laugh sounds just like his—deep and gravelly, the kind that makes people turn their heads and wish they were in on the joke.

"Well, I appreciate that, Morgan. It's nice to have student buy-in. It helps the team." The similarities between father and son are uncanny, and as his dad lets go of my hand a brief flash of how similar the two of them are physically also crosses my mind. Coach Fuentes is incredibly handsome, and maybe only an inch or so shorter than his son. While not as built, his body is equally toned, and the sharp angles of his face are clearly the same ones passed down to James. Along with his hazel eyes. And if James is lucky, the slight peppering of gray on the sides of his head will come along too.

"Are you on the volleyball team, Morgan?"

I bust out a quick laugh at his dad's assumption.

"No, I'm pretty sure I would be a great disservice to the sport by simply being on the court," I say.

"Ah." He smiles.

"She was getting her workout in. Seems I'm not the only early weekend riser," James fills in. I let my mouth hang open as he works to explain my presence to his dad, and for the first time this morning, I feel the need to retreat. His dad is pleasant toward me, but I get the sense that he's not entirely glad I'm here.

"You have a lot of early mornings in your future. We have work to do," his dad says, stepping in close enough to grip his son's shoulder. Their eyes meet in a strange quiet agreement, and I realize that James has his own set of complications in his relationship. Healthier ones, for sure. But still . . . he has some expectations to live up to.

"James is incredible with the ball," I blurt out. My random decision to bolster James's ego in front of his dad draws both of their stares. I glance between both sets of wide eyes and frozen open-mouthed smiles.

"I mean at quarterbacking, is all. He's good at it. Like, way better than anyone we've ever had. Probably because of how hard he works. You should be proud, I mean. Of his work ethic. And I'm sure he will be here early every morning. And . . ." I'm starting to panic-speak and judging by the shocked stare still fixed on both Fuentes men's faces, I'm guessing I probably should have stopped after the word incredible.

"I pay Morgan to say nice things about me," James says, letting me off the hook. I exhale, hoping my relief isn't as apparent as it feels. I feel like an overblown balloon losing half its air.

"I did your dad for free," I say, leaning in to whisper.

And this time even my eyes bug out.

Shut up, Morgan.

"All right, well, I'm about done. James, enjoy the rest of your workout. Mr. Fuentes, it was very nice to meet you. I have homework to get to. You all . . . carry on." I flit my fingers at them both before turning around and clutching my keys to my chest. I don't turn around a single time, and when I get back to my room, I avoid my phone for a full hour. This time not for the missed calls from my mother but because if I have a message from James asking if I've lost my mind I will have to answer honestly.

"Yes. Apparently I have," I will say.

I give in when my roommates come home, and only because the absence of my phone will draw questions from them. When I see a DM from James, my stomach soaks with adrenaline and my fingers tingle.

Shit, shit, shit.

I open my messages while half-listening to Brooklyn talk

about her day with Cameron. I click on James's icon and hold my breath as I ready myself to read his message.

JAMES: *For being so famous on social media you sure know how to make a conversation awkward. LOL. Seriously, though, my dad said you were delightful. His word, not mine. I don't think you're delightful. I think you're incredible. I mean, not like as incredible as I am with the ball. You know, at quarterbacking, but . . .*

I'm smiling to myself as I read his ribbing message, and Brooklyn stops speaking when she notices me.

"Who are *you* chatting with?" she teases.

I hold my phone to my chest and meet her suspicious glare. It's harmless nosiness between roommates, and these are the kinds of things Brooklyn and I talked about all the time when Anika was around. But for some reason, I feel strangely protective over whatever this is with James. I don't want to share it, and maybe because I don't know what to call it. Or maybe I'm protecting myself before it goes away, the way the good stuff always does.

"Just a meme," I answer. She studies me for a beat but buys my response and goes right back into telling me about whatever Cameron did in the cafeteria this morning.

I prop my phone on my chest and send James a quick emoji of a middle finger. It takes him only seconds to respond. And the heart he sends in return literally flattens me.

Chapter 10

James

I could tell Morgan was embarrassed when she left. I could also tell my dad was not happy to see me in there alone with her. To make Morgan feel better, I messaged her and told her my dad enjoyed meeting her. And to soothe my dad's not-so-subtle lifted eyebrow glare through his office window after Morgan left, I stayed and put in another hour of cardio and lifting. On top of the hour of work I'd already put in.

My body is limp, my muscles dead. If I had to hang onto the edge of a cliff for dear life right now, I'd be kissing my dear life goodbye. I've got nothing left. My fingers are even spent.

My mom doesn't always work on Sundays, but sometimes if she takes on too many clients, she gets behind and has to go in to wrap up a quarter for someone. Because my father and I are basically helpless at feeding ourselves without her, or maybe because our taste buds are simply spoiled and unwilling to eat the bland shit we make on our own, she always leaves us with an ample serving of leftovers.

I pull out the chicken flautas she left wrapped in the fridge along with her detailed instructions, so I don't ruin them. I'm starving, but it's worth the extra time to heat up the oven. My mom's right. While I punch in three-hundred-fifty degrees on the setting, my dad comes home and proceeds to unwrap his own portion, ignoring my mom's best advice and nuking it for a minute thirty.

"They're gonna be gross," I warn.

My dad licks the dab of sauce from his fingertip after disposing of the tinfoil then looks at me.

"It's your mother's cooking. I could put it in a blender and warm it in the sun and it would still be amazing." He grins, proud of his point, but I stick to the plan. Crispy always wins when it comes to flautas.

I fill my gallon bottle with ice and move to the sink to add water as my dad waits impatiently for his spinning plate in the microwave. He's dumped his work bag and a pile of papers on the counter, and I start to flip through them.

"Don't touch my stuff," he scolds, his back to me. That eyes in the back of the head thing is real, I swear. Both of my parents have a knack for it.

"You working on next week's game plan?" I ask.

The microwave dings, and my dad pulls out his plate, rushing it to the counter when he burns his fingers.

"Damn it!" He licks the scalded skin and I bunch my lips and raise a brow when he looks at me.

"Yeah, yeah. I'm impatient. Sue me. I'm hungry," he grunts. His mood is unpleasant, and I can't help but think it has to do with two things—Toby's family, and finding me in the gym with Morgan.

"I was thinking, maybe I should hit up Theo and run some pass plays with him today, get some extra work in. I think he's fast enough for me to hit him deep, really show off my arm."

"Toby's starting Saturday," he interjects, giving me side eyes as he passes by and moves to the kitchen table.

"I'm sorry Dad, but what the fuck?"

His fist comes down like a hammer, rattling his fork against the plate and the plate against the tabletop. I don't respond for a few seconds but eventually utter 'sorry.' My dad doesn't see a reason for me to swear, ever. Though I would bet my left nut he's dropped plenty of F-bombs when it comes to Toby. He just keeps them away from my ears. *Sometimes.*

"Only the first set of downs. And if I give him the start, it keeps the illusion of balance. I can't show favoritism in any way, and you know that. Maybe if yesterday's game wasn't such a—"

"A clusterfu—"

He points a finger at me so I stop mid-word. He rolls his eyes, though, knowing I'm right. He pushes his food into an enormous bite then blows on the forkful before shoveling it in his mouth.

"I performed well. We were missing my main target, and that's not on me. It's on Theo, and Raskin. We've gotta fix this discord on the team, Dad. There has to be a way we can get people to quit working against one another." I flop down into the chair opposite of him and stare as he devours his lunch in record time.

"Theo's out for two games. Suspended. And no practice," my dad adds after his final bite.

"Come on!" I protest.

I lean forward and rub my temples. I'm half tempted to pull the plug on everything. At least if I went back to Public I might be able to petition to keep my full season, and I would be a star there, get a full ride to a state school. Yeah, I'd probably never reopen Delgado's in the same neighborhood it started in, but we could make something work.

"I'm working on Theo. I have a meeting with the headmaster in . . ." My dad checks his watch then stands quickly and moves his dish to the sink. "Shoot, like thirty minutes."

"Should I join you? Would it help?" I move into the kitchen behind him to check the status of my lunch. Maybe I should have sacrificed quality for speed. My stomach is continuously rumbling.

"I've got this one. And sadly, it will help that I'm starting Toby. There's this weird kinship thing going on with some of the longtime families here, and I have a feeling me showing some compassion toward the Sullivans will help my case to get Theo back faster," he says.

"And what about *my* case?" My ribs vibrate with the steady drum of my heart. It's pumping with the extra *umph* of a child about to throw a tantrum. Only, I'm a six-foot-two, eighteen-year-old child. And I'm willing to throw swings.

My dad fills a glass with water and gulps down nearly two thirds before pausing, resting it on the counter and turning his head toward me.

"You'll get in on Saturday. And when you do, you'll show what you can do. But if you really want to help your case, I think you need to think long and hard about who you sneak off with in the early morning hours."

He holds my stare, blinking slowly to accentuate his point, as if I need any help understanding what he means. My raging toddler heart starts to beat wildly, partly because my dad's accusation is way off target, but more so that he's insulting a young girl he knows zero about.

"I went to the gym. Early, because I knew that would

look good and because I am fully dedicated to this," I say, my words rigid and clipped.

"Fully dedicated," my dad echoes through a breathy laugh.

"Yeah, Dad. I am. And I can't control who else shows up while I'm working my ass off." My nostrils flare with my heavy breath.

"Indeed, you can't, son," he says, emptying his glass of the remaining water and running a towel around the rim before setting it to the side. Gripping the towel in his fist, he smacks it down on the counter then turns to face me. I flinch but stand my ground. My dad and I don't fight like this. Ever. And the way my senior year is unfolding is making me sick.

My parents went through a lot last year, and I only know part of the story. I'm sure if I sat them down and asked for the details, they would share. We're that kind of family—open and honest. At least, I thought we were. I was worried about my parents getting a divorce, and I know they went to counselling for an entire year. They never hid that from me. But the abrupt move here has always left me wondering if it was really for me or for them.

"Why do I feel like you're blaming me?" I know my dad has to get ready for this meeting, but I don't like leaving things up in the air between us. There's this fog rolling in and it's messing up our relationship. I want to clear it.

My dad exhales and looks down before moving closer and squaring his shoulders with mine. He looks up and rests a palm on my shoulder, looking up the two-inch difference into my eyes.

"I'm not blaming you, James. And I'm sorry I made you feel that way." He draws in a deep breath through his nose as he holds my stare, and I find myself doing the same in preparation for whatever's coming next.

"I want to give you your dreams. At the very least, your mom and I, we want you to have better than we had. It's the cycle of life for parents and their kids. It's only that this place is, well, challenging. I'm not used to this kind of politicking. And I'm sorry that I'm not adept at how to navigate it while maintaining my integrity."

I swallow down the lump in my throat. My dad's words remind me of the many reasons I've always idolized him. I want to live the way he does—by a code. And it's so hard to stick to that path, especially when you're young and surrounded by temptations.

It's not that my father is pious. I've seen him drunk plenty of times, and I've heard the stories about his college days and the girls he dated before he met Mom. But when it comes to the important stuff, to family and friendships and people in general? I want to follow his lead. His heart is always pure. Even now as he straddles the lines in an effort to help his son earn a starting position, he still wants to do right by Toby. And I guarantee that Toby and his father don't give a rat's ass about the ethical standards my father has. They make up their own rules, and maybe that's what's got him in the mood he's in. Still, it's admirable as hell to watch him fight so hard to stick to that line.

"I understand," I say, leaning in and wrapping my arm around his shoulders.

We hug briefly, pulling apart when the oven buzzes with the sound of my lunch finally being done. My dad heads into his room to change then comes back out while I'm about to dig into my first, perfectly reheated flauta.

"All right, so it does look better your way," he relents. He reaches over before I'm able to catch him and grabs an entire roll with his fingers, taking a bite and having to drop it back on my plate and run to the kitchen thanks to his burning mouth.

"When are you going to learn?" I laugh out.

I scoot the abandoned flauta back into the rest on my plate while my dad downs another glass of water. After, he gathers his pile of papers, some of which I'm guessing will help him prove his argument with the headmaster and get Theo's sentence reduced. He stops at the table next to me, though, and pulls a photocopy of something out of one of his folders, sliding it toward me.

"I'm not passing judgement on you or your choices. I'm only looking out for you and this family," he says.

I meet his gaze and unfold the paper before looking down to take it in. It's a string of social media comments in regard to Morgan Bentley, and my first instinct is to laugh, knowing it's probably from the whole mimosa shakedown she told me about this morning. But then a certain comment catches my eye.

Coach Wallace was quietly let go after spending a lot of nights with one very popular junior who we might all know from TikTok.

I read on, scanning quickly but taking in enough to get the gist of these comments.

"This is gossip, you know. And I thought we all talked about it as a family before we came here, Dad. That's what places like this thrive on," I say, a sour taste tainting my mouth, nonetheless.

"We did, and you're right. This is gossip," my father says, pushing the paper closer to me. I assume he wants me to take it and study it more closely. "But this is the gossip that follows that young lady you were spending time alone with this morning, and there's usually a reason at the root of stories like these."

I flit my eyes up to meet his warning expression, and my insides twist with conflict. I refuse to play into the ugliness that Morgan explained to me this morning. But I don't want to start new friction between me and my dad, not as he's about to head into an uncomfortable meeting to help another one of my friends, and ultimately me.

"I understand, and I will take it under advisement," I say, choosing my words carefully.

My dad's eyes squint a little as he considers my response, but I think it's hard for him to disrespect my wish to be fair and respectful. And I hope, just maybe, a small part of him believes that Morgan was unfairly judged—*is* unfairly judged.

"I'll let you know when you can throw passes to Theo. I won't have a final decision today, but you know me—I'm pretty good at reading people." His mouth pulls into a tight smile as he gathers his papers and heads across the room and ultimately out the door.

The moment he's gone, I look down at the sordid evidence from the court of public opinion and for the briefest moment consider bringing it up to Morgan or maybe one of our friends. Ultimately, though, I decide to set the page on fire and wash the embers down the sink because like my father, I'm a pretty good judge of character too. And I think maybe Morgan Bentley isn't a distraction but rather a complicated girl with a lot of good in her heart, and one I'd really like to get to know.

Chapter 11

Morgan

It turns out that picking a place to work because you like their cute name is not the best way to land on an internship. I was right in my hunch that Opal and Jayne were, in fact, real people. What I did not expect was that they were in their late sixties and heavy smokers.

The account list for their boutique company is impressive, but their creative is very dated. When I asked who designed the cute cards and branding they had at the tent on internship day at Welles, they explained that they bought it from a pre-made kit. I bet if I looked hard enough, or maybe not even hard at all, I'd find the same pink and green leafy design and clean font treatment being used for a dozen area businesses.

Shoot! I wonder if they've resold their premade creative to some of their clients?

The young hiring manager I interviewed with is only at the apartment office for the firm twice a week, and today was my day to complete paperwork with her. She's a sweet girl named Nora, and it turns out she's Opal's niece. Or maybe she's Jayne's? Regardless, she loves the ladies. I have to admit they're fun to be around, even if the apartment smells of stale smoke and vinegar. How they handle PR and marketing for some of Boston's biggest financial institutions baffles me, though I wouldn't be surprised if it was based on some very old friendships and contracts that date back to when Opal and Jayne were in their prime and working the club scene of their day.

Nora knew who I was, which is why I got the gig, and apparently all other interviews for the day were cancelled. This tiny company needs new life, and new clients. And I think Nora wouldn't mind becoming a full-time fixture. But to grow, they need to seriously look at their billing. And that might mean startling some very comfortable financial officers who have gotten used to pathetically undervalued billing statements.

I ended up learning so much from Nora when my paper-work was done that I started working on a business plan before I left. I missed the afternoon train back to campus, so I was left taking the seven p.m. one instead.

Late train trips never used to faze me, but my guard was significantly altered after my dad's lawyer tried to feel me up. Being in a fatal car crash also shifted my sense of safety. Ever since the accident, I've found myself giving in to the constant pull of worry and panic. It's one thing to be alert, but sometimes by the time I get through something as simple as a one-block walk down a well-lit street, I'm covered in sweat and my pulse is racing so fast I fear my heart may exit my body.

The streets on the outskirts of Boston are still busy enough when I leave, but the train itself is rather empty. Only a few people take up seats on the T—two of them homeless, and a third, a man on his own. He looks drunk, and his nice suit and tie do little to offset the angry scowl on his face that he seems to enjoy fixating on me.

I pull my phone from my purse and cross my legs, glad I wore flat boots today with sharp toes for kicking. I shoot a text off to my roommates and stare at my screen, anxious for them to respond. Lily is the first to reply, asking me what's up.

ME: *I'm coming in on the later train. Can you and Brooklyn meet me at the station?*

It's a little selfish to ask them to wait around there alone at night, but there's security at the station. And they would make the trip there together. Better yet, maybe Brooklyn would drive the one block to get me.

LILY: *I'm with Theo and about to get in the pool.*

I stare at her response for a few seconds, waiting for the *but*. It doesn't come. Finally, I write back.

ME: *No prob. I understand.*

Lily has fought hard to get herself back into the water after surviving our crash. Being a part of the swim team matters to her, and I think it might help her heal. And if Theo is encouraging her, that's a good sign for both of them. I can't fully take credit for this reconciliation, but I did promise Anika in my prayers that I would nurture it.

I wait a few more minutes, hopeful that Brooklyn will chime in and offer to come get me. When she doesn't, I call. Three rings and I get sent to voicemail.

Maybe she's busy.

Brooklyn works in the Mayor's Office, so late hours are common for her. I envy her serious side. If I could somehow find that in myself, I think people would understand what I'm capable of. There are those who get it—the people I influence. At least, the ones I *used* to influence. Social storytelling is powerful. But it's not for the faint of heart. And as tough as I thought I was, maybe I'm not tough enough.

Flipping to James's profile, I send him a message in hopes that he sees it. When he pings me back almost instantly, I bite down to hold in my smile. The stranger to my right whose angry eyes have only seemed to narrow more is still staring at me, which ratchets up my guard. The old me would have live streamed this train ride and flipped the camera around on him to show my followers where I was and what was happening. I knew people would have my back. Now, I'm afraid they'd root him on. All because I haven't engaged with anyone digitally for a while. People are fickle beasts.

ME: *I'm coming back late. Can you meet me at the station by Welles?*

JAMES: *On my way.*

His quick response warms my belly, but I hold my reaction in and instead keep my phone handy in case I need to make any emergency calls. As we close in on my stop, I gather my bag close to my chest and get to my feet, opting to stand near the door. I bend forward to peer out the window, recognizing the form of the guy leaning against one of the pillars while wearing black jogger sweats and a white T-shirt. He was working out, I bet.

As the T slows, Mr. Creeper leaves his seat and moves closer to me, not quite to the door, but not taking another seat either. I brace myself, ready to kick if I need to, then pull the handle on the door to sound off an alarm and race out of here. When the stranger reaches into the front breast pocket of his jacket, my breath hitches, and a shot of acid seers up my esophagus. But within seconds, he's holding his phone up and pointing the camera at me and talking.

"It's totally Morgan Bentley, guys. I've found her. Spotted! And she's not with some mystery CEO—she's still in high school!"

Fuck you! Jerk! Creepy loser!

Those responses flash through my mind, and months ago, they would have flown out of my mouth along with a swift middle finger and then a backlash of my fans descending on whoever this guy is. But now, I merely stare at him with my mouth agape and tears pricking at my eyes.

The train inches to a stop and the doors rush open, and I begin to step off but am quickly held then stepped around by James. He must have seen my reaction through the windows, or maybe he was watching this guy get closer as the train neared. Whatever prompted him to be suspicious, I'm relieved he's here. I'm equally terrified of the fallout from his actions.

"What the fuck is wrong with you? You like making women uncomfortable? Huh? You get off on that?" James lunges at the man a few times, each time scaring him back a few steps. But the guy keeps his phone going, along with his running commentary. If I could only pause the universe for a second, I would have warned him. This is how these things go. An entire industry is built on this type of conflict. People live for it, watching it from the comfort of their pajamas while they hide under their covers at night and mindlessly scroll.

Before the doors close, James slaps the creeper's hand and sends his phone sailing across the inside of the train before slipping out onto the platform with my wrist clasped in his grip.

He's breathing hard. I know the kind of shape he's in, so it must be the adrenaline coursing through his body. As the train pulls away, I jog alongside it, enjoying the view of the scumbag who filmed me scrambling around the floor in search of what I hope are pieces of his phone. I stop when the platform ends and fold my hands over my head while I catch my breath, watching the glow of the inside train lights fade as the tracks disappear through the woods.

"That's probably going viral, huh?"

I huff out a sharp laugh and turn to face James, who is also standing with his arms over his head.

"I mean, the end was pretty epic," I say.

He chuckles as he continues to pace in a large circle. I move closer to him, stopping to pick up my bag that I discarded before sprinting—well, sprinting for me—after the train.

"Thanks for meeting me," I say, my heartbeat somehow growing faster even though my body is at rest. James holds an arm out toward me, pulling me into a hug at the side of his body when I'm within reach.

"Pretty sure I'll be riding the train with you from now on." He gives me a little squeeze as we walk, and I expect his arm to fall away from my shoulder. Instead, he leaves it draped around my neck as we head toward campus.

"Isn't your internship somewhere else entirely?" I'm not even sure what James does for his.

"I'm working with my mom's accounting firm. She's more of a freelancer, really, but under a big umbrella company. She thought it would be good if I learned how to keep books if I want to eventually open a small business." He shrugs, but his answer is nothing like I expected. Maybe it's naïve, and a bit judgmental, to assume he'd be into sports or physical therapy or something like that, but business . . . I can identify with that. Maybe I can help.

"You know, business is kind of in my blood," I say, putting on a smooth tone as if I'm a real mover and shaker. I suppose in some ways I am.

James laughs, his body rumbling next to mine with the sound. I love the way it feels tucked under his arm, and the warmth of his body makes me bold enough to slip my arm around his back. He looks down at me as we walk when my fingers run along the back of his shirt and grip the other side to hold on.

"I don't think I'm quite cut out for Bentley-sized business. Besides, from what you told me, I don't think I'm good enough at chess." He grimaces and I reflect his expression, remembering my full voicemail and the several IGNOREs I pressed on my phone today when my mom called. We still haven't talked. I'll forgive her eventually; I can't help myself. I feel bad for her because as much as she puts herself in these manipulative situations with my father, where he coerces her to trick me into doing his dirty work, she also knows no other life. I think without the vapid drama that comes along with being Mrs. Christopher Bentley, my mom's identity is vague. *Undefined.*

"So, what kind of business, then?" I tug at his shirt when I ask, the playful touch earning another laugh from his chest.

He doesn't answer right away. I keep my eyes on him as we walk and as we near the dorms, he stops and moves to stand in front of me, looking down at me with a sheepish grin.

"You really wanna know about my silly dream?"

I tilt my head to the side and put on the puppy dog eyes.

"Are you kidding me? I love silly dreams! And I bet yours isn't so silly." My belly flutters with nervous energy as James shuffles his feet nervously and breathes out a shy laugh. He's like a little kid being asked his favorite questions—so excited to talk and no idea where to begin.

"You wanna . . . I don't know, come in? My mom's at the office late and Dad's offsite with the coaching staff. Not that I'm trying to get you alone, just . . ." He drags his palm over his face and peers at me through his open fingers. "I have this knack for not being able to say the right words around you."

"Uh, I'm pretty sure I'm the one who went on about you

being good at quarterbacking, so it seems we're both bad at the English language."

His palm slides away, revealing his smile.

"Ah, yeah. You're probably right there. You were pretty ridiculous," he teases.

I step into him and bump him with my hip, but before I slip away he captures me under his arm again and glances toward his family's apartment.

"Yeah, I'd like to hang out a while. My roommates are basically nowhere to be found, and I'm feeling a bit abandoned." I feel a lot abandoned, to be honest. Brooklyn and I have hardly talked, and while I know we're all busy and the start of the semester has been rigorous, talking was always our thing. This isn't how Anika wanted things to be.

"Well, I do like taking in feral cats," James says, pulling his keys from his pocket and unlocking the door.

He steps inside but I wait on the stoop, still processing what he said. When he realizes I haven't joined him, he spins around and nods his head to the side, silently inviting me in.

"I'm sorry, but did you compare me to a feral cat?" I hold my ground, not really mad, but kind of curious how he's going to answer this.

"Huh, yeah. I guess I did. I have a feeling you'd fight like one in a back alley, so it sort of works." He shrugs and lifts a brow. I step inside and tsk as I pass by him.

"Real smooth talker, aren't ya?"

He laughs and shuts the door behind, us then leads me through the main room toward the hallway and what I am presuming—hoping—is his bedroom.

His room is very plain, which being that it's a temporary place and not a shared space with another teammate, I sort of understand. Still, there isn't much in this room that tells me about him. It feels uninspired and maybe a little lost. I spin around as he shuts his door and flips on a small lamp on top of a nightstand. His floor is clean, and a small pile of clothes sits on his desk chair. There's a boxy TV mounted to the wall above his dresser, and except for a few discarded arm bands and a water bottle, his room is pretty spotless.

"Was your dad in the military or something? Because this is a tight ship." I run a finger along the woodgrain of one of his drawers to show off the lack of dust. I'm joking, but also . . . not.

"Nah, but his dad was. And I guess the neat-freak gene trickled down. Still trickling," he laughs, patting his own chest.

He falls back onto his bed and props his head up on his elbow, leaving enough room for me. It's not my style to get nervous, but for some reason, I'm incredibly aware of my movements and expressions and sounds right now. My smile tingles into my cheeks as I work to suppress it, stepping toward the bed and sitting on the edge. I drop my bag to the floor then unzip my boots and let them fall to the floor too. I'm comfortable today, in tight black pants and a black turtle-neck. I went with my artsy look because that's the style that seems to fit the old ladies I work for.

"Cute socks," James says, pointing toward my feet.

I lay to my side and lift a leg in the air a little and wiggle my toes. I wore my long boot socks over my tight riding-style pants today, and this particular pair is covered in paw prints.

"Dog lover?" he asks.

"Dog dreamer is more like it," I say. I snuggle on my side into the bed and pull his pillow under my head, propping myself up to meet his eye line. "I always wanted a dog, but one never really fit the Bentley family lifestyle."

"That's too bad," he says, pulling his second pillow into his body so we're nearly at the same level. Lying here like this feels somehow familiar. There's an instant comfort, and I let my own vision of spending weekend mornings just like this sit happily in my chest.

"You ever have a dog?" I ask.

"Oh, we've got two right now. Rover! Mikey!" He whistles and I lift myself up and look toward his closed door, realizing too late that he's teasing me. I scowl at him instantly and flop back into my pillow.

"That was mean."

I pout for a few seconds, until he grazes my arm with his fingertips and utters an apology.

"So, tell me about this small business dream of yours," I prompt.

James rolls to his back and sighs, stretching his arms over his head until his hands touch the headboard. His legs are so long that he has to bend his knees to keep them on the bed. He seems entirely too big for a full-sized mattress. He would probably fall out of one of the dorm beds.

"You sure you want to hear my story?" he asks.

"You heard mine," I respond.

A soft smile rests on his lips as his head rolls to the side. He studies me for a few seconds.

"My grandfather—I call him Papa—he owned this cool little store where I grew up. It was a bodega, or as close to a bodega as you can get in south Boston. He had all of these strange foods in there, and he was always getting new things in for people to try. He had a whole spice section with stuff people flew in from all over the world. Some of the city's bigtime chefs sometimes stopped in and picked stuff up for special dishes. My grandpa would talk with them, and I think he even shared a recipe or two."

"Wow. I wonder if they got famous off of his recipe," I

say, a genuine question. That's my father's upbringing kicking in—always looking for reasons to get litigious.

"Maybe, but it wouldn't have been his anyhow. My great aunts were the ones with the recipes. Papa just stored them in his head. He was a decent cook, but my mom . . . she's an artist."

Seeing him talk about his mom with so much reverence, holding her on a pedestal for something so personal and domestic, fills me with envy. It's a sweet envy, one wrapped in appreciation. But envy, none the less.

"Anyway, you probably know how Boston real estate goes. Someone bought a building then changed the lease structure, so the smaller businesses had to leave, and the bigger ones expanded, and blah, blah, blah." He rolls his head in a circle then shifts so he's on his side again and staring at me.

"And that's your dream?" My eyes pull in, my focus on the weight in his. His smile dims, but it's as though it's hanging on for hope, the curve of his lips clinging to the dimples in his cheeks.

"That's my dream. I want to reopen Delgado's and add on a small restaurant concept for my mom. That's *her* dream." Those last three words seem to breathe life into his smile. It grows.

"So, your dream is making *her* dream come true," I say.

His gaze holds on to mine for several long seconds, and the farther I fall into the deep pools of blue and green, the dizzier I become. Long breaths grow soft and faint, until I'm holding mine just like him.

"Come here," he finally utters.

Our eyes remain open, locked on one another, as I scoot into him. He sweeps an arm behind my head and the last vision I have is of the strong, stubbled line of his jaw and the soft invitation of his lips a breath before he kisses me. It's soft and chaste, his lips lingering against mine, his tongue taking leisurely passes against my skin. The lust-filled neediness of our last intimate moments isn't there, instead replaced with an adoration. I feel adored by his mouth—cherished and wanted, but in a way that feels less transient. There's a steadiness in his kiss. His mouth is strong but his intimacy measured, as if he's not just taking his time but enjoying the slow dance of it all. I've never been kissed like this. And I have no intention of stopping it anytime soon.

Chapter 12

James

I t's strange to know I'm in the middle of a dream.

I'm fully aware that I am sleeping right now. I keep trying to convince my body to join my mind and will my eyes open, but the picture in my head is too sweet. The lapping of the ocean water and smell of salt in the air seems so real even though I know it's not. In the real world, I'm in a bedroom at a school I still don't quite feel at home at with a beautiful girl in my arms.

I tried to stay awake. Planned on it. I kissed Morgan until my lips were raw. And then I ran my fingers through her hair until her body stilled and her breathing evened out and I knew she was asleep. The silky feel of her hair slipping through my fingers was like some sort of physical hypnosis, and I don't know if it was an hour or only minutes after she fell asleep that I did, but I did. And now, I'm clawing my way to awake because there is no way it is not early morning.

The thump against the wall does the trick. My eyes snap open and my body jolts, which brings Morgan out of her slumber.

"Oh, shit!" she whispers, pushing against my chest and sitting up.

We stare at one another's wide eyes, somehow silently agreeing to make as little noise as possible. Neither of us breathes.

I mentally run through the sounds I recognize, matching up what I hear with what might be going on behind my door. Morgan taps the screen on her phone which is nestled between us on my bed. It's four a.m. It's not my mom we hear.

Thank God for old plumbing. The moment my dad turns on the shower, the pipes vibrate inside the wall between my room and the bathroom, and the high-pitched whine of the water coming out fades as the temperature heats.

"You've gotta go *now*," I say through a really panicked laugh.

"No shit, Sherlock," Morgan says, rushing to the foot of my bed and shoving her feet into her boots.

Her hair is a wild mess, and I help her comb through it with my fingers, which she quickly slaps away.

"Stop it. That's annoying," she whisper-shouts.

I hold in a laugh as she rolls her eyes. She's fucking adorable. I would give anything to wrap my arms around her and pull her back into this bed and continue kissing other places on her body.

But my dad will make life hell for the both of us. He has few rules, but not having a coed sleepover is definitely one of them. It's a non-negotiable, and maybe the only rule he said out loud when we were moving into this place. He was half-joking when he said it because the cheerleaders were practicing their pyramid out in the quad as we were hauling boxes in.

"Hey, no sleepovers," he said, pointing at me.

"Yeah, right." That was my response.

That was six weeks ago as fall cheer camp was underway and my dad was setting up one-on-ones with players to introduce himself as the new coach. Six weeks—that's how long I lasted.

Once Morgan is put together, her hair pulled back in some magic tie she pulled out of her bag, I make my way to my bedroom door. I stop with her behind me, pressing my ear against the slim space between the door and the jamb. The hallway is quiet, and the water is still running. I've come to know our shower, and there is a small window of perfectly hot water, so this is our chance.

"Let's go," I mouth to her. We both crack giddy smiles that break through our nerves, and it somehow calms my pulse. I think we both feel breaking this rule was worth it.

I crack open my door and apply pressure to the hinge to keep it from squeaking until it's wide enough for both of us to slip out. Our hands automatically find one another, our fingers weaving into a naturally comfortable position, and we squeeze tight as we tiptoe out of my room, down the hallway, and out our apartment door until we burst into a giggling fit in the middle the campus lawn.

"Shit! It's cold!" I high step, realizing only now that I am barefoot and still in a T-shirt. It's maybe forty-five degrees out and the sun isn't set to rise for another three hours.

"You better get back inside before you freeze," Morgan teases. She sways back and forth, her bag dangling from her arm. Bits of wet grass cling to her boots.

"I'll be fine," I say, my laughter quieting. My eyes settle on hers and I take her hand again, pulling it to my mouth and kissing the inside of her wrist.

"Thanks for picking me up at the train," she mutters, her voice soft and shy.

"*Mmm*, kinda my pleasure," I say, smiling against her wrist and dropping her hand to free my palms to cup her face.

"It was my pleasure too," she hums. My thumbs sweep along her cheeks, the space under her eyes still puffy with sleep.

"You're really pretty this way," I say.

She tucks her face into my right hand and brings her own hand up to hide half of her face.

"Stop. I look terrible. I'm sure of it."

I move her hand away and return to cupping her face, holding her focus on me so she hears me loud and clear.

"You could never look terrible. But like this? You are beautiful."

This is the version of her nobody gets to see, and it's the version that is the most honest and real. She has no idea how little help she needs to be perfect.

"Well . . ." A tiny breath leaves her nose as her lashes blink away the attention. For a girl who has spent half her life collecting viewers, my singular attention seems too much for her, which only makes me want to stare on longer.

"I'm gonna take you out tonight. After practice. Give me your phone," I say, glancing at her bag where I know she's buried her device.

She licks her lips, studying me, maybe dissecting my actions a little, and definitely flirting. God, I love flirting with her.

I let my fingers run down the sides of her jaw to the black turtleneck sweater hugging her neck. I tug at the folds and she lets out an airy laugh.

"Fine." She gives in, twisting to reach into her bag and hand me her phone. I type in my number and send a text to myself so I have hers as well.

"There, now I don't have to troll you on social media simply to talk to you," I say, dropping her phone back in her purse. "I'll message you as soon as practice is done, and I'll just need fifteen to shower and stuff."

"What if it takes me longer than that?" She juts out a hip and I take the opportunity to palm it and run my gaze along the curve of her profile.

"You don't need to change a thing. In fact, you better dress casual for what I've got planned. I'm talking sneakers and a sweatshirt." I'm going to get her away from this place, to somewhere from my world. She doesn't need to pretend to be anything other than who she naturally is.

"And . . . nothing else?" She leans her head to the side with a coy expression, and of course now that she suggests it . . .

"I would not complain if that's how you showed up." My lip ticks up on one side, almost daring her to go for it. Kissing her for hours was amazing. So was running my palms up her thighs and around her ass in the locker room. And fuck! Now I want to do all sorts of dirty things to her.

"You better get inside before you give yourself away, James," she says, glancing down at my rock-hard cock protruding from my joggers.

I laugh at myself because what can I do, and Morgan leans in, pressing her lips against mine as I'm mid chuckle. Adding to my torture, she runs her palm down my stomach until she is fully cupping my hard-on, and my dick flexes in her hand.

"Oh . . . okay," I stammer out. She nips at my lips then

backs away, leaving me hard, freezing cold, and so fucking turned on.

"I'll wait for your text," she says.

She flips her ponytail over her shoulder before looking away from me and literally swaying her hips as she walks away like some sex kitten from the movies. I stare with my lips parted, still thrumming with the sensation of her kiss. I reach into my pants and adjust myself as best as I can before bending down and brushing grass from the bottoms of my pants. I'm still half hard when I get back to our apartment, and I slip in through the door, careful to not make any more noise than I have to. When I click the door shut, I pause and listen for a moment. The shower is no longer running, which means I need to get my ass in my room. I make it halfway across the living room when the scent of freshly brewed coffee hits my senses.

"How was the sleepover?" My dad's tone is flat, lacking the sarcasm I know lies underneath his words. That's because right now he's too pissed to allow anything remotely funny to transpire.

I rock back on my feet and turn to face him. He's blowing across the top of his coffee cup, steam glowing under the light from his phone. I'm sure he was checking his email or reading the news. He has a routine in the morning, and it starts early.

"I can explain," I sigh, moving closer to the counter to keep some space between us. Not that I'm thinking about Morgan's naked flesh anymore. Now I'm thinking about the dead meat I am.

"Choices, James. That's what I told you, and that's all I have to say now. Mind your choices. Now, get some clothes on and get your ass in the weight room."

My dad clicks the screen dark on his phone and takes his mug in his other hand before heading to his room where my mom is sleeping through all of this. I'm not sure which would be better, having her awake and on my side, or having her agree with him and hitting me with a double dose of disappointment. I'm not entirely sure where she would fall on this one. She doesn't necessarily get behind my dad's all-football-all-the-time approach, but she also knows how much I need to get everything just right in order to get into the kind of college I want.

"Yes, sir," I finally utter as he shuts his bedroom door.

Fuck.

* * *

My dad got Theo's punishment reduced to a single game. That means Theo's able to join us today for practice, which makes the extra hits everyone gives Raskin on his behalf a little sweeter.

Things seem to be sorted out between Lily and him too. We're going to watch her compete next week as a team. My dad likes fostering community and supporting other athletes. He's always seen that as a natural way to build camaraderie. It was my idea, and yeah, I suggested it partly to show Theo that I truly only see Lily as a friend. I sense he still harbors some weird jealousy over her tutoring me.

I also knew if I set something like this up, I could sit with Morgan, and finding ways to be with Morgan without having to sneak around behind my father's back is proving to be a challenge.

I've been out of practice for thirty minutes now, and there's no way she doesn't realize this. I haven't texted. I'm showered and ready to go, yet here I am, sitting in my room like a grounded ten-year-old who broke a lamp. Only I didn't break a lamp. I broke a rule. And really, it's not an entirely fair rule. My dad doesn't know Morgan. I'm only getting to know her, and every new thing I learn changes the public perception I once admired online for completely shallow reasons.

The knock on my door sends a paranoid jolt up my spine and I flip my phone over on my thigh as if I have something to hide. Like seeing my phone screen will somehow pull the thread on my inner turmoil of whether to text Morgan or not, and if I do, whether that text should cancel our plans or confirm them.

"Hey, I need to talk to you about something." My dad closes the door behind him, which makes my chest tighten. He's either going to pick up where the lecture left off this morning, or he's going to start an entirely new one.

I scoot over on the foot of my bed to make room for him, and as he sits down he rubs his chin in that same thoughtful way he used to deliver news about one of our fish dying or the hamster getting out.

"Did the headmaster change his mind?" I'm taking a wild guess that this is about Theo's suspension.

"Huh?" My dad is still rubbing his chin but breaks from his trance after a few seconds to look up at me as if my question is finally catching up to him. "Oh, no. Theo and Raskin are on track. That's fine. All is fine. No, this is . . . well, it's unfair news. And I have to tell you, and this is when it is exceptionally hard being both your coach and your father."

My mouth hangs open for a breath and I lean back on my palms, dropping my chin to my chest.

"Okay. Go ahead."

I stare down at frayed hole in the knee of my jeans and prepare myself for whatever's coming.

"The coach from Brown is coming to practice tomorrow."

My heart pushes out a single, massive beat, then stops.

This isn't good news, despite how I've always imagined my father uttering this exact sentence *would* be.

"He's coming to take a look at Toby."

All I can do is breathe out a pathetic laugh and close my eyes.

"Of course he is," I say.

"Don't do that, give up like that. This has nothing to do with football and your skill versus his—"

"Of course it doesn't," I say. I roll my head until my gaze meets my father's, and I can see in his expression that he is failing to find soothing words. "That's the problem, Dad. Being great at football"—I sneer and shake my head—"None of that matters because Toby's family is so fucking rich! Dad, they probably bought a building already, or purchased this season's uniforms. And Toby might never suit up and take a snap at Brown, but he'll make their roster. They'll admit him over me. Because his family can make that happen and mine can't."

I stand and march out of my room, my chest heavy with guilt because that wasn't a fair thing to say. But what am I even doing here, trying to trick the system when it's so rigged? I hear my mom shout, "Hey!" when I slam the door behind me. She's not big on temper tantrums. I still can't sit in the armchair in their bedroom without thinking of the times she put me in time out in that seat at our old apartment. I haven't thrown a proper temper tantrum since I was five or six, though, so maybe I get a free pass with this one. And is it really a tantrum if it's a natural reaction to life mocking me?

I don't bother calling Morgan, instead marching to her dorm, taking the stairs two at a time and hoping I figured the room number right based on the names scribbled on the mailbox downstairs. The Triple-B sign on the door decorated with their names confirms things for me, and I knock before I chicken out.

Several seconds pass and I question whether she's even here. I wouldn't blame her for leaving. I basically stood her up. Their room is silent, but to be sure, I knock again and press my ear to the door. I'm about to lean my weight into it when it's yanked open and I stumble into Morgan's body. She wraps her arms around me and cushions my fall by stumbling several steps backward until she's leaning on her desk.

"Wow, look who has a sudden sense of urgency." She pushes me away and folds her arms. Her pursed lips are a pretty clear hint that she's pissed.

I sigh and hang my head, knowing I don't have a good excuse.

"I'm sorry. I had some complicated shit to work out." I don't want to tell her my dad doesn't approve of her, and I'm not in the mood to talk about Toby either, so I leave it at that and hope it's enough

Her head tilted to the side, she studies me for a beat, probably trying to decide if I'm worth the hassle. I'm not sure I am. She put on her Welles sweatshirt and is wearing black leggings with socks bunched up at the ankles with bright red sneakers. Her hair is split in two with curled ponytails resting on either shoulder. And while her lips are glossed with a soft pink color, she's not wearing much makeup besides that. Or perhaps I don't know what to look for when it comes to that kind of stuff. Whatever it is, she looks . . . well, fucking hot like she always does, only somehow more. My eyes give me away as they flit down her body.

"Are we going to get food?" Her question feels out of left field, and I'm caught staring at her hips as I laugh and blink my way back to meet her gaze.

"I mean, do you want food?" I shake my head and shrug, a bit of relief seeping into my lungs, allowing me a full breath.

"Yeah, I want food. I'm hungry, and I want *real* food," she demands.

"Like what, pork chops? Potatoes? Dinner salad?"

She grabs a notebook at her side and throws it at my chest. I deflect it to the floor but grab my chest as if she's speared me.

"Don't be dramatic. Get me a burger," she says, grabbing a small bag from her desk that she shoves her phone and keys into, then crosses over her chest and shoulders. I gawk at her as she marches to her door, which is still open from where I barreled through it. She spins around when she enters the hall and gives me the same look my mom does when I'm on her last nerve. Somehow, it's a lot cuter on Morgan's face.

She snaps at me.

"Burger."

I shake my head and follow her lead.

"Yeah, all right. Okay," I say, exiting her room and waiting in the hall for her to lock the door.

"What are you driving?" she asks the moment her keys leave the lock.

I twist my lips and feel my pocket, glad my family's truck keys are still in there. I carried them around our apartment after practice while I paced, debating what the hell I was going to do. I pull them out and jingle them.

"Ford, lifted. Glad you wore something you can climb in."

She walks up to me and stops so our shoulders touch, putting on a bit of a haughty attitude. I think she's playing now, though. Either way, I like it. She looks down at the thin space between us then back into my eyes, twisting her lips.

"I can climb into a truck wearing pretty much anything," she says, her brow set at a challenging slant.

I poke my tongue in my cheek.

"Huh," I say, my immediate thoughts of her in, well, just about anything and stepping up a two-foot lift.

"I'm hungry. Let's go." She turns and heads to the stairs, and I follow a few steps behind, wondering how I got so lucky for her to forgive me for putting her off. Of course, she doesn't exactly know that part, and I don't want to tell her. Besides, what does any of this matter if the system is set up to favor guys like Toby anyhow?

We get to the parking lot and I press unlock on the key fob, flashing the truck lights.

"Nice rig," Morgan says, giving me a sideways glance.

A crooked smile etches into my mouth. I get the hint that she's the kind of girl who likes big trucks. My dad would like that if he simply stopped to get to know her.

I hover at the front bumper while she opens her door and steps up on the running board, lifting herself easily. Our eyes meet through the windshield. She smirks as she tugs her door closed, probably knowing I was waiting around, hoping she needed my help so I could watch the view from behind. I'm so basic.

I hop in the driver's side, buckle up, and crank the engine before glancing to my side. She looks so good in that seat, nothing like a Boston socialite, but more like a college girl heading off to Texas.

"You know this area better than me. Where's good?" I ask.

She pulls one of her legs up, tucking it under her as she sits sideways and looks at me. Her cold shoulder is warming to me again. I'm glad.

"Biff's, which I know sounds so stereotypical, and believe

me—it is. But it is also amazing. Like, *uh-mazing*." She's talking with her hands, using them to mime the shape of the burger, and it makes me chuckle.

"What?"

I shake my head and shift into reverse, then check my mirrors.

"You surprise me, that's all. Here you are, Miss Louis Vuitton, and you love trucks and burgers." I press the gas and roll us back.

"You should see me haul ass in a Jeep up a steep mountain trail." She clicks her tongue and shifts back to face forward, proud of her brag.

"I'd like to see that, actually. Very much," I say through light laughter.

Morgan directs me as we navigate our way further out of town, away from the city, until we come upon a legitimate burger joint off the side of the main highway. I pull us into Biff's and park at a small intercom box to give our order. It crackles as the guy working speaks through it, asking us what we would like.

I glance to Morgan and suck in my lips.

"No clue. You're the one who demanded burgers," I say.

She unbuckles her seat belt and leans over the center console, placing a hand on the seat between my legs as she stretches across my body. "I got this," she says, her sexy confidence working its way into my veins.

"Two number sevens with extra cheese and hot pickles. Oh, and make the drinks cherry coke with the real stuff." She turns her head enough to meet my eyes, then flits her gaze down to my crotch before pulling her lips into a tight smile and easing back into her seat.

I'm hypnotized. She could have ordered live octopus with ketchup, and I'd accept it. I slip my credit card into the crusty, ancient machine attached to the call box, not sure if I'm spending twenty bucks or a hundred. I don't really care.

"The pickles are a test," she says as I tuck my card back into my wallet, then shove the wallet into the back pocket of my jeans.

"A pickle test," I reiterate, making sure I heard that right.

"Yup." Morgan slides down in her seat and props her feet up on the dash. My dad would hate that. I don't care.

"Biff's hot pickles are like . . ." She swirls her hand in front of her face with thought. "They're like truth serum. You know a person's soul based on how they handle them."

My brow shoots up and I shift, leaning against my door.

"They sound serious. What if I'm allergic to pickles?"

"Hmmm, I don't know, James. I think that's an automatic disqualification," she teases.

"Pity. I mean, I might be. Sure would hate to risk death." I challenge her stare with my own, our features trapped in a seductive dare. She glances up and to the side after a few seconds, then shakes her head.

"That is a pity. I guess I'll have to finish my dinner, then have you take me home." Her hands move to the bottom of her sweatshirt and she works it up her body, revealing a white skin-tight tank top that scoops low and displays her breasts like the fucking goddess fruits they are.

"Let's see, two sevens and cherries?" The voice behind me rattles me awake and I turn and take the bag of food from a kid who I guess is a newly minted fifteen. Fucker must like fruit too because his eyes are locked on Morgan's chest from the moment he stepped up to my truck window.

"Thanks. We're good," I say once our order is in my lap and the drinks in the truck cupholders. I flit the young lad away with my hand and press the button to raise the window before he can gawk a second more.

Morgan's laugh rasps in her chest as her head falls back and her full lips grin from ear to ear. She won this round. And even though I fucking hate pickles, I sure as shit will love these. I dig through the box until I find the small bag. I slip out a spear and lean my head back, dropping the pickle down my throat almost without a single chew.

"Oh . . . James, no . . ." Morgan's hands are on my arm, attempting to pull my hand from my face as she blurts out a panicked warning. I don't understand it until three seconds into my pickle consumption when my esophagus literally lights on fire.

"Oh, my God!" I gasp, my voice gone from the burn. I swear my insides are burning up, shriveling, and turning to dust. I don't know what the hell those things are, but they are evil. *Evil!*

"Here, drink," Morgan says, clasping one of the large drinks between her hands and hoisting the straw toward my mouth. I suck in as much cherry coke as I can in one swoop, trying to drown this awful sensation that truly may actually kill me.

"I'm so sorry," she says, shaking the drink and encouraging me to drink more.

My eyes are watering, and I'm not sure if it's from suffocating from the fire or because the burn hurts so bad. I gulp down more soda, the carbonation not really helping but the syrup doing the trick. After nearly five minutes of breathing fire, scraping my tongue on napkins, and drinking thirty ounces of cherry Coke, I'm able to use my vocal cords again.

"How's my soul?" I cough out.

Morgan blinks, then levels me with a long blank stare, clearly confused and probably feeling guilty.

"You said you could read a person's soul based on how they handle those evil little fuckers." I reach into the food bag and pull out a handful of fries. I hold them up for her to approve, sort of a safety check that I'm not going to hurt myself ingesting these.

"They're safe," she says, her mouth a regretful, pouty smile.

I stare intently at the fries for a beat, as if second-guessing her word, then pop them in my mouth and grin through chewing.

"You passed, by the way," Morgan says, pulling a napkin from the bag and leaning toward me to dab my chin. I cross my eyes to see what she's clearing from my face but stop when the thought that I coughed up pickle on myself enters my mind. *How embarrassing.*

"I passed, huh?" I say, digging back into the bag for my burger.

"Uh huh," she says, unwrapping hers and pulling the bun from the top before proceeding to layer the inside of her burger with the fire pickles of death. She replaces the bun then takes an enormous bite, giving me a triumphant stare while she chews methodically.

"Trucks. Burgers. And fire-retardant taste buds," I say.

Morgan laughs and holds a napkin over her mouth. I smirk at her while I continue eating my burger. I've never really stared at a person through an entire meal before, but that's what Morgan and I do. No radio playing. No outside chatter interrupting our quiet. Only the occasional crunch of fries and lettuce and freaky pickles until we're both left pushing our straws in and out of our drink lids.

I lift a leg up against the seat back and rest my empty cup on my kneecap while my eyes memorize every inch of her face. Her cheeks flush under my scrutiny, and her head falls to the side, resting against the seat back.

"What's on your mind?" I ask, hoping she's thinking about how amazing this simple moment is.

"Your soul's perfect, James Fuentes. Fucking perfect."

The center of my chest dents. I swear it does. Something inside me cracks open with her words, and I'm rendered speechless. I bite my tongue, smiling from the flattery. As much as I want to stay here in this patchwork parking lot with carloads of families coming and going around us to celebrate Little League games or birthdays or the simple joy of a Wednesday night, I also want to take her somewhere away from it all. Somewhere we can be alone. Maybe I take her where I wanted to in the first place.

"How long can I keep you out?" I ask.

"I've got a press release to write for two old ladies at my internship tomorrow at nine a.m. I'm clear until then." Her mouth curves up on the side closest to the window, the glimmer of light from outside highlighting the perfect shape of her lips.

"I can work with that," I say, gathering our trash and lowering the window enough to toss it into the trash receptacle.

Morgan shifts in her seat and buckles her safety belt while I pull us back out onto the highway and head toward Southside. She keeps her sweatshirt rolled up in her lap, which makes me downright gleeful because I'm certain she is not wearing a bra. Maybe it's my imagination, but I swear her nipples are hard.

It's a thirty-minute drive to where we're going, and I spend the time trying to unravel the mystery that is Morgan Bentley. I find out that she likes trucks because her half-brother drives one and he used to take her to the shore to camp and go fishing whenever she felt her parents were ignoring her. She also shares how her half-brother came to be discovered, and the countless affairs her father has had. She almost gets nostalgic when she talks about spending holidays at the country house when her grandparents were still alive. And I feel a pang of jealousy that she has those memories because my grandpa died way too soon.

We're close to our destination when I decide to let down my walls enough to actually show her some of my soul, if you can call it that. It's definitely the stuff that forms me, and something deep inside tells me it will make her feel less alone to hear how much we're alike.

"My parents almost divorced last year," I say, and hearing it out loud rather than whispered by one of my parents in a dark kitchen when they think I'm not listening is somehow liberating.

"But they seem so perfect. How?" Morgan asks.

I think about my parents, the many memories of our close family as I grew up and the way they are now.

"They do seem perfect. And maybe they are, really. Perfect doesn't mean a straight line. It's about where you are in the end, the destination and resilience of the journey," I say.

The cab of the truck hums with the sound of the heater and nothing else, so I glance to my right to check Morgan's reaction. Her mouth hints at a smile, almost the way the Mona Lisa seems to hide a secret. It's a little unsettling, and I'm not sure why. I think because I'm afraid she sees someone better than I really am right now. I almost want to challenge her to find all my faults. I'm too greedy to give up the warmth of her admiration though, so I keep my mouth shut and simply bask in it for a few more minutes until I reach our destination.

We pull into the parking garage at the perfect time, and I round the turns quickly, dashing to the top floor and parking on the south end that overlooks the busy train yard below. The cargo cranes glow in the distance as they lift heavy containers, plucking them from the tracks to stack on the cargo ship like a giant game of Jenga.

"Incredible," Morgan says, releasing her seat belt and scooting forward to rest her arms on the dash, a fist holding her chin in place as she stares. I think she's kind of incredible, but I keep that thought to myself—for now—content to watch her enjoy a piece of my youth.

"My grandpa used to bring me out here when I was little. He'd pack us a picnic and we'd take the T to the southernmost stop, then ride the elevator up here and just watch them work. He marveled at the industry of it, and I think a part of him always wanted me to grow up to be an engineer or something. You know, some job that got to play with giant toys like that." I let out a fading laugh at the memory and unlatch my seat belt to lean forward, hugging the steering wheel to take it all in.

"This is how it works. I mean, yeah, consumerism and stuff, but also life. Those containers are probably hauling shoes and clothes overseas, and then they come back with microchips and car parts," she says, and I hold in my snicker as long as I can because her wonder at it all is so sincere.

"Probably more like grain powders and maybe a crap ton of Nike Airs," I share.

"I like my version better," she fires back.

I laugh quietly to myself, glancing to check that she's still staring ahead at the shipyard.

"I do, too." I give in.

She rolls her head to the side, resting her cheek on the backs of her hands and staring at me with the same knowing smile as before.

"Why'd you want to bring me here?" she finally asks.

I sit back, twisting to rest my back on my door. There are so many answers I want to respond, and every single one of them is the truth. I wanted to share something important to me and see how she reacted. A part of me was homesick, and I didn't want to come here alone. This place was always where I went when I needed to think, and after hearing about Toby and Brown, my head is a bit tangled.

Ultimately, though, I give her the most honest reason of all.

"I knew you'd be beautiful in this light," I say.

Her faint smile stretches slowly, the shift so subtle that I would have missed it if I weren't staring at her mouth the entire time. Morgan Bentley is the only girl I've met whose insides perfectly match the image. She's a bit of a vixen, but sweet and thoughtful, and unabashedly tender when you get to know her. She feels more than most realize, and she wears her heart on her sleeve. Her heart is coated in this self-made armor that is flimsy at the seams, and I think she's desperate to tear it away but so afraid of the attacks she may face if she does. She's hungry to be vulnerable but hell-bent on being strong. And she's the sexiest woman I've ever seen—TikTok and beyond.

"Did the light live up to your expectations?" Her voice is barely above a whisper as she moves to face me, lifting the center console into the seat back.

"The light's okay, but the girl? She is beautiful." I hold her stare, loving the slight flinch in her eyes that I think maybe echoes the skip in her heartbeat just now.

Morgan moves her knees up to the bench between us and inches toward me as I twist to face her completely. She takes one of my legs in her hands and coaxes it to stretch out lengthwise, then does the same with the other, maneuvering herself until she's straddling my thighs. My cock is pulsing behind the zipper in my jeans, desperate to break free of this damn denim.

"You know, I'm pretty sure you made that freshman kid's night at Biff's with your tank top," I say, confirming my hopeful suspicions. I was right—zero bra under that thing.

"I don't think it was my shirt he was looking at," she says, flatting her hands on my thighs.

"I don't either," I admit, giving in to my impulse and covering both of her breasts with my palms. My thumbs rub over the hard peaks and she moans, her hips rocking as her own hands inch toward the zipper on my pants.

I knead her tits in my hands, pinching her nipples between my thumbs and index fingers under the knit white fabric of her shirt. Morgan's touch slides over my cock, rubbing me through my jeans and pulling a deep growl from the depths of my chest. I lunge forward, unhinged and hungry, and take the tip of her breast in my mouth, sucking it raw through the material then gripping it with my teeth.

Morgan's pressure intensifies on my dick, which fuels my need to taste more of her. I gather her shirt in my hands and lift the folds up over her perfectly round breasts, her nipples like sweet cherries on a sundae. My mouth covers it again, my tongue swirling over the hard peak then flicking it in sync with my thumb on her other breast. A tiny whimper leaves her mouth, calling me to kiss it. I taste my way up her neck and jawline until our mouths meet for a needy kiss, our tongues exploring in between sucks and nips of our lips and teeth.

She grips my bottom lip between her teeth as she reaches for her gathered-up tank, letting go of our kiss to remove her shirt completely. My hands cover her bare breasts as I kiss her hard, and she slowly works down the zipper on my jeans. My cock springs out to meet the cool air, but only briefly until her hand wraps around my shaft to stroke me up and down.

"Oh fuck, that's good," I groan into the nook of her neck.

Morgan sinks into my lap, her center grinding against my thigh as she searches for relief. My hands graze along her breasts and move to her back, caressing down her sides until I meet the band of her leggings. I dip beneath the fabric and run my palms over her round ass, soon discovering nothing there but her flesh.

"You said casual," she hums against my mouth, her hand flexing with me in her grip.

"Fucking hell." My eyes roll behind my eyelids as I let her work me into a near dream, her hand sliding up and down my dick in a steady, maddening pace.

I feel around her body until my fingers find her soaking wet center, and I tease her pussy with equally long and slow strokes until finally dipping one inside of her.

"Ah," she cries out, leaning into my touch and working her hips to push me in deeper.

I pull my finger out then push it back in simply to hear her cry again, pleased when she does. I want to fuck her so bad, but I also want to feel what it's like when she breaks apart in my hand. I'm so close to coming too, so I keep the rhythm going, pausing our kiss to flick my tongue against the buds of her tits while one finger becomes two inside her. I sink my fingers in deep, curving them to feel her tight insides, working my hand into a vibration that makes her hum.

"Ohhh, James. Yeah, James. Yeah. Yeah."

I could listen to her cry out that single word—*yeah*—for days. In fact, the thought of doing nothing but finger fucking her into delirium over and over again is enough to push me over the edge, and as she falls apart in my hands, her center pulsing with her orgasm, I explode at her touch, coating her hand and wrist. I pump the last of my climax into her grip before collapsing back against the window. She falls forward to lay on my chest.

My hand stays firmly planted on her ass inside her pants, and after we lay in languid glory for several minutes without saying a word, I dare to slip my fingers along her curves again, testing the swollen folds of her clit. Finding her wet and moaning at my touch, I slip inside her again, this time making her beg for the ultimate relief.

Chapter 13

Morgan

I feel pretty today.

I have not felt pretty for a long time. And by my old standards, I would never have considered taking a photo to mark this occasion, which is basically no occasion at all, whatsoever. Yet, I very much want to mark this occasion.

The sky is blue behind me, speckled with cotton-like clouds, and there's a crispness to the air that reminds me of those times when I was young and my mother warned it was about to snow. The chill delights me, kisses my cheeks red, and tickles my ears. I pull my knit hat lower to cover them and wrap my knit scarf around my neck one more time before holding my phone out in front of me and snapping a selfie. I mark it as a favorite and save it to a folder on my phone that I simply title ME.

Alone with my laptop and my earbuds and a playlist I haven't cracked open in months, I hike down by the river, where Cameron and his friends usually smoke weed at night. I like to come here in the afternoons, or at least I used to. This is where I get my reading done for class, and today, it's where

I intend to knock out a five-page paper on colonialism that's due by midnight.

Thing is, I'm not even panicked about it. I feel capable of pulling off miracles, and I know it's because meeting James has changed me. I've never felt more okay sharing my insecurities with someone. Not even last year when I sought out Coach Wallace to help me dig my way out of depression. I told him about my lows, but not the lowest of them. But with James? I don't feel this need to hold back. I want to tell him about my struggles, about what happened with Coach Wallace and the ugly rumors that swirled around his departure.

I want to share the good things with him too. Especially after he took me to a place that was so important to him two nights ago. I could have sat in that truck with him forever, and yes, there are many pleasurable reasons driving this feeling. But even if all we did was talk. I could watch those cranes work and listen and share with him for hours. I want to give him a piece of me like that. Maybe a trip to my grandparents' old cottage on the cape that goes terribly unused and is basically this abandoned bargaining chip between my parents. It belonged to my mother's parents, but the deed is now part of the company. *Everything* is part of the company. That's how my dad controls the pieces—aka us. Taking James there would change all of that, like bringing an old black and white memory into color.

That's what he is. He's the color.

Setting my backpack down on one end of the old wooden riverside bench, I straddle the other to create a makeshift desk for myself so I can get to work. I manage to knock out a page and a half of my essay without struggle before the buzz of my phone distracts me. I don't pull it from my bag to look right away because if it's another message from my mom telling me I'm hurting her feelings by not picking up, I might toss the phone into the river. It's not exactly my mother's best time of day, though. This is her social time, and as much as she wants to assuage her guilt of setting me up, she also does not want to miss drinks with the ladies and gossip for days.

Giving in, I pull my phone out to see a text from James. He must have sent it right before practice, and I love that he's thinking of me. I haven't seen him since he drove us back to campus and walked me to my dorm room. We've texted a lot, though. He's committing every extra hour to football, determined to not let Toby show him up ever again. I wish I could make him believe that the rest of the world knows Toby is a permanent shadow. But James isn't from my world. There is literally nothing he could have done to prevent the special treatment headed Toby's way. It's a grotesque birthright, bought and paid for with endowments and copper plaques with last names on them attached to buildings all over this state. Yet I love that James still wants to try.

I read his text.

JAMES: *Sorry we didn't get to talk yesterday or much today. But I am thinking about you. Constantly.*

I suck in my lip and my heart swells like a giddy schoolgirl. I suppose that's exactly what I am. I send him back the photo I took of myself then tack on a message.

ME: *I've decided I am no longer posting to social media. I'm posting to you. Thanks for the smile today.*

It's cheesy, but I send it anyway because it's also true. When he doesn't write back immediately, I tuck my phone away. He's probably at practice; I can hear the whistles in the distance.

I finish cranking out my essay, maybe cheating a little with the font size and margins to get to five pages, but done is done. I spend another hour looking through my old files for photos of Anika. Lily is writing a piece on her for the magazine she's interning at. They were trying to get her to write about herself and life as a competitive swimmer post-tragedy. But she's turning the tables and handing in a story about what an inspiration Anika was to her—to all of us. Brooklyn and I helped her piece some things together last night, and when the story's complete, she's crediting Theo with the byline. I'm not so sure he deserves it, but maybe none of us deserve the kind things Lily does for us. All I know is he better not be a jerk about it. I like them together, and I still owe Lily for my life. If I have to throat punch that boy to make good on things, I will.

With the sun setting, I power down my laptop and pack up it up so I can head inside. I tucked my gym clothes in the side compartment on the off chance I felt up to working out. *That's inner-voice code for if I was in the mood to accidentally-on-purpose run into James when the team heads inside.* Noticing the guys circling up to end practice, I decide I am in that mood, so I head toward the field house so I can change and maybe get lucky with my timing.

When I reach the door, I pull my backpack from my shoulder and press the side where my wallet is against the security pad. It's after hours, which means nobody is at the desk working, so I need to beep myself in with my ID badge. The scanner doesn't seem to register no matter which way I turn my bag, so I drop it at my feet and dig inside to see if maybe I left my wallet in the room. I haven't used it all day, so I wouldn't have noticed until now.

That theory is quickly proven wrong as my wallet spills out of my side zipper pocket. I flip it open and check the other pockets when I don't see my ID behind my license where it usually is. It's bigger than a credit card, so it should be easy to spot, but I look behind every card because now I'm freaking out. I can't find it.

It's not the end of the world, but getting a new one means I'll have to fill out a form and accept a detention for causing a security risk. Someone, meaning Cameron, stole a bunch of freshmen badges last year and used them to break into the computer lab and hack the system to allow porn. And to make sure the porn auto-played as soon as the projector was turned on. He also went and adjusted the volume in the computer lab, linking the sound system to the school intercom so the heavy moans that greeted that class on a Monday morning were experienced by all. I'll admit it was pretty funny at the time, but now that I can't find my ID badge and might have to spend an entire day in the headmaster's office while watching bad videos about the importance of school security rules, I'm less amused.

Giving up hope that it's in my bag, I shovel my wallet and the items I've taken out of my bag on my fruitless search back inside and hoist the heavy pack up on my shoulder. The team is marching up the hill anyhow, so I'll simply head inside with them.

I spot James easily, both because of his height and because I may have my sonar trained on him. I hold up a hand, waving, but he must not see me. He's talking with his dad and another man in a blue polo shirt. I can't make out the logo, but he may be from a university. Toby is in that mix too, him and James on opposite sides as they approach, and the closer they get the easier it is to make out the strained smiles both of them are sporting. Guys can be as catty as girls, I swear.

Steps from the door, Coach pulls his hat from his head before looking me in the eyes. I can't tell if he's pissed because of something the guy next to him said, or he harbors hostility from something that went down at practice, or a third thing that I hope isn't the case—that he simply doesn't like me. This disapproving dent on his forehead only gets deeper as he steps to the door.

"Can I help you?" His question is jarring, and I find myself unable to speak.

"Hey, Morgan. How are you?" Toby says, stepping up next to me. James doesn't even shift his gaze from its position straight ahead. *What the fuck?*

"I . . . need someone to let me in?" I don't know why my response comes out as a weak-ass question, but all of my confidence from the last two days drains out of me in seconds.

"Where's your badge?" Coach Fuentes asks. He unclips his from his belt and holds it to the security pad until it beeps. One of the other players tugs the door open behind him, and everyone files in, including James who glances my way and nods. My face lights up, ready for him to speak, but words never leave his lips.

"Your badge?" James's dad leans to the side a tick, blocking my view of his son.

I shake my head, my throat closing up and ears drumming with my pulse. My body feels hot, like I might faint, and I think it's because I feel foolish, like the butt of a joke I wasn't around to hear.

"I left my wallet in my room. I was going to run for a while and figured since you all were heading in . . ." His stare is intense, and I bet his players drop to the ground and start counting off pushups the minute he looks at them like that. I kind of want to cry.

"Go on," he finally says, nodding his head to the right in invitation.

"Oh, okay. Thank you. Thank you," I repeat, bowing for some reason as I clutch my bag to my chest and rush into the field house lobby. James is nowhere to be seen, but Toby lingered behind, and I can tell he did that so he could walk with me. What is this stupid ego challenge happening between these two? I mean, I get that James needs this for college, but Toby can go anywhere he wants. Hell, his parents can buy him an entire school.

Now that I'm inside, I can't really turn back around and leave, so I head into the locker room and follow through with my original plan. I change out quickly, no longer in the mood to time things so I can run into anyone. If there was a treadmill in the women's locker room, I'd use it, and then I would tunnel out of here so I never had to see a soul.

Since that's a fantasy, I go ahead and pop my earbuds in and push my overstuffed bag into a locker before heading to the weight room. It's empty, which is normal for this time of day. I flip on a row of lights, leaving the room dim, then pick the treadmill by the window so I can watch the players—*James*—leave. I start on a low level, but within minutes, I've cranked the speed up to a sprint. My half-brother calls this my angry run, but it's really more of an all-encompassing emotional run. That works, because I'm feeling a whole lot of things right now.

Most of the players have left, and for a while I was counting as they passed, as if I somehow knew the magic number I needed to see to be completely alone. I'm approaching my second mile, and my legs have gone beyond burn and are nearing that Jell-O state. I press my finger on the minus button and cut my pace in half just as I spot Coach walking away with the mystery man in the blue polo shirt. I slow to a walk so I can follow his path for any insight into where he's headed, and why James isn't with him. It takes a few seconds for my eyes to adjust, and when I see James's reflection in the glass, I slap the emergency stop button and grip my chest.

"Jesus! You scared me!" I shout as I yank my earbuds from my ear. I hold them in my palm like dice and lean against the back of the treadmill, my skin beading and red from exertion. Running is the only truly physical activity I'm good at, but even that sprint was a lot for me.

"Sorry," James grunts. He moves toward the window, slipping into the space between my treadmill and the glass. He's watching his dad, too.

"You know who that is?" he says.

"No clue. Don't care." My answer comes out harsh, but I'm a little hurt. He treated me like I was a ghost, or worse, like I was some fangirl who was stalking him. And his dad was rude.

James lifts his shoulders high, holding them there for a few seconds before exhaling heavily and letting them fall to his sides. He turns around slowly, and I wait with my arms crossed over my chest.

"I didn't mean to ignore you, Morgan. I'm sorry." His expression is soft, lips turned down and eyelids heavy. He holds out his palms and shakes his head.

I want to maintain my cold shoulder, but he looks downright pathetic. I hold on to his gaze for a full breath, mostly to make him suffer a little. It's not nice, but my blood is still boiling.

"Who's the guy in blue?" I ask, my lips pursed as I wait for his answer.

"Penn. Here for, *duh duh duh duh!*" he sings.

His jaw works side to side while I put together the fairly easy puzzle thanks to his brand of sarcasm.

"Toby."

"Bing, bing, bing!" His voice echoes in the room, and I

spin around to check the door, almost expecting someone to rush in to see what the noise is. "Relax, we're alone. Everyone is gone. My dad left to meet with Toby's dad in the headmaster's office, along with Penn's recruiting coordinator. Toby went to run his mouth off to his friends about how amazing he is."

My back to him, I let the quiet fill in after his tantrum. My chest hurts, partly out of pity for his situation, but also, I'm still hurt. And yeah, he apologized, but it was rather pathetic. And he waited to see me—he waited for us to be alone. *Why?*

"Why are you here now?" I ask, turning slowly until our eyes meet.

His brow drawn in, he shakes his head a tick.

"You want me to go?" His response is meek.

"I didn't say that. It's just . . . are you ashamed of me, James?" I level him with it because I've been through hell and back a few times. There's a reason I don't fall for boys. It's the pretty ones who hurt the most.

His laugh comes out almost immediately.

"Are you kidding?" James grabs one side of the treadmill and swings around so we're both standing in the tight space. I feel a little trapped so I back into the opposite railing and shuffle my body until we're both equal parts standing in this stall and able to escape.

My body trembles from the mix of emotions rushing through my body. I want to forget all of it, step up on my toes to hold his face in my hands and kiss his worries away while he does the same for me. But at the same time there's an edge of fear trying to break into my head. It's a feeling I haven't had in a long time, that inkling of something being wrong. And no matter how badly I want to, I can't seem to ignore it.

"Morgan, I'm a joke compared to you. I'm a joke, period.

I don't even know what the hell I'm doing here, and honestly, I can't stop worrying about when you're going to realize you're too good for me."

His confession slams into my chest, and it takes me a moment to catch my breath.

"I worry you're going to realize the same thing," I admit, choking down the emotion threatening to soften my resolve. I'm not ready to be soft just yet. I still have questions. I'm still wounded. "I don't think your dad likes me."

He flinches at my words, and his reaction, though pained, is telling because he doesn't dismiss my observation. Not immediately. Not even close to immediately. His expression and actions morph through all of the appropriate phases—creased brow, forced incredulous smile, fluttering lashes, roll of the eyes, and a breath of a laugh. But I see right through it. And he knows I do.

"It's not you," he finally says.

"Ha!" I huff, stepping off the treadmill. James grabs my wrist before I leave our tight space completely.

"Morgan, listen. It's football. It's the pressure and this place," he says, glancing around the room—around Welles. There's desperation in his eyes when his gaze comes back to me, and I swallow hard, feeling the weight of everything he means. "It's hard on us. My dad has coached for years. He's won state titles with teams that are ten times the talent of this place, yet the Browns and Penns of the world don't show up at those schools.

"We came here for the opportunity, and my dad is laser-focused on getting me to that next level, not just on a field but in a classroom that can make something of me. And when shit happens like what's gone on this week, when colleges I have dreamt of getting into show up to look at some . . . some . . . fucking joke? I guess it turns both of us into royal assholes.

I'm not proud of it. I hate that I let this get to me so hard. I want to run into the headmaster's office and spout off all of Toby's weaknesses. I want to beg him to look—*to really look!*"

His hand slowly loosens its grip, finally letting my wrist go, but I quickly snatch his hand and work our fingers together.

"It isn't you. My dad is just intense, and he's intense for me. He wants one hundred percent of my focus on the mission. But I am focused. And being with you . . . it balances out the garbage on the other side."

"Are you saying I'm anti-trash?" I joke. *Sort of.*

A hint of a smile tugs at his mouth. He steps into me and takes my other hand, bring our tethered fingers up to the space between us, clutching our fisted hands against his heart. My skin beads with chills from the air conditioning, the sweat from my run cooling me quickly. Too quickly.

"My dad sees you as a distraction. I see you as a necessity."

Well, damn.

The rage that held me up for the last thirty minutes is gone, and I think if James let go of my hands, I'd collapse at his feet. I'm charmed by his incredibly effective apology. Running my palms up the front of his shirt, I gather fists of cotton at the center of his chest and jerk him the final few inches into me. He lets out an exhausted laugh then cups my face, stroking the skin over my cheekbones before letting his forehead fall forward to rest on mine.

"Thanks for waiting around for me," he mutters.

"Hmm, what makes you think I was here for you?"

He presses his lips to my forehead, and I feel his mouth stretch into a smile.

"You normally run two six-minute miles on a Friday night?"

I open my eyes and follow his gaze over my shoulder to the numbers blinking on the treadmill. *Shit. That's fast.*

"I'm a real party animal," I say, bringing my gaze back to his.

"Right," he laughs out. "Well, party animal. How do you feel about taking a walk to the juice bar and getting a recovery smoothie with me? I need every edge I can get if I want to draw that Penn guy's eyes my way during tomorrow's game."

"Do those smoothies come with new legs so I have something to walk back on?" I'm half joking as I bat my lashes and look up into his amused grin. My feet are numb, and I truly believe my knees will buckle the second I leave this room.

Shaking his head and laughing, James kneels then twists around, patting his shoulders.

"Go on. Hop on and I'll carry you."

"The whole way?" I question, already moving to climb onto his back. He sweeps his hands under my thighs and hoists me up like a backpack. I giggle, feeling ridiculous.

"Yes, Morgan. The whole way." He leans across the treadmill and snatches my phone, handing it to me over his shoulder.

"I have things in the locker room," I inform him when he reaches the door.

"Awesome. More weight," he deadpans.

I wait until we're in the hallway before I reach down and swat his ass, yelling, "Yaw!" His feet stop in their tracks, and he cranes his neck to look me in my eyes.

"Are you serious right now?" His brow arches.

My mouth settles into a timid smirk.

"I have never been more serious in my life."

About anyone.

Chapter 14

James

I don't care what Theo and Cameron say, playing football on Saturday mornings is not the same as under Friday lights. There's a charge missing. This energy that a quarterback gets when the sky is black and those yellow posts glow against the dark night.

There are birds chirping right now. Lots of them. A whole damn flock. And it's so loud I keep looking at the trees when I should be watching our defense.

"This game is yours. You ready?" My dad leans into me and pulls my shoulder pad toward him as he speaks right into my helmet. I leave the birds and meet his eyes, or what I think are his eyes because I can't see them behind the sunglasses. Because the sun is out, and it's not night.

"I'm ready," I grunt. My dad moves on, shouting down the line at our defense as they force a third down.

I'm not ready.

I'm distracted, and while I'd like to blame the sun and the birds, they have zero to do with it. I'm sure my dad will want to blame the girl wearing my initials in glitter on her face for the lack of spirit I fear I might showcase when I get out there. But it won't be her fault, either. All I can think about is Toby and the fact he got the ball first . . . again. And he scored in two minutes. People went nuts. The Penn guy nodded and wrote shit down on his pad of paper then made a call to someone, probably the university president. In my head, the conversation went something like this:

"Hey, Larry. Yeah, it's me, Clueless Scout Man. We have to get this guy. Now look, I know his dad is basically our boss, but I still think we need to offer him a full ride. He needs to know how much we want him, otherwise he'll go somewhere else. What is that you ask? Do other people want him? Larry . . . *everybody* wants him."

In this fantasy, the president of Penn is named Larry. I'm not sure why I manifested this nightmare with a Larry at the helm, but I think it has something to do with latent resentment I harbor against the kid who stole my entire piñata from my fifth birthday. His name was Larry, and my mom made me invite him.

I try to amp myself up as our defense forces a kick. Our return team isn't very strong, but the school we're playing is shit, so I get to come in with decent field position. My dad flattens his hand on the back of his clipboard as I run out, his fingers spread wide to indicate play set five. I knock on my helmet to signal I'm ready and got his sign.

My dad wants me to show off my passing strength, but I'm missing Theo's hands, so I turn to Devin and Cameron in the huddle and tell them run their asses off and get open.

We break and get to the line. I position myself, ready for the shotgun snap for a bit of running room. I start my count, and for whatever reason, our center, Jake, sails the ball over my head before I finish the sequence. It catches our line off-guard, which means I have about a second and a half to land on that ball before a thousand pounds of high school football player weight piles on top of me to punch it away.

"Damn it!" I growl, eyes scanning the field behind me, tracking the ball as it bounds left, then right. I dive on top of it and brace myself, praying my ribs don't crack as the tackles come. It takes the referees nearly a minute to pull everyone off, fists beating at me to get to the ball the entire time.

I leave the pile shellshocked, tossing the ball to the referee as I jog toward the sideline, the world a little fuzzy.

"Can you go?" My dad makes a throwing motion with his hand. I nod, ignoring the trainer moving closer to the sideline, wanting to push for concussion protocol. My head is actually the only thing that doesn't hurt. My lungs feel like pancakes, and my arms took about three dozen fists to the forearms and biceps.

My dad fans his clipboard toward me, which means run it again. But something doesn't feel right. I scan the line and stop at Toby. He's standing with his helmet dangling from his hands as he rocks side to side, a smug grin on his face. Realization slaps me in my face.

I don't have the team.

I tried to convince myself that I could win them over, and maybe in time, I will. But as of now—*right now*—I have a handful. These are Toby's guys. They're the same. It's a good ole boys club and my membership application has yet to be accepted.

My mind runs through options as I run back to the huddle, and I'm still not certain how to handle things when I pull everyone in tight. Again, I scan the faces of the guys here with me. I look for the weak links, but they're all so deceptive.

"Come on, what's the play?" Devin demands. I meet his stare, his eyes as hungry as mine. Maybe it's not a matter of sorting out who is against me but finding the ones who are with me. Devin wants the ball. If I throw it, he'll be there.

"Devin, you get open on the route for the long ball. They're doubling coverage on Cameron since Theo's out, so let's use that. I want you to really break." Devin nods and claps his hands, his hot pink receiver gloves glowing in the morning sun. I bet they would look even better at night.

"All right, let's do this!"

We break, the play clock running, and I manage my time carefully, spending only one second on something more important to this play than anything else. I flatten my palm on Jake's back and lean into him as his hands push the ball into the grass.

"Don't fuck me again," I grunt.

I slap my palm down with enough force for my true message to sink through—so he *gets* it—then I back up and start my count. I'm ready for the ball to come at me instantly, but I hold on to the faith that my southside grit will wear Jake down. My pocket is going to give me up fast so I ready myself to move and burn as much time as I can before Devin hits his stride.

Jake snaps the ball on time and target, and our O-line leaves holes for the defense almost immediately. I swing back and to the right, leaving myself a good ten yards of room to run into my throw. I manage to break one tackle, but I don't know that I'll be able to get through the next one. Hoping I've given Devin the time he needs, I tighten my core and step into the throw of my life, launching the ball down the field a good sixty yards. I barely have time to witness it crest at the arc before I'm flattened on my back. I don't expect to get a flag for roughing the passer, and if my pass fails I may shrivel up into the earth anyhow, so I lay with my hands wrapped around my facemask and my ears tuned to the reaction of the

Welles home stands. If they explode, I can get up knowing I executed the biggest mic drop of my life.

The world switches to slow motion, and my eyes catch my dad's movement first as he leaps and pumps a fist into the air, his mouth shouting, "Go!" The hundreds of students and alumni in the stands behind him all get to their feet as their hands shoot into the air, and then the frenzied wave of cheering breaks through and turns time back to normal.

"Dude, that's the longest pass in Welles history, I swear," Cameron says, leaning over my body and stretching out his hand. I grip it and let him yank me up.

"Did it look as good as it felt?" I ask him as we jog off the field, another six points added to our score.

"I'll let you decide for yourself based on his reaction," Cameron says, pointing toward Toby, who is now sitting by the water cooler, his helmet on the bench next to him as he chews on his mouthguard like a rabid pit bull.

"Damn, I should have watched. It must have been good," I say.

Cameron laughs and we slap hands as we cross over the sideline and leave Toby to stew on his own.

I didn't expect everything to magically turn around in my favor. Toby went back in for more running plays the next set of downs, and he led one more scoring drive before the game was done. But Orland Homan, the recruiting coordinator for Penn, did stick around after the game and ask to talk to me and my father separately from Toby and his dad. And Jake gave me knuckles on his way out of the locker room.

* * *

"It's not an offer, but it is interest."

Those are the last words my dad said before heading out

for date night with my mom. He repeated them about a dozen times after our meeting with Penn. While I'm sure he wanted to keep me grounded, I think he was also reminding himself to not get carried away. Still, he was proud, and seeing him proud made *me* proud.

Things were beginning to feel tangible and within reach. It was exhilarating, but at the same time, it was all so terrifying. Interest is not an offer, and interest isn't going to get me the kind of money I need to be able to afford a school like Penn. I need more games like today's, and I need to convert more Jakes into Camerons and Theos.

I slip into the archive room after everyone else has arrived, and there's a beer in my hand within seconds. It's not quite the speakeasy-style whiskey and bourbon from the last few parties, and that's primarily because I'm too chicken to swipe more liquor using my dad's access key. I crack the can open and take a big gulp, glad I took my mom up on her offer to whip me up some dinner before she and my dad left.

A few guys congratulate me on my game as I wind my way through the desks toward the back of the room where Theo and Cameron are laughing about something. Lily and Brooklyn are huddled on the old leather sofa, and Morgan is nowhere to be found. I edge toward my friends while I scan the room one more time, then pull my phone out to check for a text from her. Nothing.

"Dude, if you keep throwing the ball like that, we might not be a joke this year. Shit, we may get a trophy out of this or some shit," Cameron says. His red eyes and half-awake demeanor clue me in to how high he is, and I wonder how Theo lives with him.

"Thanks, man," I say, bracing myself for his oncoming hug. He holds on to me a little too long, and I start to worry he's sleeping on me or working this into a slow dance when he laughs in my arms.

I back away and screw my eyes up, a little worried that he's about to be sick or something, but then I notice his gaze locked on something behind me. I follow the direction of his pointing finger.

Fucking Toby Sullivan standing in the middle of our secret. *This is bad. This is really bad.*

"Shit," I grumble a second before Theo does behind me.

"Maybe he won't come talk to us," I say, trying to reason my way out of this nightmare. Theo laughs, then lays his hand on my shoulder as he steps up beside me.

"Dude, we are the entire reason he's here. At least, *you* are." He pats my shoulder a few times before picking up his beer and ambling his way through the haphazard clustering of desks toward our unwanted guest.

I put my beer to my lips and tilt my head back, draining it completely and leaving the can behind. I'm going to need some sort of buzz for this conversation, and I don't have time to get on whatever cloud Cameron's floating on.

"So, this is where you moved things. Classy. Respectful too. I get it," Toby says, earning a hard stare from Theo. I glance down to catch his fist tightening at his side while he calmly holds his beer with his other hand.

Theo's sister died after a party in the woods. I guess that's what prompted Welles to completely close the campus and enforce strict security for the late hours. Morgan told me the only reason we were able to drive in and out late the other night was because my father's truck has a faculty sticker.

"I don't think you're on the guest list, *Tobes.* Sorry, but we have a strict policy," Theo says, circling his finger as if to suggest Toby simply turn around and leave. But Theo's right. That's not happening. Because he came here for me.

Theo sets his beer on a nearby desk and inches into Toby's space, his chest puffing up as he nears his face until they're almost nose-to-nose. I have my own battles with Toby, but for Theo, this moment is about his sister. And something in my gut tells me Toby is itching to push my friend over the edge. Before that can happen, I step between them and strong-arm Toby backward a few steps, not fast enough to knock him down but with enough force that he gets my point.

"All right, that's enough," I hiss. My eyes lock with Toby's. He blinks to look over my shoulder, lunging forward to fake Theo out, but nobody is fooled. I put my palm on his chest and our gazes lock again.

"Let's get this out of the way," I say, nodding my head to the side, to the far corner of the room away from the people having a good time.

Toby hovers for a moment, a front I recognize quickly because that's how the guys back home always intimidated people instead of having to get into an actual fight. Knowing he's not going to demand I fight him right here and now, I roll my eyes and leave him standing alone as I head to the back of the room. I slide up to sit on a metal desk and wait for him to finally join me. He only lags a few seconds. He leans against an opposite desk and folds his arms, his T-shirt sleeves cut short to accentuate his biceps. It makes him look like a cartoon.

"How do we get past this?" I offer first, figuring if I wait for him he'll choose to stare at me and flex his jaw all night.

"I don't think we can."

I appreciate his honesty, and maybe he's right. But I have to try. If I want any shot at all, I need to get the guys behind me. *All* of them.

I nod slowly.

"Here's the thing about that. I know I can. So, what

you're *really* saying is you don't think you can get past this."
It's twisted logic, and I can tell he's a little confused by it
thanks to the squiggle on his forehead.

"Whatever. Listen, this is my senior year. Me and the
guys have plans. We want to make memories, and you
coming in with your big fucking head is just messing up our
rhythm."

Big fucking head?

I laugh and quirk up the side of my mouth, and maybe it's
subconscious but I also drag my hand through my hair,
sampling the size of my noggin. I think he was being
metaphorical, but also, I don't think Toby's that bright.

"You know what? You're great at the run," I say, a total lie
because he's average at best. And our running backs are slow
compared to most of the public schools. The only thing great
about our running game with Toby at the helm is he doesn't
have to throw so there's a lower chance for an interception.

"I am great, and you're shit. So how about you stop taking
favors from daddy and quit the team?"

Wow. That escalated quickly. I wonder if he's like this
when he sits down for college interviews. Those checks his
dad writes must be enormous.

"Right. Okay. Well, Toby"—I run my palm over my chin
and get to my feet. It's a total power move because I'm much
taller—"I'm not going to quit the team. This is everything to
me, and I am going to work my ass off to see it through. So,
like I said, either you can get past this and maybe I'll let you
run the ball a little here and there, or *you* can quit the team.
How's that sound?"

Okay, my buzz is hitting my head. Nothing too strong,
but enough to drop my filter and let my inner thoughts loose.
It's kind of nice saying those things you really want to say out
loud.

"That might be hard when your dad gets fired," he says, and suddenly I'm stone cold sober.

"Excuse me?" I tilt my head and step into him.

"Oh, you must have heard the stories. You know . . . about Morgan Bentley and the last coach? They had a thing." Toby actually holds up his hands, making a fist with one then moving his fat finger in and out of it with the other.

"Watch yourself," I seethe. Theo is on the other side of the room, so I'm in charge of stopping myself from going too far. I know what he's doing. He's provoking me. Maybe I'll take a swing and get expelled for assault, and he can report Theo's secret lair and ruin life for everyone.

Keep it together, James.

"Just, I noticed her in his truck the other day when I was working the security booth. They were coming in pretty late, just the two of them. I could show you the picture if you want." His lips can't hold back his gleeful smile as he grins at me like a psychotic clown.

"Maybe I ask your dad about their relationship? Or I could ask around campus, see if anyone else has seen them together."

I hold his stare, studying his eyes and looking for the weak link in his game. This school is toxic. These people are toxic. And more than his accusations ruining my life, they'd implode my parents' marriage.

"Go ahead, ask around. Ask my dad, or his assistant coaches for that matter. My father can't stand Morgan Bentley. And you know what? Neither can I."

The words leave my mouth before I have a chance to evaluate them. They inflate on my tongue and choke my windpipe. I smell the way they burn up in the air. It was a pretty harsh lie, but I sold it. Only problem is that lie was Toby's end goal all along. I was too furious to see it coming, too proud to slow down and simply stand my ground. I let him take me low.

"I see. Whatever you say, James. Hey, nice game today," he says, his lips puckering into a pretentious and tight grin that dimples his cheeks like the sour of a lemon.

I stand pinned in place, my feet lead on the floor as he winds his way back to the exit, not bothering to provoke another soul on his way out of the fire. The only thing left for me to do is look down at the floor and follow the trail of glitter to the glass office door, shades drawn and lights off.

I hold my breath. I hold out hope. And then I hear the click of the lock.

Chapter 15

Morgan

He isn't going to leave.

It would have been better to run out of here in front of everyone, under the cover of a small gathering. It might have caused a scene, and James probably would have gone after me or tried to make me stay so he could explain, but if I had just left, this would be done by now.

Instead, I waited. I cried—*I hate crying*—and nothing is done. Everything lies ahead. I'm considering living out my days in this old office and digging out that weird bag of pot to get by.

"Morgan, please open the door."

It's four in the morning. His parents have to wonder where the hell he is. My roommates are wrapped up in their own happiness and probably don't even miss me. Not that I've been there much for them. Lily's big swim meet is soon. I should be doing those little things Anika would have done— leaving little notes of encouragement for her to find, stopping by her practice to cheer her on and embarrass her in that loving way, or organizing a party for after she competes. And Brooklyn . . . I think she's hooking up with Cameron, which scares me because he takes absolutely nothing in life seriously. I haven't been a very good friend. I've been busy wasting time, thinking I was falling in love with a stupid boy.

I can't very well sit in here for an entire weekend, and I really want to take a shower. Lifting my tired body from the floor where I have been wallowing for the last hour, I use the door handle to stand the rest of the way, flipping the lock as I do. I step back and a second later James pushes it open an inch.

"Thanks," James says. He's resting his head on the metal frame. I wonder how long he's been standing there like that. I was too afraid to peer through the drawn blinds.

"You can come in," I relent, turning around and heading to the rolling chair that I had my first good cry in hours ago.

James takes measured steps into the office, the archive space behind him an eerie kind of silent. He stops at the desk, his fingertips tapping the wood as he looks down with a thoughtful expression. He sucks in his lips and nods before slowly making his way backward to the wooden chair on the other side of the room. I think he's afraid I might hurt him.

"What? Can't stand being close to me?" I mock him with a bitter tone as I throw his own words back at him. I've been practicing that for hours. It didn't feel as good as I thought it would.

He lifts his gaze to mine, his eyes heavy and the corners of his mouth weighed down.

"You know I didn't mean that," he croaks.

Deep down, I do. But hearing something like that said about me out loud is hard to shake off. I can't parse it out just yet, because while he'll probably deny it, there was some truth in those things he said to Toby. His dad can't stand me. And I know why.

"Why did you blow me off at the field house the other day? Remember? While your dad was sort of letting me in the door?" He remembers. His dad's mood wasn't entirely about football.

He shakes his head and draws in his brow, but I keep my gaze locked on his face, my eyes narrow and drilling into his. After several seconds, he exhales and leans his weight back, flitting his eyes away.

"It's not like you think," he relents.

"But it is." My quick response takes him off-guard, and his eyes bolt to mine for a brief second before looking away.

Shaking his head, he leans forward to rub his temples.

"Morgan, the last couple years have been a battle for our family. My parents were in a bad place, and as much as we came to Welles for my benefit, this move was kind of for them, too. I'm not saying you can outrun your demons, but where we lived before, the things tearing down the trust between my mom and dad were everywhere."

He pauses to sit up, a short, sad laugh lifting his shoulders.

"I don't know for sure, but I think my dad was seeing someone on the side, or at least flirting with the idea of it. I don't think it progressed to an affair or anything like that. And I'm sure there's a lot more to it than the small pieces I put together, but where we were, our routine and our environment, it all fed into the story. It was this story that just wouldn't end. Bickering in their room that I heard through the walls. Days of silent treatment. They put their energy into me by coming here, and maybe it's unhealthy to be their distraction, but it's my family, Morgan. I haven't seen them this happy in a long time. And my dad . . . I think he's afraid of anything shaking up their new beginning."

I let his truth simmer. He has no idea what demons are, what consequences from decisions looks like.

I breathe out a laugh as I sit back and fold my arms over my chest, my gaze off to the side so I don't look him in the eyes and lose my way.

"You know, I'm used to people not liking me. I mean, the first time people started trashing one of my photos on social it was kind of hard to take, but the older I got the more I realized they do that for sport. They don't really *know* me."

My gaze shifts to him, and my teeth gnaw at the inside of my cheek.

"But you? You know me." I swallow the hurt that comes with that statement.

His focus dips below my gaze as his Adam's apple moves up and down. A single tear slips from my right eye, and I swipe it away, my sniffles giving me away and bringing his attention back to my face. I'm so angry and hurt, but more than that . . . I feel betrayed.

God, I was really falling for him. And I *know* he has feelings, too. I can tell this is hurting him—that hurting me hurts. But he still did it. And yeah, maybe I wasn't meant to hear him say that awful truth to Toby. And Toby's a real dick for luring it out of him the way he did. But when his back was pushed into a corner, he chose football. He chose to believe the rumors.

He didn't ask me.

"Remember me telling you about the last time my dad had me 'entertain' some of his clients? How things didn't go so well?" I can feel the tears welling in my eyes, but I won't cry over this.

James's mouth is closed tight, his jaw flexing and eyes pained, the weight dipping his brows.

"My family has this big yacht. It's more like a company yacht, really. We've been on it as a family of four once, and we never left the dock. But my dad's on it all the time. Some of his biggest acquisitions were negotiated on that thing while floating out in the Atlantic."

I pause to gather my thoughts, my mouth growing dry. James's breathing is growing heavier, his chest slowly inflating as he takes in my words. I can see it in his expression, in the locked focus of his eyes— he's trying to get to the end of my story before I do. He won't get it right. The only person who knows their story is the one who lived it. That's why it's so important to listen.

My teeth graze against my bottom lip as I let it slip from my nervous hold.

"My dad has had the same lawyer since he made his first million. Edwin Hague. He's good. Probably saved my dad millions by now, and I'm sure he's kept him out of prison for shady financial shit. If it's an important meeting, he's in the room."

James shifts in his seat, folding one arm over his chest to prop up the other so he can chew at his thumbnail. I close my eyes and shake my head.

"Don't work ahead. Let me tell this story," I say.

I draw in more air through my nose, my pulse oddly even. It's strange how I haven't had a panic attack since my accident. It's as if that trauma rewired the damage from all the ones before.

"My dad invited me to join him for a business dinner out on the boat, asked me to invite some of my girlfriends from the city. Not Brooklyn or Lily, but old family acquaintances.

187

People I grew up with and often ran into at society events. The ones you see on my social media pages."

I shrug because my digital life looks nothing like my real one. There's nothing wrong with those girls. They played the same kind of part I did in our world—rich girl, daddy's girl, brat, influencer, the list of titles goes on. None of us were ever close. We were pleasant to one another. Every now and then one of us would start some drama about the other on Twitter, but even that was more about the attention than the relationships within. Meanwhile, my real friendships—Brooklyn, Anika, Theo, and now Lily—those were off the page. Protected. *Not salacious.*

"I knew what my dad was up to. He wanted to make this dinner party seem hip. He was courting Silicon Valley guys and their startups, which he would eventually buy for cheap and fold into his empire. Having me and my friends hanging around meant buzz, and buzz made young business types make poor decisions and sell themselves short. The deal was done by the time dinner ended, but we were in an ocean and drinks were flowing. Everyone was having a good time."

I shrug, pursing my lips in admission.

"Nobody was running off and hooking up, but there was plenty of flirting. Mostly innocent stuff like dirty talk in a corner while the guys watched me and my friends dance and simply be young, reckless teenagers."

I smile at the good stuff, the fun of being in such a privileged position. It lasts for a second before it fades into a soured line.

"I never liked Edwin. Something about him has always given me the creeps, even when I was a little kid. He was that guy who always handed out money when he came over, like he was buying me. When I was five, he'd slip me twenty bucks and tell me to buy a bunch of junk food. When I turned sixteen, he gave me a grand and told me to party hard. My parents laughed and said he's like an uncle."

I stare ahead into James's eyes, my mouth watering with sickness.

"I was catching my breath, drinking water to sober up and hydrate from all the dancing. I'd only stepped off to the side for a minute when Edwin placed his hand on my bare back. I stiffened under his touch, and when he tried to slide his hand lower inside my dress, I tore away from him. Almost nobody noticed. One or two of the girls I invited saw me jerk away, and without asking, they knew. Things like that had happened to them—they happen a lot. My dad saw it, too. And the worst part was I thought he would get mad at me for running off, for making a scene and ruining his party. For offending his best lawyer, his faithful friend."

"He blamed you?" The first words James has uttered come out coarse, angry. His jaw is rigid, his molars pressed together as his nostrils flare.

I spit out a breathy laugh and shake my head.

"He said it didn't matter because it all turned out fine in the end." I swallow down the bile that comes up when I quote him. I can still picture the movement of my father's lips as he says those words to me.

"It was the next morning, and I was trembling as I stepped up to join him on the patio over a late breakfast. I wasn't hungry. I wanted to throw up. And all I could do was force myself to apologize for ruining his party, knowing I wasn't to blame at all. That his lawyer was a piece of shit for a human, and that a real dad would do something on his daughter's behalf. But he closed a deal, and Edwin got a bonus. *It all turned out fine in the end.*"

My tongue presses behind my front teeth as my mouth hangs open in a hostile, faint smile. I haven't talked to my mother since she conned me into helping my dad again, and honestly, maybe life will be better if I cut both of them out of it. I'll keep Braden, the half-relative the universe must have thought I needed. The universe was right. But I needed Coach Wallace too.

"Morgan. That's . . ."

He swallows, and I laugh softly then shrug.

"Awful? Yeah, it is. Common? Yep, that too. Sexist? Assault? Probably." I have many labels for the shit I've worked through. I'm still learning how to assign blame to others, and I'm getting better at it.

"It is. It's all of those things," he answers.

The quiet takes over for nearly a minute. We endure long stares, and he begins to speak a dozen times or more. He wants to apologize on behalf of everyone, but that's not for him to do. He can, however, apologize for himself.

"My depression hit a pretty serious low last November. And I remembered Coach Wallace's talk about mental health during one of our workshops the year before. The school hosts those things to tick off boxes and brag about being proactive. But Coach Wallace's talk was really good. It was enough to help me recognize when I needed to talk to some-one. And he's the one I talked to."

James blinks, his face a clean slate, expressionless. I know he has heard the rumors around campus. For a while I braced myself for him to bring it up, but when he didn't, I simply figured he didn't buy into them. Maybe he hasn't. But his dad has heard those rumors, too, and for him, rumors are every-thing. He fits in here better than James thinks.

"I confided in Coach because I had nobody else, and he kept everything in confidence. But he worried. And he worried enough that he finally made a phone call to my dad. So, my dad had him fired."

By the time I finish my tale, James's eyes are closed. His lids tremble, and his mouth swells into a deep frown. I know that look. I've worn it myself many times. I've left him with my burdens, with the weight of them. I feel lighter. I'm sad. I'm still hurt. The edge of anger remains too. But I know who I am, and I know who I am not. And I'm worth more than the consideration I've been given.

I get up from my chair and walk over to James, lifting his chin with my fingertips. He keeps his palms flat on his thighs. They twitch, and I think he wants to reach for me, but he feels it in the air. He can't. Not right now. Maybe . . . one day. But not right now. Not when his father can't stand me.

"You should have asked me. I would have told you," I say.

His eyes become glassy, and he sucks in his lips along with his guilt.

"Morgan." My name floats from his lips and the sound dissipates into the quiet. The room is cold, and my arms are covered in goose bumps and flecks of glitter from the bright way the day began.

"You were good today. On the field? Quarterbacking?" I let out a tiny laugh that he matches, and I let my thumb rub across his chin that's still in my hand. He's terribly pretty. And I think inside, he's also a good man.

He reaches up and wraps his hand around my wrist, holding on—holding me here. He stands slowly and my hand falls away as his comes up to sweep what I imagine is smeared, crusty glitter from my cheek. His eyes dip to my mouth, briefly, and I see the flash of guilt in his eyes that he would even consider a kiss from me right now. Thing is, though, I still want one.

Lifting up on my toes, I catch his face between my palms and press my lips to his for a soft kiss that lingers, our mouths motionless yet teeming with electricity. I fall back on my heels and look away before he catches the tears threatening my eyes. I don't run out of the archive room, but I don't waste time leaving him with his thoughts, either.

Damn me for giving in and tasting him one last time. I like him so damn much—at least the parts of him that are brave enough to be with a girl like me.

As angry as I try to be at him, as much as I want to say no, my body refuses. I'm always left breathless. And alone.

Chapter 16

James

I've come to learn a few things about places like Welles. Grand schemes and manipulations are everywhere, and they come in all scales and sizes. There are students undermining teachers, and the same goes for the reverse. Some families use their name to hold the school hostage, and the school uses those names to bully other people around.

Toby got what he wanted. He never had some grand master plan to get me off the team so he could take over, though I still don't believe he wouldn't squash me like a bug if he had the chance. He only wanted me to hurt. To look bad. To expose a blemish on my character like the rest of them.

And I think a part of him wanted Morgan. She would never give a guy like him a chance, though. Her standards are far too high. They're too high for me, too, and I accept that. Barely. Begrudgingly. At least, I do for today.

It's been two days since she walked out of that office. Forty hours since I sent her the longest text of my life, rife with apology and empty on excuses. She hasn't responded, and I'm honestly not sure how to speak to her face to face. She's right to wait me out. What she deserves is more than an "I'm sorry," and she deserves it in person.

I'm distracted, for sure. It's showing on the field. Yesterday, I hit my targets maybe fifty percent of the time, and today I can't seem to quit soaring the ball ten yards past the end zone on the special play we set up for this weekend's game. Toby's dad is hovering in the stands along with our athletic director, and I know they're going to give my dad an earful after practice about letting him take a shot at running this since I seem to be such shit at it. He won't be able to make the pass either, but at that point we're both garbage quarterbacks.

I take a snap, roll back a few steps, and turn to spot my target. Theo cuts through the end zone and I fling the ball toward the corner. He manages to hang on to my missile and keep one foot inbounds, but not two.

"Fuck!" My frustration echoes off of the stands on the hill. I glance over in time to see Toby's dad leaning into the athletic director and covering his mouth to share some comment that I'm certain is about me.

"All right, let's stop there for the day. Theo . . . James . . . Toby!" My dad waves the three of us over and my insides crumple. I'm literally handing this job to Toby.

"Cameron, close us out!" My dad sends him off to circle everyone else up and pack up for the day while he pulls the three of us to the side.

"Gentlemen." My dad's stubble is growing out, and it sounds like sandpaper when he runs his palm over his chin. Clipboard hugged to his chest, he looks down at the grass between our circled-up feet. "We've got to do better.

Saturday is a big game, rivals and all that, and we can't come out there with the kind of shit I saw today."

Toby snickers, and my dad's head snaps up to stare at him.

"I said *we*, Toby. Your footwork is sloppy and you're going to get our running backs killed if you can't hand the ball off tighter. And forget about making the run yourself. You're too slow."

Toby's mouth hangs open and for a second his eyes flash in offense. My dad keeps his glare on him, though, waiting for him to argue. My father's done kid-gloving him because he's special. And he's right; all three of us were shit today. Theo should get a free pass, though, because it's my fault he couldn't pull anything in.

"James, you're going the entire first quarter how I have it now—"

"Uhm, what?" Toby cuts my father off. My dad's only response is to move his clipboard to his right and hold it against Toby's chest.

"Unless you can't sort through these yips you seem to have with hitting your target. Lipson Prep is going to be tough. They're our only real competition as far as I'm concerned, and we are going to have to be our absolute best if we want to win." He turns to me, taking the clipboard away from Toby's chest and spearing mine with the corner. "Game time is not the time to practice hitting your targets. Got it?"

My dad's brow lifts, and he keeps his focus on me a few seconds after I say, "Yes, sir." This is bigger than him showing favoritism. If I don't get my shit together, he can't afford to lose the game taking a gamble on me.

"Theo," he barks, the clipboard leaving my body as he hands it to Theo instead. "You were great today. I want you to learn these routes. We're going to need them, assuming someone can throw the ball to you."

"Yes, sir," Theo says.

My father turns around and heads up the hill to the locker room where he'll bury himself in his office and pray that Toby's dad and the AD don't come knocking.

"Something in your head today, Fuentes? You were all over the place," Toby snarks. It's nothing new from him, and honestly, I was expecting it. Maybe I even wanted it. Because I shove him backward on his ass in a blink and land with my knee in his stomach, pinning him to the ground.

"Hey, cool it! That's not gonna help anything. James, come on," Theo pleads at my back. I feel the tug of his hand jerking my shoulder pads upward. I give my knee a little nudge, just enough to let Toby feel it, as I flinch at him.

I get up but he stays on the ground for a few seconds, his usual laughter in the face of my intimidation not there this time. His sneer is tinged with fear, which I like.

"I don't like being manipulated," I say, spitting on the ground next to me before turning my back on him and walking toward the locker room with Theo. He doesn't say a word to me until we're well out of Toby's earshot.

"That have anything to do with Morgan?" he asks.

I chew on my tongue and when I feel his eyes on me I shrug.

"Kind of," I huff.

He chuckles and echoes me in a super unflattering voice. "*Kind of.*"

I shove his shoulder and knock him off balance.

"What, are you Cameron now?" Cameron is constantly parroting shit people say to be annoying. He likes to get under people's skin, and that method is really effective. I glare at Theo and roll my eyes. He's completely unfazed, and steps back up beside me, still laughing.

"It's a lot more fun when you're on this side of that shit. Believe me," he says.

"Oh, I do. Because that's super annoying," I huff.

Theo bites his tongue for a few seconds but busts out a laugh at my expense when we get to the field house. I stop at the door, holding my hand on it to keep him from opening it.

"Dude, sorry. Your tantrum is funny. That's all," he says.

I sigh and fling the door open, stepping through and not holding it for him. He catches it before it swings closed and follows me down the hallway.

"Hey, wait up a minute." He tugs on the back of my jersey, and I spin around and flatten my back to the wall with a grumble. I let my head fall back against the brick and blow up at my sweaty-ass hair. I lower my gaze and meet his face, relieved he isn't smirking or trying to hold in more laughter. I'm miserable, and I feel as though everything is falling apart.

"What?" I relent. I'm exhausted. I'm not used to playing games for everything in life. You show up, you work hard, you do a job, and maybe if you're lucky you get to do something you want at the end. That's what I thought life was. This isn't like that at all. It's a winding route with tar pits and dead ends.

"Morgan is . . ."

I must react to him saying her name because he throws up his palm to stop me, as if I'm going to take a swing at him. My trigger-like temper is touchy right now, and frankly, I'm tired of hearing people talk shit about her . . . though I did, which is why I feel like this.

"Morgan is resilient. That's what I was going to say." Theo's head tilts to the side, his mouth a flat, sincere line. I consider that word and how it aligns with everything I know about her and decide he's right.

"Yeah, okay," I say.

"Of every student in this school, she's the toughest. My sister and I grew up with her. Our families went to the same boring-ass parties, and we had to endure a lot of the same shit. That world made me angry, and it made my sister feel small. Morgan wears the wounds from it, too. She takes more shots than most of us. But that girl—" He pauses and puffs out a quick laugh. I meet his eyes and take in his admiring smile. "She was twelve and figured out that if she was going to have to live in that world she may as well profit off of it. You know that her brand alone, nothing to do with her dad, is worth millions? *Mill-ions.*"

I swallow at that thought. I've never really thought about that side of things with her. Before I knew her, she was this semi-famous personality that yeah, I definitely wanted to brag about to the guys back home. And then I got to know her, and she was this smart, beautiful creature. She's a genuine force, though. Theo's right.

He pats my chest a few times with a heavy hand, and I cough out a laugh.

"I'm sorry my passes were shit today. I'll be on when it's game time. Promise."

Theo points at me, finger right in my face.

"I know you will. Because Toby can't even throw a party, so if you let your moody ass get you benched, we're getting our asses kicked Saturday." His eyebrows shoot up to punctuate his point then he heads into the locker room.

I head inside a few seconds later, not wanting to wait around for Toby to drag his ass in here. Theo's right about everything. And I don't have a lot of time to fix shit on the field. Tomorrow's practice was cut short so the team can go to the swim meet to cheer on Lily. Looks like I've got an early morning ahead of me.

* * *

My mom is deep into somebody's tax forms at the table when I walk in. I can always tell when she's dealing with a difficult client because she doubles up her reading glasses, forgetting that she's already got a pair on her head.

"Leftovers in the fridge. We still have some of the carnitas left too, if you want that. Nothing fancy, but I'm going to be in these files for a solid week." She pulls the glasses from her eyes and rubs the bridge of her nose. I step up and take the pair from her head, then kiss her hair. She laughs when I hand the spectacles to her.

"That's how you know *shit has gotten real,*" she jokes.

We both laugh. I head into my room, dropping my stuff by the door and grabbing the fresh T-shirt and sweats from the basketful of clean stuff I still need to put away. I tear off my sweaty practice shirt and toss it on the chair but do a double take when a blue and gold card catches my attention. I lift my shirt back up and Morgan's ID card slides from the chair to the floor. I stare at it for a few long seconds, trying to figure out what this means and who left it here.

I pick it up and carry it out to the kitchen, my stomach sinking as I assume my dad left this for me as some little reminder to stay focused. I'm so tired of the needling from every direction. This is not the way I want to kick off a conversation with him about how wrong he is about Morgan, and how I can be both focused and close to a girl like her.

"Hey, do you know why this card was on my chair?" I hold it up, figuring my mom won't have a clue. She pulls her glasses away from her face again and tilts her laptop halfway closed.

"Yeah, I found it in the truck. I was thinking maybe you could tell me?"

The weight of her question swirls in my belly for a second or two, and I try to respond but the only thing that comes out of my mouth is mush. Is she fishing? She can't think Dad has a thing going on with a student.

"She's . . . a girl," I stammer.

A loud belly laugh escapes my mom's tiny body as she taps her laptop completely closed then leans back in her chair.

"Well, duh! She's a very pretty girl. I can see that from her picture." She's mocking me, and she doesn't look upset. I relax a little, but now my cheeks are burning. "James . . . do you have a girlfriend?"

I roll my head at her tone. She's enjoying this, which would be sweet if it weren't so complicated. I drop my chin and meet her anxious expression.

"I don't know anymore. I maybe blew it," I admit.

My mom frowns, at first playfully, but the longer she studies my face, the more the gravity of it must set in.

"Oh, son. Come here." She slides her chair out and drags another toward her using her foot. I shuffle her way and slump down next to her. She pats my knee.

"Tell me about it."

I pull my mouth into a tight-lipped smile with a single laugh. I don't even know where to begin.

"She's . . ."

Our mother-son session is cut short as my dad enters the room, bringing with him the massive weight I got a short reprieve from. I blow out through my mouth and shift to get up from my seat.

"No, stay. Honey, our boy has girl trouble. He needs advice," my mom says. My dad stops just inside the door and levels me with the same *Oh, shit* look I'm pretty sure I had when he walked in the door.

"I'm pretty beat. And you should be focused on football, not girls. Penny, I've got a lot to do tonight." He gestures toward their bedroom, but my mom leans forward with her elbows on the table and rubs her hands together, challenging him.

My dad sighs and moves to our table, dropping his bag in one chair and sliding the other out, away from both of us. He takes a seat as if he's in a meeting with a discipline problem, leaning forward with his arms on his knees, cracking his knuckles. The air in the room is instantly thick. I glance from my dad to my mom, her forehead creased with worry. The sense of déjà vu makes my stomach turn. The last time the three of us sat at a table wearing expressions like these and showing body language like this was when my parents told me they were going to counselling.

"I can't do this," I say, getting up and tucking Morgan's card in my pocket, hoping my dad doesn't notice. But the man must be former CIA because I swear he misses nothing. *Nothing*.

"What was that?" he asks.

"Nothing," I lie.

My mom slaps my arm and I flinch, then look at her.

"Why are you lying to him? Dave? Why is your son afraid to talk to you about this?" My mom's eyes bounce between her husband and son, and I don't know what to say to get out of this mess, so I do what I probably should have done all along. I go with the truth.

I pull Morgan's ID from my pocket and toss it on the table.

"I took Morgan out the other night, on a date. And I took the truck off campus, which *I know*," I nod, as if that's the thing my dad is going to be pissed about. "She must have left her ID in there, which is why she couldn't get into the field house the other day. You remember when you basically put her through an interrogation?"

I probably could have left my editorializing out of that answer, but I'm just so sick of it all. And if I'm going to be honest, I'm going to be *totally* honest.

"I did not interrogate her," my dad defends.

I puff out a quick laugh and mumble, "Bullshit."

"James! Language," my mom chastises.

I sigh because seriously, me saying *bullshit* is so not the point right now.

"I'm having girl trouble because Dad doesn't like her. He thinks she's a distraction," I level.

"She is." His answer is swift and offensive.

"Because you say so. But you don't know her," I defend.

Now my dad's the one to punch out a laugh.

"What does that mean?" my mom cuts in, something in her tone sharp and pointed, piercing enough to get my dad to shut his mouth and me to sit down. She reaches forward and pulls the ID toward her, holding it between her thumb and index finger. Nobody in the world takes a good ID photo, except Morgan Bentley.

My mom shakes her head, the lightness gone from her face as she stares at Morgan's picture. She sets the ID back on the table and folds her hands over it before lifting her head and staring my father in the eyes. His movement is slight, but he shakes his head at her almost in a warning, like he's begging her to leave this alone.

"The girl had inappropriate relations with my predecessor," he finally utters, and I can't take it.

I spin out of my seat so fast my chair tumbles to the floor, both of my parents jolting back in their seats and staring at me wide-mouthed and wide-eyed. I point at my father, shaking my finger, my body vibrating with anger.

"That's a rumor that you *chose* to believe. And it's—*I'm sorry, Mom*—but it's bullshit. She came to Coach Wallace in confidence to get help with her depression. Her life—my God, *her life!* The pressures that come with her family are almost unreal, and I'd think they were made up if I didn't see them. If she didn't confide in me and show me some of the insanity she has to go through. You want to know why Coach Wallace got canned? Because he cared about her, and he dared to question the Bentleys' parenting skills.

"You've seen it, Dad. You know how people are around here. They are mighty quick to react to criticism, and it's never in a good way. Mr. Bentley had him fired."

I'm out of breath by the time I'm done, my fists at my sides as though I'm ready for a fight. Sometime during my rant my dad looked down, and his gaze is still on the floor. My mom's is on nothing, her focus almost on my face, but more like she's looking at a ghost somewhere over my shoulder.

"Say something," I implore my father. "Anything. Maybe apologize, even though I'm not the one who needs to hear it."

"I'm just keeping you focused. This is what you wanted, I thought. This school, or one like it. A scholarship to a big fancy school. Am I wrong?" My dad twists his head, giving me a sideways look as he opens his palms out in front of him as if presenting a prize.

"I'm doing the work," I argue.

My dad shifts in his chair, turning to rest an elbow on the back, his trademark move before making a point. But my mom speaks first.

"That's not what this is about, Dave. I thought we were over this," she says. My dad's gaze bolts to hers.

"Penny—"

"No," my mom interjects. She stretches her hand out toward me with Morgan's ID pinched between her thumb and fingers. I take the card and look at Morgan's sweet face, the forced smile that I've seen on her social media so many times.

"James, sit down." My mom's voice is calm as she motions to the chair I tumbled to the floor. I glance to my dad, his expression stoic, and sad.

I put the chair upright and sit in where it lies, suddenly wanting to be on an island. I want a way out if I need it. Nothing in my way.

"Your dad and I . . . we're good," my mom says.

"We're better than good," my dad adds. His tiny tacked-on statement brings a brief smile to my mom's face. They exchange glances, my father's eyes softer than they've been all night.

"There was a man, one of my clients, actually. And James, nothing happened between us. It's important to me that you hear that and know it. I would never betray your father that way."

My heart is pounding, and I think I utter, "Okay," but I'm not sure if it was aloud.

"I did develop a relationship with this man, though. Not romantically, but we began talking regularly. Your dad and I were struggling at the time, so I turned to him and leaned on him for support. I met him for coffee the morning after our first counselling session, and I broke down in front of him. My emotions were a mess, and that first session was a lot to process. He comforted me. We hugged, and he . . . he got carried away. He tried to kiss me. I rejected him, but it still

204

changed everything. I came home and told your father immediately, and he reacted as you'd expect."

"I went to the man's house." My dad's response is direct
and curt, and he glances to me briefly, almost as if to prove
he's not kidding.

My mom sighs.

"He did, and it was a really bad time. It set us back, but
also—and tell me if you agree, David—I think it made us
stronger." She looks to my dad, her arm outstretched across
the table. My father gets up from his seat and steps in next to
her, kneeling and taking her hand in his. He presses it to his
mouth.

"Why didn't you tell me?" I ask.

My father chuckles.

"You really want to know every detail about your parents'
marriage?" He lifts a brow. It takes me a few seconds to get
his insinuation.

"Oh. I mean, no. But something like this? Yeah, I
think so."

My dad shakes his head then stands, helping my mom to
her feet so he can hug her.

"Your father is being modest, but he didn't want you to
think poorly of me. I was afraid you would, so he promised
we would never talk about the details with you, and that we
would work hard on *us*. We put in the work," my mom says.

Effort.

That's what I've been missing. I'm so good at wringing
myself dry for football and my own goals. I need to give
Morgan that same kind of attention. I need to make her feel
like a priority. It's not something that will distract me. It costs
zero time. It's in the effort, in the ways I spend my time with
her. I need to make her feel the way she makes me feel.

"I'm going to get this back to her. She's been missing it," I say, flashing her badge then turning to head out the door. I stop with my hand on the knob and turn to look at my dad. "Don't worry about practice tomorrow. I'm going to hit every pass. You can start thinking about how you're going to let Toby know he'll be on the bench a lot more moving forward."

The slight smirk that ticks up the side of my dad's mouth lets me know he likes the fire I'm showing. I don't push things now, but I'm also going to need him to actually sit down and meet Morgan. He owes her an apology, which is not his strong suit. I think he'll make the effort, though.

Chapter 17

Morgan

I would almost rather spend the night here in this smoke-scented apartment than go back to my dorm tonight. I didn't mean to stick around and work so late again, but my mind is soaking up the distraction. And maybe I'm starting to really fall for Opal and Jayne. They're old school, and I don't think they're aware that their way of doing things is incredibly rare in today's digital age. They're just missing a bridge to pull today's world together with their attention to detail.

Turns out their biggest client, Boston Financial, is the one that basically pays the bills. It's the reason they can do so many cool boutique jobs for businesses—well, like the kind James wants to open one day. Boston Financial asked for a meeting, and being a Bentley I'm privy to the insider shakeups that my gut tells me are the reason for the meeting. Boston Financial is undergoing a transition from father to son at the helm. My father and Roderick McCoy, the outgoing CEO, have had a standing annual golf trip to California going on thirty-years, and knowing what I've gleaned about

Ginger Scott

his son Noah, he's out to really prove himself. Show he can not only hold his dad's position but shake it up. That means out with the old ways and in with the new when it comes to things that don't startle investors, and marketing and brand management is low-hanging fruit.

Opal and Jayne are about to get plucked. And discarded.

I channeled my energy today into coming up with an entirely new pitch for Boston Financial's brand awareness, and I got so invested in it, I found myself still neck-deep in design files when the ladies told me they were heading out for their dinner party. They left me with a key to lock up, and having my own office key—albeit to a musty apartment office trapped in the seventies—gave my mind the jolt it needed to power through.

Now it's nine at night, and I have to find a way to get home. I've alienated Brooklyn thanks to my sharp tongue and inability to hold it when it comes to sharing my concerns about her dating Cameron. Lily has the swim of her life tomorrow. And then there's James. Who *can't stand me.* I know he didn't mean it. I even understand the pressures and circumstances that forced him into saying it. But that was two days ago. I haven't even read his text. Well, that's not entirely true. I skimmed it for the highlights. I counted three *very's* and four *sorry's.* Lots of *so's.* Nothing about it was the James I thought I knew. That James? He wouldn't send a text. He'd show up.

Left with little option, I call the one person I know who is most like me—Braden. He's been spending a lot of time in the city thanks to some recent acquisitions, so there's a good chance he's still in his office. I give him a ring as I close down my laptop and pile my research into my canvas bag to take back to Welles. I can continue distracting myself with Opal and Jayne's business future back in my dorm.

"Hey, favorite sister! Let me guess, drunk in the city and need a ride?"

I mock laugh at his greeting, though it is warranted since I have requested his car service for such an occasion more than once—*twice*.

"Your *only* sister is in the city, yes. She is sober, however. I just really don't want to take the T alone at night." I bite the end of my pen, hoping he can rescue me.

"Well, first off, we don't know for sure that you're my *only* sister. I mean, there could be dozens of us running around out there." We both laugh at my father's infidelity. It's easier than taking it personally.

"But yes, I'm finishing up now. Where are you?" he asks.

"I'm on Fourth and Adams. Fifth brownstone from the corner," I answer. "I'll wait by the door."

"Okay, should be there in ten."

I end the call and gather my remaining things, a little excited to spend more time working on my presentation. I'm not even sure the ladies knew what I meant when I offered to put a pitch together for them. They laughed it off to an extent, probably because they haven't had to work this hard to keep a client in a long time. Long-time relationships can be that way—steady and easy to get lax with until all of a sudden they're not.

Deciding to mark this occasion, I pull my phone out and hold it high above my head to capture a photo of myself weighed down with a bag full of meaningful work. I glance at my first take and immediately see flaws in the way my smile doesn't quite reach my eyes, which are puffy from two days of feeling upset and being exhausted.

Before I delete it, however, I pause and think about my point of taking the photo in the first place. This is me, right now. This is the way I look, and it is certainly the way I feel.

Why would I want to erase that? Maybe there's value in looking back on this moment and remembering how it felt. It's good to recall that the journey was hard when you come through the other side. It makes the work more meaningful.

I make a note about the image in the caption area and save it to my ME folder along with the one from a few days ago when I felt pretty. Seeing the two images side-by-side, I'm suddenly struck by how different the girl in them looks. I'm the same person with two, and probably more, very different sides. Something about that thought settles in my chest and relaxes me. I put my phone away and wait for Braden to arrive, but that thought lingers with me until his black Tahoe pulls up outside the brownstone.

I climb into his car and tuck the key Opal gave me into my purse. My brother notes the enormous fluffy pig on the keychain as I do.

"This keychain is just the tip of the iceberg. You should see the things in that apartment." I tap the pig's head into my purse to make sure it's secure. then buckle up as Braden shifts into drive.

"And why are you at a strange apartment with stuffed pig chains?"

I realize how little he knows about my life, and for a second it makes me sad. I wish we were closer. It would be nice to have someone feel like family the way other people have family.

"Internship. I'm working for these two PR ladies who run their business out of their shared home. It's a real scene, believe me," I say.

Braden waves his hand at me and bunches his face.

"I will take your word for it. Did they turn you into a smoker? You know you can get that stuff in bubblegum scent now instead of Marlboro, right?"

I sneer, then pull my shirt collar to my nose and inhale to discover he's right.

"They're a bit seventies, as is literally everything in their place. Unfortunately, so is most of the material they produce," I admit. I feel good about the direction I'm taking things for them, though. I hope they'll get into it, or at least let me run with it.

"You know, that stuff is in again. With a twist, of course. But there's a lot you can do with that seventies' vibe," he says. I love that he's taking an actual interest, and I beam at his response.

"Maybe when I finish this pitch I'll run it by you because that is *exactly* the thing I'm going for." I lift my bag to my lap and hug it, glancing at the notepads and folders. This is something my parents wouldn't understand. I don't think my mom has ever held a paper and pen in her hands that wasn't a checkbook, and my father hasn't been one doing real work for years—decades. He delegates. And he barks orders. What I'm doing is real, and it feels good.

"Hey, you know I don't like to get into things between you and your mom and dad and all, but—"

"Please say Mom is not trying to get to me through you?" It wouldn't be the first time my mother has wormed her way back into my graces using Braden as bait.

He grips the wheel and purses one side of his lips, glancing at me with a wry, guilty look. When he doesn't follow it up with an explanation, or even a message from my mom, I start to get worried.

"Braden?" I prompt.

He looks back to the roadway, resting his elbow on the window ledge and rubbing his palm over his chin. Something's wrong.

"Dad had a stroke. It's been about six days, and he's going

to be okay. But he's going to need a lot of rehab, and my time-line at the businesses definitely got sped up."

"What? I'm sorry." I shake my head. "I don't understand. I was with him days ago. He was fine! I mean, he was a complete asshole and I wished to the world that I'd never need to speak to him again, but still—"

"Yeah, right after you had that breakfast meeting, which I promise I was not involved with, by the way." Braden holds up a hand in a scout's honor swear, and I push it down imme-diately because I know he wasn't involved. There's only one man who operates that way, and he's apparently in a hospital recovering from a stroke.

"Why didn't anyone tell me?" I protest.

"Your mom told me she was handling it, even though I offered. She said she called you, but you kept hanging up." He grimaces and I sigh, fluttering my eyelids in disgusted disbelief.

"She set me up and I was pissed, but seriously . . . she could have left a message," I grumble. This is so typical of her, using something like this to spin a pity party she can tell everyone else. I can hear her in my head now: *Oh, and my daughter, Morgan—she hung up on me!*

"I'm no one to talk because Libby can be a real pill, too," Braden says, referencing his mother. "But your mom has a real flare for the drama. You know the more times you hang up the more times she will call and not leave a message."

"Oh, I'm sure it's to the point now that she's doing it in front of her society friends to show off how unfeeling and awful her daughter is. Damn it!" I sulk into my seat and bite at my thumbnail, wanting to crunch my front teeth down hard enough to break a finger. "You know what? Next time she calls I'm going to answer and act all sweet, and if I find out she has me on speaker phone, I'm going to call her out in front of her friends."

"Way to focus on the big picture, Morgan." Braden has always been good at pulling me back from the edge with his special brand of sarcasm. I'm still fired up with anger, but I take a breath at his comment and center myself on the real point like he said. My dad is in the hospital recovering from a stroke. Braden is taking on more of the work.

"Sorry," I apologize, my tone still a little begrudging.

Braden reaches forward and turns the music up a few notches, knowing I'm not quite ready to be rational. He's intuitive that way, and he's probably also doing it a bit for himself, so he doesn't let his temper get the best of him. His relationship with our dad is much better than mine. I have no doubt he feels differently about things, and my reaction is admittedly a little insensitive.

"Should I go see him?" I finally blurt out when we have less than two blocks to go from campus.

Braden straightens his left arm against the wheel and leans into the center console as he sighs.

"I think that's up to you, honestly. And I'm not being passive aggressive about it, I promise. He's going to be okay. I don't think this was one of those personality-altering moments where after six months of rehab he's going to come back and suddenly want to look into philanthropy."

We both laugh.

"But this knocked him out of the game for a bit, Morgan. And he's your dad, so it sort of depends on you and how you want to shape that relationship moving forward."

Braden pulls up to the circle drive at the front of campus and shifts into park. I unbuckle and shift to stare at him, a little in awe.

"How'd you get to be so smart?" I ask.

213

He chuckles, then glances to his side in thought.

"Maybe because our dad wasn't around much during my formative years. Less for him to corrupt?" He shrugs and I do the same. I think we both got the same amount of damage, only in different ways.

I scoot across the console and throw an arm around his neck as he does the same. I love my brother, and I'm grateful for him.

"I'll see him when I know I can be an adult about it. I promise," I say before kissing his cheek. He nods to me, clearly glad to hear me say that, and I grab my workload and slide out of the Tahoe.

Braden drives away, leaving me alone at the front of the school, steps from the Fuentes' truck. I indulge in staring at it for a few seconds, remembering everything James and I did in that cab. I blush a little at the thought, but heartache creeps in quickly. I miss him.

My heart in my throat, I peel myself away from the parking lot and drag my heavy bag up to our dorm room. Music is playing on the other side of the door, and I pause for a second to steel myself. With a deep breath, I regroup my hold on my bag and push through the door to find my room-mates sitting on their beds studying.

Lily's hair is wet, which means she probably finished training recently. She pulls an earbud out as I enter and smiles.

"There you are! I just sent you a text, so feel free to ignore. We were worried about you," she says, her smile forced. Lily is a bad liar; not that she's lying about *her* being worried, but I think that *we* should have been a singular pronoun.

"I got caught up on a project. I'm really enjoying the PR stuff," I say, twisting to glance to Brooklyn. Her face planted in an open textbook on her lap, she doesn't even look up as I talk. Her earbuds are in, but I know she can hear me. That girl never likes to block out full sound. It makes her nervous not being able to hear.

I wasn't very nice to her at lunch yesterday. I was bitter, and a lot of that had to do with James. After sending me an essay of an apology, he showed up to the cafeteria during our lunch hour but instead of sitting with us—*with me*—he took a seat alone across the room. He crammed his food down his throat and left without a word, and it pushed my pain to the surface. It's possible I retrained all of my indignation onto Brooklyn and Cameron. I said some awful things, and I didn't mean them.

I tap Brooklyn's shoe to force her attention. She glances up and pulls one earbud out, giving me half of her attention. All right. I accept that.

"Yes?" Her tone is flat, mouth soured.

"Nothing. Just wanted to say I'm home." I shrug, my spine pricking up with that familiar fire.

She scans the room before bringing her eyes back to mine.

"Yeah, I see," she says, putting her earbud back in and dropping her gaze to the text-heavy pages in her lap.

I work my jaw side-to-side before breathing out a short laugh and muttering, "Okay." I drop my work on my bed and kick off my slide shoes before sitting down to pull off my tights. I feel to the side to brace myself as I pull one leg free, and my hand lands on a hard plastic something. I grip it and inspect it once I'm sitting straight again, and the sight of my ID badge brings an odd wave of relief over my body.

"Oh, my God! Where did this come from?" I shout, holding the ID up.

Lily looks at me and shrugs.

"Did you leave it in bed or something? I've done that," she says. She's been at the pool all evening, and I haven't told anyone I misplaced my badge so I nod as if she could be right. I know that's not the case, however. It's been missing for days, and the odds that it's been chilling out on top of my comforter throughout nights of tossing and turning are basically nil.

I glance toward Brooklyn and decide my curiosity is worth braving her ire . . . again. I wave my hand emphatically until she looks up from her book and pulls her earbud free . . . again.

"Yes?" she grumbles.

My stomach sinks. I've really fucked things up here.

I hold up my badge and lift an eyebrow.

"James dropped it off," she says, moving to put her earphone back in. I wave my hand again quickly, stopping her.

"James was here? He dropped this off?"

"Uh, yeah. That's what I said," she grumps, holding a palm out as if to add in a little *WTF*.

"And he didn't say anything? Did he ask me to call him? Did he wait around for a while?" I stare into her eyes, feeling my emotions give and force them to drop at the corners with the weight of hope. She blinks a single time.

"No. He said, 'Give this to Morgan,' and then left. And now you have it, so . . . job done." She doesn't smile a single time, and when she pushes her earbud back in this time I don't stop her.

I want to throw my heavy bag at her and make her engage, but that would only be because I want someone to fight with—someone who isn't James because I don't want to fight with him.

But I want him. I want him to *want* me . . . to have stuck around and waited for me to get home. But he didn't, and

Brooklyn has unfairly been my sparring partner enough today. So instead, I tuck my ID badge into my wallet and pull out the work I brought home to distract me for the night. I spend an hour and a half reading through everything I wrote during the day, mentally not retaining a single word. The only thing I think about is James, and how much his dad hates me.

Chapter 18

James

I'm the first from our team to walk into the aquatics center at the field house. The space is pretty packed for a swim meet, at least in my experience. We never had enough to field a full team at Public. Sharing lanes with a dozen different teams at the Y didn't really lend to strong competition. I guess at schools like Welles, however, swim is big.

I'm not sure how many seats to save, so I climb to the top, figuring that's the best view. I pull my sweatshirt off and stretch it out to hold a few spots, then sit at the end and prop one of my legs to the side to cover more ground.

My dad isn't going to make it. He wanted to, and not only for the team, but I think for me. Things have been strained between us since our huge truth session. I think my father's embarrassed. He prides himself on family and how close we all are, but having to talk about the times when things weren't great between my mom and him meant he had to expose the cracks. If that all had happened when I was younger, maybe in grade school, it would have hit me differently. But now it only makes me admire my parents and their relationship more. There's comfort in seeing people handle curveballs. And my curveball just walked in.

I take a deep breath and sit up tall, hoping Morgan spots me. She stops in the doorway for a few seconds, so I stand up to make it easier for her to spot me. She wasn't home when I left her badge last night, and Brooklyn seemed really busy with her studies, so I didn't wait around like I wanted to. I asked Brooklyn to tell Morgan to call me, but she must have gotten in really late.

I lift a hand above my head and mentally will her eyes to look at me. She seems to be scanning the stands, so I wave a little more emphatically. Her arms fall heavy at her sides the minute she spots me, and she looks down at her feet as she trudges forward.

The bad feeling in my chest grows the closer she comes. She abruptly stops in the front row of the student section, about twenty rows in front of me, and plops her bag down along with a sweatshirt before she sits on the very end of the row, kind of like I did. Only she's twenty rows away.

I look to my right, to my empty bench that is not even remotely under threat of filling up as people file into the lower rows first, and decide it's probably safe to abandon my row and move down to join Morgan. I snag my sweatshirt and take the bleacher seats two at a time until I'm standing behind Morgan. I hover there for almost a full minute without her turning around, and the longer I stand the more I feel like a total jerk with absolutely no clue what to say.

I may as well cut my misery in half. Sitting down behind her, I'm enough to her right that I have a clear view of her profile. She's wearing an intense expression, her lashes kissing her cheeks every time her eyes dart to a new focus. She seems nervous, and I'm not sure if that's for her friend or due to the fact we are sitting close enough to touch yet not saying a word. This is silly.

"Did you get your badge?" I ask, leaning forward enough to catch her eyes. She shifts a little, startled, and meets my gaze.

Flashing me a quick smile, she utters, "I did. Thank you." Her attention immediately returns to the pool and the door on the other side, waiting for anyone else to join us and save her from this. I find myself wishing for that too.

Leaning back, I rest my shoulder blades on the bench behind me and pull my phone out to see when Theo is coming.

ME: *Dude, where are you?*

He doesn't write back right away, so I waste a little time flipping through social media. I pause on Morgan's profile and notice that things have changed. Most of her images are gone, maybe only a handful still posted. And those are the images from important dates like her Sweet Sixteen party, and the photo of her with Anika, Lily and Brooklyn. My eyes dart up to catch the side of her face. She's chewing on her bottom lip.

My chest gets heavy, my stomach sinking with an over-whelming sense of dread. I feel like I've lost her.

I lean forward, holding my breath because I'm so damn nervous to speak. But that's the only way to figure this out, to fix things. Eventually, I'm leaning so far over my own knees that I enter her periphery and she tilts her head to the side and lifts a brow as if asking, "What?"

"I was hoping maybe we could talk. Not now, of course, but after. If you want." I meet her stare, and she blinks a few times, the way she does when she's baffled by someone, and not in a good way.

"You want to talk." Her statement is simple. Short. Maybe a little mean.

I swallow down the acid climbing up and pray my heart steadies. She makes me so fucking nervous.

"I do. Yes. I want to talk. With you," I say.

Her mouth forms an instant smile. Again, not in a good way.

"Is that why you dropped off my badge and ran last night?" she asks.

I look on for a moment, not sure how to answer her. My tongue gets more tied when Brooklyn steps up to her row, then proceeds to move up one step to sit next to me. Morgan makes eye contact with her friend for maybe a second before Brooklyn turns to her side and begins a conversation with a faculty member across the aisle.

"Unbelievable," Morgan utters, turning around in her seat and effectively ending our conversation.

I'm missing major context clues, but from the little I've gathered, Morgan and Brooklyn aren't getting along. I have zero experience with siblings and wouldn't presume I'd be able to step into a situation that's more like sisters, but if Morgan's beef with Brooklyn is getting in the way of resolving the one with me, I have to do something. I wait for Brooklyn to finish her conversation, and the moment she turns back into our row, I pounce with my own questions.

"Did you tell her I dropped the badge off? She knows it was me, right?"

Brooklyn stares at me as if I spoke Latin.

"Did you tell her—"

"Yeah, I told her. She got her badge. All good," Brooklyn cuts in. She turns her attention to her own purse, pulling out her phone and flipping through social media. I keep an eye on her screen, totally invading her privacy, and when she gets to

Morgan's account she stops. Like me, she must notice the drastic change in her feed. The followers are still near a million, but the content is sparse, like a purge. And for a girl who has spent years honing a digital universe that she could basically retire on, it's weird to see such a huge remodel underway.

"Hey! Let's get this crowd going!"

Cameron raises his hands as if he's trying to rev up the crowd. He gets a few whistles as he climbs a step and takes a seat on the other side of me. We pound fists, and I relax a little with his presence. It doesn't last long. Within minutes, Brooklyn and he are carrying on an entire conversation across my lap. Eventually, I convince Brooklyn to switch with me, which puts me directly behind Morgan, and being here, unable to see any hint of her expression, is absolutely worse.

The team streams in, and eventually Brooklyn and Cameron move to Morgan's row to help hold open a spot for Theo. Devin and a few of the other guys from the team fill out my row, and Toby sits on the opposite end with his shrinking group of friends. He glares at me every few minutes, and between the laser eyes from him and the cold shoulder from Morgan, I strongly consider leaping in the pool.

The aquatics center is buzzing, and it's awesome to see the turnout to support Lily. I know that's why most people are here. It's a little voyeuristic; this is her first big swim since the accident. But the overall vibe is basically a *Mighty Ducks* level of positive.

I shoot Theo another text, worrying he's going to miss things, and I know how important today is to him. Other than Lily, he has the most invested in this moment. I don't think she has a parent in the room, and that thought brings me back to my own and the realization of how special they truly are.

I cradle my phone in my palms and type as they announce the members of the team.

ME: *You better hurry. This place is packed, and Morgan is threatening to sell your seat.*

That's not true. I mean, it could be. I wouldn't know because she won't talk to me. But the point is he needs to get his ass here.

THEO: *Just got here. Be there in a second.*

I focus my attention on the door, and when I spot him rushing past a few parents from one of the competing schools, I lean forward to point him out to Morgan.

"Theo just walked in," I say, my mouth at her ear. Her shoulder lifts, maybe from the tickle of my breath, and I fight the urge to sweep the loose hairs away from her neck.

"Thank God," she breathes, and I smile, both because I'm glad Theo made it and Morgan spoke to me like I'm human.

Theo climbs into his seat a few minutes before the meet gets under way. He and Morgan have an intense discussion about something, and I'm tempted to invite myself into their small circle, but I get the sense this talk has nothing to do with me. When Morgan hands Theo her phone, I lean in enough to glimpse the words on her screen. It looks like it's a story in *The Affiliate* with his byline, which is crazy cool. I stop short of patting him on the back in congratulations, realizing just in time that I'm not really a part of this conversation, and instead sit back and continue searching for openings for the talk I really want to have.

By the time Lily is at the pool's edge, the entire field house is roaring. My palms are sweating as she takes her mark, and when the beep sounds and she doesn't move from her starting blocks, my heart breaks. It's as if I'm on those blocks with her, scared and frozen, my dreams swimming away from me stroke by stroke. The water in her lane is calm while everyone else's is complete chaos.

Oh no.

I lean forward.

"Dude, this isn't good," I say to Theo.

He shakes his head, but within seconds, he bolts into action, diving into the pool and willing her to do the same.

"Oh, my God!" Morgan shouts, and she's on her feet in front of me, willing Lily to swim to Theo. In the moment, I grab her shoulders and bounce on my toes in sync with her while she claps and we both beg the universe to give her this breakthrough.

The entire field house chants her name, and when she finally jumps in the water and begins to swim, there's a swell of hope that makes everyone practically high. Morgan turns into me and clasps my hands, her face lit up with pride for her friend while my chest cracks open with thanks for this moment. It's about Lily, but I steal Morgan's singular attention for myself. I covet it and pretend, for a blip. And then she leaves me to rush to her friend and celebrate something I have very little to do with.

* * *

The cold crept back in—literally *and* figuratively—the moment Morgan and I were outside the field house together waiting for our friends to join us.

I walked out here during the final relay, pretending to take a call from my dad. Really, though? I was suffocating. The longer I sat on that metal bench, now an entire swimming pool away from Morgan who opted to stay by the team and with Lily, the more I felt like a helpless fool. I kept comparing myself to her parents, finding parallels in the way we treat her. It didn't help that Toby and his friends seemed to be constantly laughing within earshot. My paranoia kicked in and made their cackling about me . . . every time. I'm sure some of it was. I removed myself before I made life more complicated with my fist.

I leaned against a pillar, across from the main doors, and aimlessly scrolled through my phone until people began to stream out after the meet finished. Morgan came out after the crowd left, and we've been out here alone, wordless, for almost ten minutes.

There's a hint of electricity happening between us, like a misfiring conductor. The spark flickers briefly every time our eyes meet. Each time she catches me, I promise myself I'm going to stop looking at her, but deep down, I have no intention at all of stopping. I like the spark. It makes me feel as if I still have a chance.

Morgan is leaning against the wall by the door, and she keeps recrossing her ankles, swapping dominant feet. I stretch my legs out and do the same, following her lead every time. She finally catches on after the sixth or seventh time and sighs, instead placing the sole of one shoe against the wall. Her lip ticks up the tiniest fraction on one side, though, and I know I've wormed my way in.

She's wearing her red canvas shoes with black tights, her school uniform, and an oversized Welles sweatshirt with sleeves that cover half of her palm. I'm sure she stole it from some guy, and I hate him, whomever he is. I've been working on getting the courage to ask her about it and am about to when one of Toby's mouthy friends runs to the door and slides to a stop, slapping his hands against his pockets.

"Fuck! I left my wallet upstairs," he groans, glancing over his shoulder to me, I think expecting me to let him in. I shrug because no way I'm getting up for that asshole.

My focus drifts to Morgan next, her eyes suddenly on mine. Without peeling her focus away from me, she reaches into her purse and pulls out the badge I returned last night and presses it against the security pad. It beeps, drawing our stranded visitor's attention and he tugs the door open fast, tossing out a dismissive, "Thanks, bro," as he rushes through the door.

Morgan bends her wrist and drops her badge back into her purse, all the while our eyes lock, and after a few long seconds, she grins. I breathe out a laugh and start a dramatic slow clap that finally pulls a bona fide, out loud laugh from her lips.

Our moment is busted up when Cameron bursts through the door, Theo, Brooklyn and Lily tagging along behind him. I get to my feet and position myself so Morgan is forced to look at me, unless she decides to close her eyes, which at this point wouldn't shock me.

"I am starving! Morgan had Biff's the other day and now I want it, too," Lily proclaims.

Morgan's eyes flit to mine, and the same smirk she wore a few seconds ago after flashing her badge appears.

"Ugh, I hate those fucking hot pickles," Theo exclaims.

Again, Morgan's and my eyes meet. I lift a brow and she shrugs. Seems I'm not the only one who can't handle that mystery spice.

"Please? I really want their fries. I'm kind of hangry!" Brooklyn grumbles.

"Aw, shit. Save us all, this girl is hangry," Cameron jokes.

Brooklyn punches his arm, and he swiftly swings it around and catches her in an awkward bear hug that lasts longer than something should between two friends. They're flirting, and again, Morgan and I exchange glances.

"It's Lily's night, so what Lily wants, Lily gets," Morgan

announces. Her point is hard to argue with, especially after the moving moment we all shared thanks to Lily.

We all make our way to the parking lot and split up, Brooklyn and Cameron climbing into Brooklyn's SUV and Lily and Morgan joining Theo in his car. I make a rash and desperate decision and hop in the back seat next to Morgan, and she doesn't seem to protest, which only builds my hope.

We pull out of the lot and onto the dark side road that leads to the main highway. Theo and Lily clasp hands as he drives, and I envy the little things between them, like the way his thumb strokes the edge of her palm. Looking down, I glance to Morgan's lap where her hands are clasped together on literal lockdown, and I breathe out a sigh. It comes out louder than I expected, and she gives me a sideways glance.

"Just dreading the pickles," I say.

She doesn't laugh at my joke this time.

I spend the next few minutes thinking of something else to say, eventually sharing that she left her badge in my family's truck. I mention it to hopefully draw on that night in her memory. I do it for a reaction. But all she says is, "Ah."

Lily must see me struggling because she eventually takes over leading the conversation.

"What was your grade on that paper I read, James?" she asks. It takes me a few minutes to transition my brain to talking about my lit course and Lily's tutoring, especially because all I can seem to think about is how far away Morgan is for being so close.

"I got a B, I think. I don't really remember," I say. I got a B minus, actually, but I don't want to talk about my English homework right now. I want to talk about why Morgan and I *aren't* talking.

"I'm sure you will do better on the next one. It was a hard work to compare. I think the next piece is a short comedy."

Lily turns to catch my attention and I try to piece together what she said.

"I like comedy," I come up with. *Fucking idiot.*

She smirks and sits back in her seat.

"Well, that's good, then," she says.

We travel another two blocks in complete silence, and I would give anything for Theo to turn up the volume on his stereo. As it is, it sounds like I'm listening to some pop song through a bathroom door, most of the sound pushed to the front speakers, and the volume set to low.

"My dad had a stroke," Morgan blurts out.

Theo punches the brake at a stop light, and we all fling forward. I brace myself with a palm on the back of his head rest, and Theo and Lily twist in their seats to glare back at Morgan. Her gaze is fixed out her window, the only thing visible a cluster of metal guard rails that seem to have been used to stop a dozen crashes in the last year.

"Are you all right?" Theo asks.

Morgan slowly turns her head and meets his concerned face.

"About my dad? Yeah, I'm fine. He's all right. I just . . . thought I'd share," she says.

Theo's eyes flit to mine and I offer a quick shoulder shrug. Lily reaches back and holds out her hand, and Morgan stares at it for a few seconds before taking it in hers.

"I'm so sorry," Lily says.

"Don't be." Morgan's response is fast and it catches Lily a bit off guard. She lets go of her friend's hand and looks to Theo who whispers, "Long story."

The light changes and Theo returns his attention to the road. Lily turns back to the front, too.

I'm still leaning forward, my safety belt snug against my chest and hips as I continue to study Morgan's face. It's practically void of emotion, though I know in my gut that underneath the surface is anything but calm. She may hate her father for many reasons, but a health scare still triggers a reaction in hearts and heads. Given her history with her dad, she's likely struggling even more.

Mustering the courage to take her wrath if that's how she decides to react, I reach my hand over slowly until my fingers brush against her arm. She looks down as my hand wraps around her forearm, and her gaze pops up to my eyes soon after.

"Why didn't you tell me?" I ask, my voice hushed as I work to make this as private as possible in the back seat of our friend's car.

She looks at me and blinks, her mouth a straight, unfeeling line.

"You didn't stick around to talk," she says.

My brow furrows, and she seems to give up on explaining but then suddenly turns back to face me, jerking her arm from my touch.

"I waited all night for you to show up. You brought over my ID and left, and I thought *surely, he wants to talk.* Why would you bring something so trivial over late at night only to run away before I got home? Unless you were sneaking out and keeping me hidden from your dad, who thinks I'm a terrible, horrible person. Or maybe you needed to get to the field to throw a hundred passes at midnight for your precious football. Or maybe you just wanted to show me off to your friends back home, brag about hooking up with *Hot TikTok Girl.* I know what people call me. I thought you were better than that, though. I guess I was wrong. You're just like Toby Sullivan, only he's bold enough to know he's a dick. You're still pretending not to be."

She's panting when she finishes her verbal assault. My

pulse stopped somewhere around the part where she said *precious football*. None of this is going the way I want it to, and I feel like I'm running out of opportunities to get things right.

"Morgan, I'm sorry," I say in a whisper, leaning toward her. As if Theo and Lily aren't hearing every word of this. Hell, Morgan was so loud I'm sure somehow Brooklyn and Cameron had full audio in their car behind us.

"You're sorry," she says through a heartbroken laugh. "Tell me, James. Does your dad know where you're at right now? And who you're with?"

My eyes widen at her indictment, only a hint, but it's enough for her to notice and tear my reaction apart.

"Why are you even here? Nobody wants you. *I* don't want you. In fact, I can hardly stand you," she says, her eyes narrowing with a special kind of hate.

My chest grows hot, my heart twisting at her fury and pain. I know she doesn't mean any of this, but as poor as her parents are at showing affection, she's only ever known the dramatic pushes and pulls. Before she can say more, I lean forward and undo my seat belt.

"I'm getting out here. Don't worry. I'll be fine," I say at Theo's ear. His eyes meet mine in the review mirror a second before I open the door and step onto the roadway.

I push the door closed and stare at Morgan's profile, her arms crossed over her chest and her legs crossed as to close herself off from me as much as possible. I'm so angry at myself for losing her like this. And I'm angry at myself for falling for her in the first place because now I know how good she is, and unrequited feels fucking terrible. And I'm mad at my father for passing judgement on her so fast, for thinking that she, of everyone in this damn school, would be the one to ruin my shot. Not the Tobys of Welles, or my own damn self, but Morgan Bentley.

Theo pulls through the intersection as the light changes and I step back a few feet to wait for Brooklyn's SUV to catch up, letting the two cars that were between us on the roadway pass. Brooklyn flashes her hazard lights and pulls to a stop right next to me, the car behind her blaring its horn.

"What's wrong?" she asks out her window.

I grab the handle for her back seat and hop in before we hold up traffic for too long.

"Morgan kicked me out of the car," I say as I buckle up and get settled in my new ride.

Brooklyn laughs for a second then looks up to peer at me in her mirror.

"Dude, you and me both."

I give her a wry smile that quickly fades, then sink into the back seat and practice everything I'm going to say at the restaurant when I see her again. She may think I gave up, but I'm just getting started. There is no way I'm letting her get away without bleeding my heart dry to prove to her how sincere I am.

Chapter 19

Morgan

Theo keeps eyeing me in the rearview mirror. I wish he'd just say whatever is on his mind. He and I aren't so different. It's the reason we always got along so well. It's also the reason we sometimes loathe each other. When you're so similar to someone, you understand their motivations and bad behaviors as much as you do the good stuff.

We pull into Biff's parking lot and Theo backs into a spot. Lily opens her door, and I move to escape the back seat. But before my hand hits the handle, Theo holds up his palm.

"Lily, can you give us a second? Maybe order me a seven? Cherry coke?" he says.

"I'm fine. We can go in," I protest.

"Nah, you're not. Sit tight," he scolds.

I'm not sure what pisses me off more, his sarcasm or that he's parenting me.

"No, really," I reiterate, moving *again* to leave the car.

He turns in his seat, his eyes leveling mine with a look that pins me in place and cuts through my layer of bullshit.

"I'll just order for all of us. Morgan, seven for you too?" Lily knows my order.

I swallow and mutter, "Sure."

Lily escapes the tension-filled car, and the moment her door closes, the space inside gets tighter. I flop back into my seat with a heavy sigh and match Theo's expression, one of defeat and embarrassment and resentment.

"I'm sorry about your dad," he says.

I laugh out once and fold my arms over my chest, glancing out the window to my right. When I look back at him, he's still staring at me with the same pitiful, straight-lined mouth and sad eyes. I shift in my seat, uncomfortable in my own skin, and a tear pricks the corner of my eye. I wipe it away with the back of my palm.

"It's fine," I say.

"It's not fine, and I get all the reasons it's not." Damn him for understanding.

I meet his gaze again and allow myself to break for a breath. Sniffling, I nod, keeping my chin up to guard against letting too much of the messy feelings slip in.

"The last time I saw him, he was using me to set up one of his targets for a media hit," I say, knowing Theo won't need the details. He probably saw the blitz that hit the tabloids and websites. Fewer people saw the retractions that came out a day or two ago. Nobody cares when people get shit wrong. They like the scintillating lies.

"Did you say some things to him?" Theo asks. I get what he's asking—whether I left my father that day on bad terms. But I didn't really. I left him the way we've always been.

I shrug.

"It was the same as any other day with Christopher Bentley. He bought some mimosas, I drank half. I mentally swore I'd never talk to him again, but who knows."

Theo nods, probably having sworn the same thing about his mother more than once.

"You should probably see him, ya know? For yourself. You don't have to linger around the hospital and visit. I mean, he'd probably try to get you to help him take over a hospital system."

I bust out a loud laugh and we both smile at the truth to his joke.

"I know I should," I admit. "Maybe I'll go with Braden. Not sure I can take my mother's drama over it right now. I'm sure the sky is falling."

"Her husband did have a stroke," Theo counters.

I wobble my head.

"And I'm sure she is telling all of the ladies in her club about it. While not visiting often," I add.

Theo's mouth tugs in on one side with a short laugh in understanding.

"Wanna talk about James?" His brows rise.

I meet his stare for a breath, then look away.

"Not really," I lie.

Theo lets me wallow quietly for a long minute before finally tossing his keys in my lap. I look down then flash my gaze back up to him.

"In case you want to go pick him up off the side of the road," he says, finishing with a tight-mouthed grin, the kind that blends an *I told you so* with a *you know you want to.*

He exits the car, leaving the driver's door open and waiting for me. I spin in my seat and scan the parking lot for Brooklyn's SUV, but we're the only new car to arrive. They could have made a stop somewhere or gotten behind us.

I slip out of the back seat and walk the long way around the front of the car, glancing to the inside of Biff's where Theo is standing behind Lily in line, his arms around her and chin over her shoulder like two people in love. My heart squeezes with envy, and I turn around to guard the entrance for several seconds, wishing for Brooklyn's SUV to appear out of nowhere. The longer I stare with zero traffic passing, the stronger the visual in my head becomes of James walking along the dark roadway.

I pull my phone out and pull up his contact info. Swallowing my pride, I hit the call button and let it ring. When it goes right to voicemail, I do it again with the same result. Dialing a third time, I get into Theo's car and shut the driver's side door. I lay the phone in the passenger seat and wait for it to go to voicemail while I crank the engine and peel out of the Biff's parking lot.

His voicemail beeps as the tires hit the main roadway.

"Hey, it's me. Morgan. Look, I'm sorry. I shouldn't have bit your head off like that. I'm just still pissed, and this thing with my dad is . . . I don't know. Anyway, I really would like to talk. And I don't want you walking here or home on a dark road so call me back so I can pick you up, okay? I'm heading that way now."

I fumble for the phone and press the end call button at my side as I lean into the steering wheel to cut the window glare from the sparse streetlights and few passing cars. I scan both sides of the road while cruising along at a very slow thirty miles per hour. I earn four honks from various cars doubling my speed and probably wondering what the fuck is wrong with me, and I'm back at the school parking lot within ten minutes. James is nowhere in sight.

I shift into park at the school exit, everything at campus quiet. Baffled, I glance to my phone to see if I maybe missed his call. I pick it up and check my texts, but the only thing I have from James is his apology that I've basically ignored for four days.

I press the call button again and put it on speaker, setting my phone on my thigh and circling the parking lot to make sure I didn't miss anything before doubling back on my route.

"Hey, so, it's me again. I just drove back to the school, and I can't find you. I'm a little worried. Call me." I end my call and pick up speed, slowing only when I hit the roadway where I forced James out of the car. He was wearing jeans and a sweatshirt and Vans without socks underneath. Not exactly running attire, so I can't imagine he got very far. I don't pass any cars on this trip through, and before I get to the Biff's turnoff, I flip around to drive the area one more time.

He's nowhere to be found. I pull off on a side road and send him a text in all caps.

CALL ME!!!

My pulse is racing and my stomach is a twisted stress knot as I weave in and out of back-countryside streets that lead to strange off-the-grid neighborhoods. I give up this quest after about ten minutes, my panic and mania hitting a soaring high. I pick up my phone before turning back onto the main road to race back to Biff's, this time dialing Theo.

He picks up on the second ring.

"Hey, I can't find him. I'm kind of freaking out." My words rush out, and the sound of laughing and families eating burgers and having a good time in the background of his line only fuels my ire. "Did you hear me? Theo, I can't find him!"

I pat the wheel with my nervous hands as I lay on the gas and speed up to seventy.

"Hold on, I'm stepping outside," Theo says.

I shake my head and get ready to shout my panic, but before I can, Theo speaks.

"Morgan, it's okay. He's here. He got a ride with Brooklyn and Cam. You can come back."

I punch the brake, fishtailing to a stop, burnt rubber smoke stinking up the air.

"You're fucking kidding me!" I shout.

Theo chuckles, which amps me up more.

"Theo! I couldn't find him. I was worried. I thought he got hit by a car or something or . . . I don't know."

I shift the car into drive, grinding the transmission as I do, which Theo must hear because he shouts, "Hey" into the phone.

"This is your fault! You told me to find him."

He laughs harder.

"I'm sorry, but this has nothing to do with me. You kicked him out of the car. I only guided you to what you really wanted, which is to fix whatever the hell is going on between you two. I can't help that you had visions of a six-foot-two man getting thrown into a pillowcase and held for ransom."

"Shut up!" I retort. *I did think that.*

"I'm coming back," I grumble, ending my call with Theo and pushing his car up to eighty. I get to Biff's in minutes, most of the spots full now. I end up making my own by the dumpsters, and I fly out of his car and march toward the patio seating where I find Theo, Lily and James. I throw Theo's keys at his chest, and they deflect off of him and land on the ground.

"Morgan, calm do—"

I shoot him a glare and point, daring him to finish that sentence. He holds up his palms and lets me stomp the rest of the way toward James, who is now standing and bracing himself for me. Undeterred, I press my palms into his chest and shove him back a step. I do it again, and again, hoping one of those times it will make me feel better.

"I went looking for you, asshole!" I shove him again, maybe feeling a little relief.

I make another attempt at him but this time he grabs my wrists and holds them tight against his chest, rendering my upper body helpless. I kick his shin, pissed off at being tethered.

"Oww!" he howls, a slight laugh coming through along with his wince. His grip tightens on my wrists, and I bring my foot back to kick at him again, but he preempts me, holding me out from his body like some wild animal he's rescued.

"I couldn't find you!" Tears prick the corners of my eyes, and I hate that I can't wipe them away.

I suck in my lips and try to breathe them away with a long draw of air through my nose. But it only makes them come faster, falling down my cheeks. I shake my head and tuck my chin before my body deflates and I give in to one big sob.

"Morgan, hey . . ." James says, his grip loosening. I no longer want to run away, but I can't bring myself to collapse into him, either.

I cover my face with my palms and cry a little harder, my body shaking. Everyone sees this, and the silence around me makes everything feel worse.

"Morgan, I was getting you these," James says.

My stomach squeezes at the sound of his voice and I uncover my eyes to see him holding a bouquet of yellow roses. Half of the twigs of baby's breath poking out from the sides are snapped and dangling from the stem. My lip trembles as I blubber out a short laugh and take them into my hands, picking away the dead garnish and smelling the yellow blossoms.

"It was the best I could do in a pinch. I made Brooklyn drive me to a gas station, and they dropped me off here." I don't miss the fact Brooklyn didn't stay for this, and I know it's because I have work to do there.

"They're not *that* ugly," I say, which draws a sweet laugh from his chest.

"You're such a snob," he teases, taking measured steps closer to me, inches at a time, until I finally give in and flatten myself against his chest.

"I'm not a snob," I defend, knowing very well that I am.

"Okay," he says, kissing the top of my head. "Whatever you say."

* * *

For the last hour, I let life feel normal. We ate burgers and listened to Lily share things about the story she wrote for *The Affiliate*. I can't wait to get my own copy in print. There's something about seeing Anika memorialized that way that feels like closure. It was a beautiful tribute Lily wrote, and the fact she let Brooklyn and me add our own words was special. I don't think Theo is going to let her give him credit for it, and I love that he doesn't want her to. Seeing how they are together is inspiring.

The drive back to campus is nothing like the trip to Biff's. We all talk and laugh in the car, and when the subject of Toby comes up, we are merciless about his lack of talent and class. Lily and Theo slip away when we walk toward our dorms, leaving James and me alone with our new awkward.

"I'd invite you up, but I think Brooklyn is up there and she and I aren't exactly okay right now," I admit, sucking in my bottom lip.

"Maybe you should do something about that?" James leans his head to the side and reaches forward, taking my free hand.

I hug my flowers to my chest and smell them just as he

reaches toward them with his free hand and prunes away a dead stem.

"They really aren't that ugly, are they?" he jokes.

A soft laughter brews in my chest and I shake my head.

"You can come hang with me for a while, if you want," he says, tilting his head the other way, toward his family's apartment.

"What if your dad is there?" I ask, a sharp pang taking aim at my chest.

James shrugs and looks down at me with soft eyes as he steps in closer.

"I told him he needs to get to know you. And he can't do that if I don't bring you around, so . . ."

I exhale, my lungs opening to take in more air than I think I have in four days.

"You want him to get to know me?" I say.

He nods.

"I do," he says, dropping his lips to mine for a soft, gentle kiss. "And he owes you an apology. As do I," he adds.

I lift my flowers up between us.

"Pretty sure you're covered. Yellow means you're sorry," I say.

"I know," he smirks. "I read the cheat sheet at the Kwik Trip.

I huff out a quick laugh and hug my flowers tighter. They get less ugly by the minute.

"Come on," he says, tugging my hand toward him, urging me to follow him to his apartment. "And don't worry. My dad is with the coaching staff all night. They'll be late."

I nod and we walk together to his door. The windows are dark except for a dim light filtering through the front blinds. He unlocks the door to an empty space, the only light on is the one above the sink. I stare at it for a moment as we come inside and remember making popcorn at that counter for the Wallace girls when I babysat them.

"Your mom isn't here," I note.

He shakes his head.

"She said she might be out late. It's girls' night with my great aunts. Those ladies are twenty years older than my mom, but they can drink like frat boys," he jokes.

My mouth tightens into a smile at that thought.

"I wish I had family like yours," I admit.

"You should meet them," he says over his shoulder as he heads toward the hallway and his room. "They'd probably get you drunk too."

"Be right back," he adds as he disappears down the hall. I hover around his kitchen table and turn in a slow circle, examining the space. This place has always felt so safe for me, and it does now too.

I turn to face the hallway again, seeing a faint light come through James's cracked door and the occasional shadow of his movement. No longer wanting to be alone, I steal my way down the hallway until I reach his door. I push it open cautiously, without him hearing me at first as he's slipping his sweatshirt and T-shirt from his body. He reaches down and picks up a clean long-sleeved tee shirt from the chair by his bed and turns before putting it on. He stops with his hands barely inside when he sees me and drops it to the floor before letting his eyes rake over me. His jeans are low on his hips, his abs defined, and the black band of his underwear taut against his stomach. I lick my lips at the sight of the V that forms on either side.

I bring my gaze up to meet his and work my shoes from my feet without breaking our connection. His chest flexes with his breath, which grows more rapid by the second. I lift the sweatshirt I stole from one of the linemen last year over my head and toss it to the floor then follow it with the black baby tee I am wearing underneath.

The one thing I indulge in always, no matter how sad or hopeless I may feel, is dressing in a nice bra and panty set. I was given a lot of nice things from a sponsor when I was a freshman, and it made it impossible to ever wear anything that didn't make me feel beautiful underneath. Of course, my body has grown to fill things out differently, and now I don't just feel beautiful in the black satin and lace from Fleur du Mal, but I feel powerful.

"You know, boys have these schoolgirl fantasies . . ." James begins, his hands wringing at his sides as his eyes haze and focus on my breasts. The demi-cup bra covers half of my nipples, which are hard as diamonds.

"Girls have those fantasies, too," I say, inching toward him.

He keeps his hands to his sides as I close in, letting me press a hand above his belly button and slowly paint my fingers lower to the button on his jeans. I look up into his hooded eyes. He's biting his fat bottom lip, his breathing measured.

I pull the button free and drag the zipper down without looking. His eyes dip, his attention on my touch. His body trembles, but before I move again, he grabs my wrists and holds me still, forcing his gaze up to meet mine. His eyes are full of want and conflict and something else I can't quite read.

"Is this . . . okay?" My heart begins to pound.

A nervous laugh dashes from James's mouth and he nods.

"Yeah, Morgan. This is *very* okay. I wanted to tell you first, though . . . this thing with me and you? This isn't some hookup for me. I don't see you like *that*, I mean. I see you like long-term. Like the big G word."

My mouth slips into a crooked smile and I arch a brow.

"Girlfriend, Morgan. Girlfriend," he breathes out, play rolling his eyes.

"Ohhhh," I say, leaning forward and pressing a kiss to the divot in his throat before slowly nipping my way to his jaw. He turns into my kiss until our mouths meet and his lips cover mine, his tongue probing my mouth and his teeth grazing along my bottom lip as he pulls away.

"What I'm saying, or *trying* to say," he continues. I step up on my toes to kiss his mouth again, mostly to tease him. He laughs through our touch then brings a hand up to press two fingers to my lips.

"Damn it, let me talk," he protests. His mouth shifts from smile to letting out a trembling, nervous breath. "Morgan, I'm . . . I'm falling for you. I'm falling *in love* with you. And I have no intention of sneaking around and ignoring you in front of my father or any of that. I have every intention of beating the shit out of anyone who is mean to you. Or looks at you like you're theirs. Or . . ."

I pull his hand away from his mouth.

"I'm falling for you too. In love with you. And I'm shit at trust and come with loads of daddy issues. But if you can get past that, I think you and I might end up being pretty great for each other."

James stops breathing for a beat, his eyes locked on mine as his head falls to the side a tick.

"I think so, too."

His hands move to my arms, drawing feather-like lines up them to my shoulders where he flirts with the strap of my bra. I give him a coy smile and move my hands back down his chest and stomach until stopping at the band of his underwear.

"I'm okay sneaking around this once, though. How about you?" I ask.

"Oh, fuck yes," he breathes out.

My hand slides into his underwear and I find his hard cock waiting to be touched. It flexes in my palm when I wrap my fingers around it and his head falls back with his groan. I stroke him a few times, teasing the tip of his dick with my thumb before pushing his pants down enough to pull him out completely.

He brings his gaze back to me, his thumbs hooking in my straps again and tugging my bra down my shoulders and chest while I work him with my hand. My breasts fall out of the small lace shelf holding them up and James moves a hand to my back to unclasp the bra and free them completely. In a single swift movement, he braces the arch in my back and lifts me as he dips his head and sucks my hard nipple, his tongue swirling around the tender tip as he coaxes me backward until my legs hit the foot of his bed. He pushes me back and I fall into his mattress, letting my hands cling to the blanket beneath me as I bring my feet up.

James grips his cock in his hand, stroking it as he looks down on me as I squirm, feeling my center get wetter at the sight of him standing above me so dominantly. He steps out of his jeans and underwear then grabs his length again while running a hand from my knee down the inside of my thigh until his thumb finds my swollen middle. I writhe at the touch, needing the relief as he presses his thumb against me.

"You are very wet, aren't you?" he asks.

I nod, a small cry leaving my lips. He presses his thumb against me again, stroking up and down a few times, only pushing me more into desperation. I move my thumbs to the waist of my skirt and work it down my hips, hooking the top of my tights as I do. I lift my hips and James tugs the material down my legs until it's a pile on the floor with the rest of our clothes. I'm in nothing but a black lace thong, but when I bring my hands to slip it away, James covers them with his palm and shakes his head.

"Leave those," he says.

Cock in hand, he rests a knee on his bed between my legs, bringing his mouth to my aching breasts to kiss each of them again. He suckles my hard tips so hard that they feel raw, then he soothes them by pressing his tongue against them and blowing the air cool on my sensitive skin.

I scoot back wanting him to have more room to be closer to me—to touch me. When my head rests on his pillow, he completely covers me with his body, one arm holding his weight up by my head as the other holds his length and guides the tip to rub along the soaking wet lace between my legs.

"Ahhh," I cry, quickly biting my knuckle to muffle my sound.

James sits up on his knees at my sound, grabbing my legs and dragging me toward him. He licks his thumb, then runs it along the tight lace strip that cuts into my swollen pussy. His thumb teases my center to the brink before he abruptly stops and steps back from the bed, leaving me there so needy and wanting him so fucking bad.

"Where are you going?" I pant.

He chuckles then moves to the drawer beside his bed, pulling out a condom and tearing the package open with his teeth.

"Oh," I sigh, my hips rocking as if he's already in me. I'm so close to coming that I know when he touches me again I'm going to fall apart. I press my own hand on my stomach and slowly inch it lower as he strokes himself, then works the condom on.

"I'm going to watch for a minute, if that's okay?" he asks,

his eyes intensely focused on my hand that is moving lower still.

I bite my lip and curl my toes just as my index finger slides against my own slick skin. My center throbs, vibrating from the touch, and I arch my back and squeeze my eyes shut as I continue to pleasure myself in front of him.

"Fuck that's hot, Morgan. Fuck, that's so . . ." His voice falls away, which only drives me wilder, imagining him worked up at seeing me. I look down to where he stands, stroking himself slowly as his eyes burn into me. I slip my finger underneath the center strip of my panties and push the tip inside, crying out and wishing it was him there.

"Yeah, I need to be inside of you now. Are you ready?" he asks, moving between my knees and spreading my legs wider.

I nod but keep stroking myself, liking both the way it feels and what it seems to be doing to him. Within seconds, his thumb is working me as well. His fingers thread into mine as our joined hands rub my wet center and work to open me up for what's coming. I leave him to do the work and grab at the blanket again, taking fists full as he tugs my panties to the side and moves forward, pressing the tip of his cock into my entrance.

My eyes flutter closed and my back arches at the sensation of him stretching me. He pushes in slowly, letting me accept him and get used to the feel of his hardness inside. He rocks his hips slowly at first until I move mine with him, pressing up as he pushes in, wanting to take him deeper and harder.

He grunts with every thrust until he's pounding me so hard that my tits shake with the movement. He leans down and takes one in his mouth as his hips swivel and punish me in new angles that coax my orgasm to the brink. Unable to hang on for much longer, my hands leave the bed and grip at his hips, urging him into me faster and harder until I feel it build.

"Morgan." He hums my name into my ear.

I whimper, my hushed cries trembling with the unrelenting waves of pleasure that burst between my legs. My hips rock into his as he swells inside of me and buries his mouth in the crook of my neck, groaning with his own orgasm as he thrusts a few more times until he's completely empty.

He collapses on top of me but rolls me so I'm lying on him as he swells inside of me still. I've never been able to come from fucking. I've only had sex with two guys, and both were boys. James fills me in a way I never would have imagined, but more than that, my body is at ease under his control. I trust him. I *want* him to please me. I want to please him. I want to love him. And I think, maybe, I already do.

Chapter 20

James

I think maybe it's hard for a guy to hide when he's having sex. The smile is undeniable. I've been grinning like a fool since I felt what it was like to be inside of Morgan Bentley. She's the sexiest creature I've ever seen, and I'm not sure how many sets of lingerie she has, but I intend to see them all. So far, the black set she wore that first night is my favorite. Maybe I'm simply sentimental.

I'm smiling over more than getting laid, however. It's a different kind of happiness. It's a complete sort of feeling that I have with her. I insisted my parents have her over for dinner the night after we . . . *made up*. And by the end of the meal, she had my father in stitches with her quick wit and charm. I think he might also be a little afraid of her, which my mother likes.

The unthinkable happened too. My father uttered the words *I'm sorry* in earnest. Morgan had every right to drag that moment out, but I think the entire history of it embarrassed her. Her image is a source of conflict. It breaks me because she's such a special person. But she's been so inun-

249

dated by criticism and assumptions and judgement, She's lost sight of the good that can come from the power she wields.

Morgan makes people fall in love with her.

My parents were taken with her enough that they didn't question me being out late after. And I was glad I made an extra key for Theo's stupid party lair. Seeing Morgan spread out on that desk in our secret office was a whole other level of fantasy for me. Still, though, I like it best when she's in my bed. I imagine her being there in the morning, and when I wake up throughout the night. I could get used to seeing her always. Everywhere.

It's been two days now since I've seen her. She spent yesterday with Cameron and Brooklyn, and I haven't asked her for details. Brooklyn is important to her, and they needed some time together. I'm not sure why Cameron got to be there but I didn't, but I'll question that later. For now, I'm glad to know she feels she's earned back a friendship. She texted me about it some, and I know she'll open up more.

I get to be her person, and I like that. She's mine. I would tell her anything now. Trust her with anything.

We have a big game this week. The one from this weekend was a tougher win than it needed to be. Two weeks in a row of having a player kicked out is not the record we want to set, First Theo then Cameron. I wonder if I'm next on the list, only if I get booted, Toby gets to run things on his own. I'd fight the refs bloody to keep that from happening. Probably would not be very effective given they're the governing body that can eject me, but still . . . rationality would go out the window if it looked like Toby was going to take over QB1 alone.

He got zero time Saturday, and I know it's because the game was close. I also know how that looks for me and my dad to the people pushing from the other side. I've already heard the whispers about a few meetings with the league chair. Private schools aren't like public; the governing boards for athletics are made up of people just like the ones who don't really want me starting in Toby's place. If this becomes a case that has to be settled in front of them, my chances are slim. My only hope is enough people realize how close that game was Saturday and they consider the fact the only score was a passing play from me to Theo. Toby's running game would have been clobbered by those guys.

"You're throwing the ball pretty good today for a total princess," Theo teases me as he shoves the ball back in my chest before lining up to go out for another deep pass. I chuckle and remind him that he's a princess too. We decided we are definitely not kings because Lily and Morgan completely own us.

I toss the ball to Jake, whom I've noticed is not speaking to Toby at all lately. He's an important convert for *Team James*. I can't do this well without a good center.

He snaps the ball and I drop back, then sprint to the sideline before zipping the ball into the end zone where Theo hangs on for a touchdown. Or what *will* be a touchdown on Saturday.

The whistle blares, and we all jog in.

"All right, get some recovery time in today guys. I've gotta cut short. Coaching staff has a meeting," my dad says, his eyes meeting mine with a warning-type look.

My stomach tightens and I force myself not to look in Toby's direction. I don't want to confirm any suspicions. I'm too happy not knowing, and I'd rather not ruin it. Besides, Morgan has been pacing at the top of the hill for the last thirty minutes and I'm dying to race up there and carry her off to a dark corner somewhere. She's dressed in this cute short dress with her knee-high leather boots on, her hair pulled up into a tight ponytail that I kind of want to wrap around my hand and hold while I torture her body a little.

I put that thought to the side long enough to count down for our break for practice, then I help the field crew clean up and load the cart with our water and discarded cups. I notice Toby jogs right to the locker room, and I can't help but think what a lousy leader he is.

Lingering behind the rest of the guys, I peel off when I reach the top of the hill. I'm tempted to race toward Morgan, but I don't want anyone calling me out for not sticking with the team, even though I did help everyone with the work. Instead, I saunter toward her as she does the same in my direction. I don't see the strain in her expression until we're about ten feet apart.

"Hey, what's wrong?" I say in a hushed tone, reaching a hand toward her.

Her lip puffs out and her forehead crinkles with stress and sadness. I run my thumb across the tiny divots then cup the back of her head and bring it toward me to kiss her forehead.

"Is it your dad? Did you see him?" She's been working herself up to make a visit. Last she told me, he was talking and doing well, looking to move to rehab at the end of this week.

She shakes her head.

"I have to tell you something, and this is hard, and I'm maybe afraid of what will happen. So, I need you to just let me get this out, okay?" She's clutching her phone to her chest, which I can't deny doesn't set me on edge. I nod slowly anyhow.

"I promise," I say. I'll keep that promise, but I might get sick while I'm waiting.

Morgan hands me her phone. I turn it for landscape view

as I take in the photo on the screen. It must be the image Toby threatened me he had—a clear view of my dad's truck and Morgan in the passenger seat. I told her about his threat after we made up, and she blew it off, assuming Toby was probably talking out of his ass. So what if he wasn't. He can't threaten me or my dad. I shake my head and hand her the phone.

"It's fine. My dad won't let him get away with trying to say there was something between you two—"

"James, it's video," Morgan says, shoving the phone back in my face.

I hit play, noticing the movement inside the truck. I zoom in, easily recognizing the two of us. I drag my finger on the timeline to watch it again. We kiss in the truck and again when we get out. It's disturbing, especially when we thought we were alone, but still . . . who cares? I'll kiss her in the middle of a school assembly. I don't care what people want to make up and say.

"It's creepy for sure, but if he wants tapes of you and me kissing, I say we make him a whole damn library," I say.

Morgan takes her phone back and levels me with a hard stare.

"It's time stamped. And they'll pull the real tape. James, we were off campus way after hours. I'm sure you can see the truck leave and come back. And while that might not sound like a big deal, it is since the car crash. The closed campus after midnight is a hard rule. I'm not sure me or Theo could get out of being caught without some serious consequences. But you . . . you'll be—"

"Expelled," I finish.

Fuck.

I take her phone and play the video again.

"I thought you said we would be okay because of the

253

faculty sticker," I plead, gnashing my teeth because I know how shitty it sounds, like I'm blaming her.

"I didn't know they had video surveillance. Not there, or like that. I always heard they captured plates and windshield stickers and that was all." Her voice quavers. I reach my arm around her and pull her into a hug.

"It's going to be okay," I say, stopping short of promising because I don't really believe that. My dad and the coaching staff are meeting, and I'm pretty sure this is the reason Toby didn't stick around long. I don't know how far along in the process this is, but I have a feeling time is short, and if I have any argument to make on my behalf, I should probably get started on it.

"I'm going to fix this," Morgan says.

I laugh a little and hand her back her phone.

"You have a time machine?"

I'm joking but she doesn't smile. I shake my head, pull her head to my chest, and kiss the top of it again.

"I have faith. Good will win over evil." And I think maybe Toby really is evil. He wants things he doesn't deserve —things he hasn't earned. I'm not naïve enough to believe life doesn't work that way for the rich, but it doesn't make it right. It doesn't make it ethical.

And yeah, it makes Toby evil. I'll stand by that.

Chapter 21

Morgan

I have the power to fix things for James. It means I'm going to have to play by Bentley-style rules, though, and I'm struggling with that.

The only reason I found out about the video is one of Toby's friends leaked it. A lot of his inner circle is jumping ship, looking ahead to college life when they won't be this insecure little group of rich kids pushing other people around. Toby may very well become an adult who does that, but some people want better for themselves.

I do know one man who doesn't, though. He was a Toby when he was in high school. Hell, he probably came out of the womb with manipulation stitched into his DNA.

"I'm here to see Christopher Bentley. I'm his daughter," I say to the floor nurse at the main desk for his wing of the hospital.

I talked to Cameron, of all people, the other night about my struggle in coming here. I know more about Cam than he thinks I do, like the fact his grandparents are the headmaster and his wife. My family's reach carries to many social circles.

There's not much about the heartbeats in Boston that the Bentleys don't know. I've kept his secret, though. Even he doesn't know I know his roots. I figure maybe one day he'll tell me. And after listening to me and helping me sort out what to do about Toby's threat, after I shared my idea with him, I wouldn't be against getting to know the real Cameron better. He gave me the courage to come here.

"You can go on back. Room seven," she says after putting down the phone.

I hope he's alone. I'm not quite ready to handle *both* of my parents. I slowly round the corner to his room. It's a large single—of course—with flowers on every flat surface. So many fake friends. I rap my knuckles on the door and he sets down the drink he's holding after pulling the straw from his lips.

"Oh, thank Christ. Morgan, please get me some real goddamn food. I'm getting sicker eating this shit," he says, pushing the rolling table away from the side of his bed.

I breathe out a small laugh and shake my head. This is exactly as I expected.

"Maybe it's good to be humbled," I say, moving to his side. I don't reach for his hand or lean forward to kiss him. That's not how this family works.

"Horseshit," he says.

That. That's how this family works.

I nod.

"Okay. Hey, listen. I actually came here for your advice, which I know you love to give out even when nobody requests it."

My father shoots me a sideways glare, and for a moment I feel connected to him. We have the same sense of humor, for the most part.

I drag the chair from the corner to the side of his bed and plop down, bringing my phone up to give him the visual aid.

He might not understand how tech works, but he gets the power of it. He definitely understands the potential to earn.

"You know the Sullivans? Toby?" I ask.

He grunts, his mouth contorting into a sick expression.

"Yeah, that guy. Well, he's threatening me and a friend of mine, misusing his power in the security booth."

"Why the fuck is he working at the school?" My dad is diverting, so I pull him back on point.

"Because he's a fuckup and got caught smoking pot last year. He has to volunteer hours."

My dad nods, then flits his hand for me to continue.

"He got video of my friend and me leaving campus after hours, and no, I was not going out to party or anything like that. We went to dinner and then just off campus because sometimes that place is stifling," I say, filling in the details with a bit of truth and some fabrications before he asks. My dad wasn't really upset after my accident the way mom was. It was maybe the only time my mother truly *felt*. Of course, she got over it quickly when I wasn't hurt the way Brooklyn was. What I don't need right now is my dad doing a deep dive into who I was leaving campus with and why. He doesn't care that I date, but he'll want to dissect James and his connections, and he'll get super critical. He'll use James as a piece in his game, something to needle me about. I'm done playing on his chess board.

"So, he's blackmailing you?" He's fairly familiar with how this works. I know, and I also *don't know* things my father has done.

I lean my head against my shoulder and pull my lips in tight.

"Uhhh, sort of. He wants attention, and me and my friend are in his way," I say.

"So let him try to pressure you. I'll just sue his family and get your punishment overturned and ruin his little life. It's fine, it's fine." My dad grabs the TV remote from a fold in his blanket and presses random buttons in an attempt to turn on the television. I grab it from his hand to force him to focus. Plus, I can't stand watching him fail.

"I'd rather do this more delicately if that's okay. My friend isn't used to big fights like you are, and I might have an ace in my pocket," I say.

My dad's eyebrows perk up at my mention of an ace. That's a term he likes, one he uses when he's in the middle of a messy takeover. There have been times when I was the ace.

"I have some incriminating evidence because my father taught me never to permanently delete anything." I'm stroking his ego a bit, but it's true. And that little life advice might come back to save me—and more importantly, James.

"Good girl," he says, his praise the thing I longed to hear when I did ballet or won the cookie sales contest. Not a Bentley girl, though. No, she gets a *good girl* for being good at extortion.

"What do you need from me?" he asks.

This is where my ask gets hard. I lean back and let my shoulders fall as I attempt to exhale and relax. Every muscle on me is tight. My stomach is turning, the bile crawling up my esophagus.

"I need you to ask your lawyer for a letter, one that authenticates what I have and sounds . . . serious." Showing Toby what I have might be enough, but in case it's not, I need him to know I've gone a step beyond. That I'm prepared. His family won't want to go down this road with me, and if he can keep what I have from his family, he will.

My father laughs and puts his glasses on then snags the remote from my hand, studying the various buttons until he finds POWER.

"Just call him yourself. It'll be fine. Everyone at the office knows who you are." He begins changing channels, stopping on the news. He's not watching for anything other than the business part, mostly the market. He can't get away from it, not even in a hospital bed.

Meanwhile, my insides have died a little. I won't call his lawyer.

"I'd really rather you asked for me. I'm asking for this one thing," I plead. My voice breaks a little, but my dad doesn't notice.

"Why?" He flips to a different channel.

I don't answer, hoping that maybe somewhere in the depth of his mind he'll recall things. He's not that blind. I know he's not. He's heartless, but blind? No, he sees.

He takes his glasses off and breathes out a frustrated sigh, then looks at me again. He blinks a few times before shaking his head, but then his lips part and he chuckles out an, "Oh." *He chuckles. Hardly the right reaction.*

"Morgan, I fired Hague months ago. He's gone. Probably unemployed," he says, turning back to the TV and hitting the volume, turning it up.

"You . . . fired him," I repeat.

How did I not know this? Why didn't Braden tell me?

"Yeah, yeah. I let him go about a month after that . . . you know," he says, waving his hand. My mouth is dry, but I know in my gut that this is his way of saying *sexual misconduct. Assaulting his daughter. Crossing a line.* He's uncomfortable saying the words, and maybe because I'm his daughter, or maybe because he's surrounded by a world filled with people who push and blur those lines all the time. Maybe because deep down he knows he blurs them too.

"You have a new lawyer." I rephrase, making sure.

"Yeah, Jeremy. Just call the office. Page will put you through."

My father settles back in his bed, intently watching the small TV bolted to the wall near the ceiling. I don't think he's really interested in anything the news is reporting. I think he's uncomfortable talking with me about this subject. None of that matters, and I'm not blown away and touched that he did the right thing for once. Pleasantly surprised? Perhaps. Shocked—definitely. But there is no big hug or pat on the back for having a conscience once in his entire life.

"Thanks," I say, leaving it at that. I get up from my chair and drag it back to its place, knowing nobody is coming to sit in it after I leave. I scan the board on the wall, taking in the information I recognize. It looks as though he is going home soon. I'm sure he won't follow a single order his doctor gives him. And he'll probably be back here soon with another stroke, or a heart attack. I'll deal with these feelings then. I've done enough today. No grand forgiveness, and our relationship is what it is. A very Bentley relationship.

And Toby Sullivan? He's fucked.

* * *

I got Cameron to let me into the guys' dorm. I feel a little strange walking through here alone. I haven't done that since I was a third form, and I was super boy crazy. Anika and I once dared each other to kiss a boy on every floor in a race. She said I cheated because I kissed Theo for one of them, and she knew he wouldn't make a big deal out of it. But I kissed a few boys I wish I could take back now.

And then there's the boy I refused to kiss, which is why Anika won. I knocked on Toby's door, and something about his expression when he saw me said he knew I was coming, and he was waiting to make sure he was the one in his room who answered. It could have been Jake. I would have kissed Jake. Probably. But I saw Toby and then stepped back and said, "I quit."

Maybe that's why he sent me what he did. Or maybe he is just a real piece of shit. Either way, with Jeremy's letter in my hands, I'm ready.

I knock on his door and lean against the wall outside. I know he's in there. I can hear his music, and I saw his room-mate Ethan leave for study hall before Cameron snuck me in.

He pushes the door open and pops his head out by stretching his neck, his snake-like smile spreading on his face when his eyes spot me to his right.

"Aw, Morgan. I thought I might hear from you," he says.

I push my hands into the back pockets of my jeans, feeling the sharp edges of the envelope in one and my phone in the other. Toby shifts his weight, leaning against his door jamb and crossing his feet and arms. His expression is smug, sinister. It makes everything that's coming sweeter.

"I don't think you were expecting me." I tilt my head to the side and temper my smile. I don't want to give this away too quickly. It's been a long time coming, and my father always did like the art of the reveal. I'm a bit like him in that respect.

We both revel in this little stare-down for a few seconds; Toby the first to break with a snicker.

"Come on, Bentley. What are you doing here? You come to let me know daddy is going to push me around if I don't do what you want?" His nostrils flare as he puffs his chest. That's fake bravado right there.

"Oh, fuck no. My daddy isn't doing shit unless he can make a million dollars off of it," I say. It's a true statement.

Toby's eyes narrow, his brow lowering.

"What's your deal with the new guy? You slumming it?" That was a low dig, even for him.

"Ha! I'm pretty sure this conversation we're having right now is me 'slumming it.'" I give the quotey fingers and all.

"You broke code. Not my fault. And you of all people should know why we don't leave campus," he says. His sanctimonious lecture pushes me more than I'd like.

"Fuck off, Toby," I bite back. "You leave campus all the time, and I don't remember you really giving a shit last spring. You can kiss my ass."

"Oh, I've wanted to," he says, showing his tongue off through his teeth. It's revolting, and it cuts my little dance with him short.

"Okay, here's the deal, Tobes." I step into the middle of the hallway, emboldened by the fact Cameron is waiting in the stairwell and will bolt in here if things go sideways. "I don't know if you remember the night you were either exceptionally bitter about me denying you once or just plain fucking creepy, but do you remember this little beauty?"

I pull my phone from my pocket and open the image he sent me a few years back. Of his dick. Along with the one of him posing and flexing his scrawny, transparent arm in the mirror while holding his dick.

"I get a lot of these, and I save them all because you never know. Turns out, though, I maybe kinda knew about you." I stop to let Toby have his moment, his eyes glued to my screen, my phone clutched in my hand. I can see his mind working as his eyes dart millimeters back and forth. He flits his gaze up to me and steps back with a laugh.

"Nobody will buy that," he says.

"Oh, I think they will," I muse. I cup my phone and slide to various screens where I have captured all of the steps, including the metadata behind him sending that image to me.

I turn my phone around and let him have a good look as I scroll with my finger, flipping it like a nightmare slideshow cooked up just for him. It kinda is.

The tendons in his neck distend as he sucks in his breath and clenches his jaw.

"You're bluffing. Besides, you couldn't post that if you wanted to. I'd sue you so fast. It would be fun for my family to take your millions. All that money you made from smiling and pushing perfume and yoga shit." He purses his lips with a faint smile, so proud that he thinks he's insulted me.

"Yeah, I did make a lot of money talking about perfume and yoga shit," I say. "But—"

I pull my second weapon from my pocket, opening the envelope and unfurling the letter Jeremy wrote for me. I hand it to him and wait while he reads, but after a minute I start to explain it to him because I know he doesn't understand.

"See, I also did my research before I got *into* business. And when I set up my platforms, I had some opt-in in place. You probably got the screen when you clicked follow. You definitely got one when you opted to send me a message. Oh wait, I have a copy of it."

I hold my phone up and scan back to the screen where he clearly got the disclaimer, terms and conditions.

"*Anywho*, when someone sends me content through one of my platforms, they give up the rights to that content. It states so before and after every opt-in you do. When you followed me? Opted into that. When you messaged me? Yeah, opted in. So, this dick pic? I own it. And I can do with it as I please."

That part is a bit of a bluff because I'm sure extortion is not written into my terms and conditions. Jeremy did try to explain that to me, but I didn't want to lose my nerve so I made him power through so I could get here.

"Anyhow, I'm sure your daddy wouldn't want to see how liberal you are sharing the family jewels. Do you?" I level him with a stare, casually pushing my phone back into my pocket, ignoring the thumping of nerves in my chest.

His mouth tightens before he bursts out, "Fuck!"

He pushes the letter back to me, but I shake my head.

"No, that's your copy," I say.

Toby rips it up and throws the paper bits in my face. I don't even flinch. I do laugh, however.

"You probably have some phone calls to make, so I'll leave you to it," I say, spinning on my heels and marching down the hall with a sway in my hips. I haven't felt that sway in a long time. I've missed it.

When I step through the stairwell, Cameron is waiting for me a few feet from the door. He holds his finger to his mouth and nods for me to follow him down to his and Theo's room. We wait until we get inside and he shuts the door, then we dance like childish fools because we just pulled off a massive crime. I don't feel the least bit guilty.

Chapter 22

James

It's never good when my dad says he wants to meet. It's even worse when that meeting is one-on-one—and the day before *game day*. The fact Toby was not at practice today does not help. Our biggest game yet is tomorrow, and if I'm benched or suspended or whatever the hell is in the works, I'm going to be sick.

I'll be more than sick.

I'll be devastated.

"Hey, good work today. Good work today. Keep it up. Bring that tomorrow. Bright and early." My dad pounds fists with every single player as they exit the locker room. I'm on the bench by my locker, fiddling with my shoes.

"What's up with this?" Theo asks, leaning into me and keeping his voice down as he passes by.

I shrug.

"No clue. Kinda dreading it, though," I admit.

Theo pinches his brow then looks at my father as if he'll somehow read some clue that will enlighten us all. My dad's a lockbox. Whatever he has to say will stay in this locker room, for my ears only.

"It's gonna be just fine; I know it," Cameron says, practically singing the words. Theo steps into his space and sniffs him, then looks at me.

"I don't think he's high," he says.

I laugh lightly, but Cameron simply lifts his shoulders.

"Just high on life, fellas," he says, then whistles and drops his hands in his pockets on his way out of the locker room.

Theo shakes his head as our friend walks out, then looks back to me.

"Text me if it's something big. If I need to make some people feel uncomfortable, I can do that too." He nods and I nod back, though I don't think he's going to need to do any of that. Whatever that means. The way people put pressure on each other around here is beyond me, and I don't think I will ever be good at these mind games. I'm fine with that, though. I've been true to myself, and my papa always said that's what mattered in the long run. I hope that means I'll be able to run a business someday.

The locker room empty, my dad walks back into the main area and glances around. His eyes are full of distrust, and I get it. The way things have been lately, it feels as if there are microphones—and apparently cameras —everywhere.

"Let's just talk in your office," I say.

He nods and I follow him into the small room where he closes the door. He sits on the edge of his desk, and I take one of the chairs against the wall, bracing myself for whatever news he has.

My father twists his lips, looking down at the floor as he crosses his arms over his chest and nods, almost like he's still processing whatever it is he has to share.

"Toby Sullivan withdrew from Welles this morning," he finally spits out.

I cough. No, I choke.

"I'm sorry, he what?" My eyes are wide, my heart thumping and mind whirling at what this all means. I don't want to get excited yet because I've been conditioned over these last few weeks to always anticipate another shoe dropping, and those shoes are usually spiked.

"The coaching staff was supposed to meet with the headmaster this morning about some complaints brought forward about one of our players. Honestly, I was expecting them to pull out some bullshit about you, attacking whatever they can because that's basically been their constant obsession since day one. But then I got a call this morning from the headmaster saying the meeting was off, and that Toby Sullivan would no longer be on my roster."

My mouth hangs open, my tongue planted behind my teeth as my mind races through this freaking karma marathon I've somehow possibly won.

"Toby . . . is gone," I simplify.

My dad shakes with a single laugh.

"Seems so. Which would mean you're running the show. But don't think this means you get to relax. It's the opposite actually, James. You need to work even harder, prove to everyone that Toby isn't going to be missed. You need to show off your run game and your passing, and probably get up even earlier to put in the work.

"Not a problem," I say, still blinking as I try to make sense of everything I just heard.

"Oh, and one more little thing," my dad says.

I shift my gaze to meet his and try to read his poker face. This is the shoe. The spiked shoe is coming.

"Penn is coming out again to take a look. No pressure," he

says, leaning forward and patting my shoulder twice. He rounds his desk and takes a seat, pulling out his playbook and thumbing through the pages, probably to shift some of the things he put in place to help support Toby. He pulls his glasses off his desk and slips them on, stopping at the tip of his nose and looking at me over the lenses.

"You can go. Mom made enchiladas. Try to save me some scraps," he says.

I feel weighed down in my chair, or maybe the feeling is gone from my legs. Whatever it is, I find it hard to get to my feet, but I manage. I leave my dad's office, pushing his door closed gently and sliding my feet to my locker where I grab my bag and click the door shut. I'm still in a state of shock when I exit the locker room and find Morgan sitting on the nearby bench waiting for me.

"You are not going to believe what happened," I crow, dropping my backpack on the ground and striding toward her. She sits up tall. I scoop my hands under her arms and swing her around, loving the way she giggles but also pounds me lightly to let her down.

"What am I not going to believe? Tell me, James Fuentes. Blow me away!"

I set her down on the back rest, her feet on the bench. She playfully flings her hair over one shoulder, and I pause for a second. If she hadn't done that, the moment would have passed. But she did, and there was something in that move that felt like a hint. I hold my smile in place and study her, my eyes darting from hers to her mouth and taking note of every single nuance.

"Morgan?" I tilt my head, but she holds her ground.

I wait her out, my mouth holding its half smile in place, my expression dripping with suspicion. I don't want to have to ask, but I think I'm going to need to.

"What did you do?"

I pull my mouth in tight and hold my breath as she blinks slowly and gets to her feet. Placing her hands on my shoulders, she slides them around my neck as she leaps down, knowing I'll catch her. She wraps her legs around me, and I give in and embrace the soft stretch of her leggings and the candy-scent of her sweater.

"I told you I would fix it, right?"

She shifts so our heads rest against one another. Our noses touch.

"I said you didn't have to," I say, taking a heavy breath. I don't want her putting herself in any trouble. I don't want her feeling like I'm using her for my own game. I'm not her father.

"I know you did, but here's the thing, James. I'm not just falling in love with you. I *love* you. And I have learned that when you love someone you do things for that person, maybe irrational things."

I stop her with a kiss, a hard kiss that makes her tighten her grip on me and pull herself up higher so I can deepen it more. Our lips part thanks to our growing smiles.

"I'm sorry, all I heard was you love me," I say against her lips.

She leans her head back and giggles, dropping her chin again and meeting my gaze. Her eyes dazzle, picking up the gaslamp lights that glow along the nearby walkway.

"Guess I can admit to loving you too now, huh?" I say.

Her eyes flicker and she sucks in her bottom lip before nodding.

"Yeah, I guess you can." Her voice is caught between her normal tone and a whisper.

My head falls forward again, resting on hers, and I shut my eyes as I hold her to me. It's cold out. We'll be able to see our breath soon. But I can't seem to will my legs to get us inside. I don't want to leave this place, this moment.

This girl.

"So, are you going to tell me what exactly happened to *fix* things?" I ask.

"Hmm," she ponders.

I sway her in a slow circle, my lips tingling with the need to kiss her again.

"Do you trust me, James?" she finally asks.

It's my turn to consider. I hold my breath and sway her in my arms as if we're slow dancing. She's so warm against me. I can feel her pulse against my chest, and the weight of her arms and legs around me, holding me. Loving me.

"You know, Morgan. I do trust you. Implicitly. And if you ever want to tell me the backstory of today, I'll be here to hear it. But if you don't think it matters or that I need to know, I'm good with that too. Because yes, I trust you. With my everything."

Her hands slide to cradle my face and she leans back enough to meet my gaze.

"I trust you with my everything, too," she says, bringing her lips to mine.

I rotate us so I'm sitting on the bench holding her, and we remain outside until we do in fact see our breath turn to fog in the air. And then we stick around a little longer, neither of us wanting to give in first to the bitter cold. It's a little bit about being stubborn for sure. But also, it's a lot about falling in love with someone you trust.

For me, it's about chasing what my parents have, and for her, it might be about being as different from hers as possible.

For us? It's about taking what we want. What we deserve. What we've earned.

Epilogue

Morgan

H i, everyone! Thank you so much for tuning it and watching me live today. I know a lot of you can't be here to hang out in the middle of the day, so I promise I will force James to do another one of these with me later. But I thought you all would want to watch him officially sign his commitment to Penn State. I'm so proud of him. He's the first Welles quarterback to go to a big Division I school where he may actually get to start.

And don't worry. I will be at every game. I got into Penn, too! This is the official letter. It just came, and I'm going to tell James after his signing. Okay, I'm going to set this up on my tripod, so you don't miss a thing. I'll be back on later. Love you, stay positive, aim big, and if you are struggling and need someone to talk to, please reach out. I will be here. And if I'm asleep, well, that's why I started my foundation and why we have hundreds of volunteers. Mwah!

"What do you think? Lame?" I always cringe when James watches my posts after they happen. It's easier for him to see them live because then I don't have to watch along with him.

He squeezes me as I sit on his lap.

"I'm so proud of you. That's what I think of that," he says.

"Proud of what? Of Penn? Because that's a miracle. Daddy did not make any phone call for that to happen. That was all this girl's persistence," I say.

I am rather proud of my own media kit. I sent my entire revamped brand to Penn, figuring I would take James's advice and leave it all on the field in my effort. It turns out I'm pretty good at this PR stuff. And Opal and Jayne have invited me to continue working with them while I get my degree.

I know what got my foot in the door for Penn, though. And I have Anika to thank for it. Sometime after the football season ended and my father was back on his feet and ignoring doctor's orders so he could boss people around, I sat down and took a hard look at my social media business. I closed a few things, making sure to point everyone to one place before I did, promising something new and exciting. I wanted to simplify, but also, my life was worth too much to obsess over things that only gave me stress. If my stomach turned at the thought of opening an app, I deleted it. Then I focused on the content. It all started with that one photo—the one of the four of us. Brooklyn, me, Lily, and Anika. I remember when we took that photo, all of us happy and full of hope.

"You should make more posts like these," Anika said.

At the time, I figured she meant of the four of us. But looking back, I see that's not what she meant at all. She meant *real* posts. Not pushing things for people to buy or places for them to be seen. Simply the real me and my real friends and our real challenges.

I took the photos I'd been saving for a few months and made them into an intro post, and then I recorded my first live video in months. I got real about depression, about my struggles and how so many of us are afraid to talk about it when we're low. And I didn't stop there.

I talked about my regrets for constantly pushing myself to look older—sexier. About the way I felt when men twice my age hugged me a little too long, or when their handshakes felt more like suggestions. I talked about the trolls who commented on my posts after my accident. I didn't blame them for being cruel, but I did remind them of the outcome of their actions. I let their words bury me, but I was done hiding. I will get hurt, but when I do, I'm going to talk about it.

My followers doubled within a week. I crossed two and a half million last week, and the numbers continue to grow. I partnered with a mental health hotline, recruiting volunteers and volunteering time myself. There's something soothing about talking to someone who sounds like you, your contemporary. I wanted young voices for young people who were feeling boxed in and afraid.

When James says he's proud, I know what he means. He's proud of all of it—every piece of me that I've become. I feel the same way about him. And seeing him sign his commitment to play football for Penn today was a dream.

"I got you a little something, by the way. I thought maybe you could open it now before we meet your parents for dinner." His mom made a special meal, and making them wait to eat is a big deal in James's house.

"You didn't have to get me anything," he says, but I can tell by the way he's holding his hands out that he wants it.

I hop down from his lap and move to my desk drawer to pull out the envelope and the box. I hold them both to my chest and bunch my lips.

"Hmm, I think maybe this one first," I say, handing him the envelope that is his *actual* gift.

He gives me a sideways glance, suspicious, and probably

for good reason. We've always been playful with one another, quick to tease, and each of us giving as good as we get. It's unlike any relationship I've ever had—family, friend or romantic. I think it's the same for him.

"Okay, but if something pops out at me," he warns.

I hold my breath as he tears open the yellow manila envelope. He reaches in, sitting back and holding the envelope away from his body as if something might truly leap out at him. Eventually, he slides the paper out and begins to read. I can tell by the way his eyes widen that he's gotten to the meat.

"Morgan?"

"I know," I say, a proud smile resting on my lips.

"I can't," he says, clearly not handing the lease document back to me. He can. He will. He must.

"It was mostly Braden getting it done. It's his building project. But that storefront is there for you when you're ready. And the lease is locked. You'll be grandfathered in at the current rate—forever."

"Morgan," he croaks. His eyes are glassy, and he reaches his hand out, calling me to him. I fall into his lap and hug him tight as he continues to look at the lease over my shoulder. I brought the idea to Braden, and he loved it. My brother is into mixed-use developments, and he talked my father into making a division of the business just for him. He revitalizes old properties then fills them with things that the community needs. This particular project is near the docks where James took me to watch the cranes move items from train to boat. It felt like kismet.

"Thank you," he says, pulling back and kissing me. His body is trembling, and I don't want him falling apart on me now—not before dinner. I change the subject with present number two.

"You have one more gift," I announce, pushing up from his lap.

"Oh, God," he jokes. I smile to myself because this time, he should probably be prepared.

"Now, *this* one is going to make the lease seem like nothing. I can almost guarantee that this will be the most favorite, best present you have ever been given."

I hand the garment box to him with a flourish, as if he's won a prize on a game show. Again, he leans back, timid, and unsure what I'm up to. I cross my heart.

"Nothing will leap out. I swear." I bite my thumbnail in anticipation as he pulls the lid away.

It falls to the floor as his head falls back and he howls with laughter. In the box, in all of its now framed glory, is the motivational poster to end all motivational posters.

"Don't wait for opportunity. Create it," I say, reading those incredibly corny yet powerful words to him out loud.

"I love it," he says.

I take it from the box and hold it up, imagining it on a wall.

"I feel like this definitely needs to be in Delgado's one day," I say, squinting an eye.

"Oh, it will be," James says. I turn to check his expression, and he holds his mouth in a serious line for a few seconds before continuing. "In the bathroom!"

I set the poster on my desk and leap at him, letting him catch me as I straddle his lap and kiss my way up his neck and jaw until I'm suckling his fat bottom lip. I will never get tired of kissing him. But I did promise my viewers a live, and we are due for dinner soon.

"Gah!" I push back.

He tilts his head and puts on pouty lips because I broke our kiss.

"I promised we'd do a quick live. It won't take long. And then we can go to dinner, I swear. I need to keep people's attention, though. Especially if I want to make this work."

I get up from his lap and snap my phone back into the tripod and flip on the light, returning to his lap and swinging my arms around his neck. I hold the remote in my right palm, then look James in the eyes.

"Tell me when you're ready," I say.

"One minute. I want to look at you first, all on my own," he says. I blush in an instant, but I let him look, his gaze taking time on every inch of my face. I start to giggle, and when I move to tuck my face against his chest, he lifts my chin with the tip of his finger until our eyes meet again.

"I'm done. Just wanted to remind you of something," he says.

My eyes haze.

"And what is that?" I question.

His focus dips to my mouth and his tongue peeks from his lips before he bites the tip and smiles, his gaze popping back up.

"The only attention I want you to need is mine," he says.

My mouth spreads into a wide smile and I give him the only answer left.

"It is."

And then we both smile for the camera, and there's nothing fake about it.

THE END

If you enjoyed this series, you might also like:

The Varsity Series

A New Adult Sports Romance Trilogy

Free in Kindle Unlimited

Begin Your Binge with Varsity Heartbreaker

Lucas Fuller is a lot of things.

He's the boy next door.

He's the first crush I ever had.

He was my first kiss.

He's also the only person who has ever broken my heart.

For two years, I've wondered what happened to the us I used to know.

We were best friends, and then suddenly...we weren't.

I tried to run away from it. I even changed schools just to make the hurt disappear.

But no matter how hard I tried to not think about Lucas, I just couldn't stay away from the high school quarterback with perfect blue eyes and so many secrets.

I'm back. We're seniors now. We've grown—all of us. And Lucas Fuller might be different, but I'm different too.

This is my time to take risks, to experience life and to fall in love for real.

I want Lucas Fuller to be a part of my story, but I know for that to happen, I need to know the truth about our past.

BUY NOW ON AMAZON

Acknowledgments

As Morgan would say, *real talk*.

Life got pretty messy for me as I was finishing this book. I struggle with some always inconvenient yet ever persistent anxiety on an average day, but as I was making my way through James and Morgan's story, my family got some not so great news about a loved one. It tilted the world a little—some days a lot—and I had to rely on my support system more than I want to. That statement right there says a lot, too. *Not wanting to rely on the support system.* I'll get back to that.

I'm normally pretty disciplined. I'm a goal-setter down to the grocery shopping list. I love checking off to-dos and meeting my own expectations. Sometimes, I aim a hair too high, but that's alright. It's cool when I hit the milestones. Other times, I aim *way* too high. I'm good at the whole nose-to-the-grindstone work ethic thing. But when the everyday plans get thrown out the window without my permission, mental short-circuiting ensues.

I definitely had to rewire my brain as I finished *Habit*.

I had to lean on my team. I had to say no to things I may normally be compelled to say yes to. I had to delete the desire to be lazy sometimes in the morning and commit to an early day, one without distractions . . . *sound like anyone you know? James, LOL.*

But as I dove into Morgan and James every day, every night, most mornings, I found a kinship unlike I've ever had with my characters. I think we taught each other a lot in the end. Like, when you have great friends on your team that are begging to help you, it's okay to say *yes*. And when you're struggling, it's okay to tell them. And when you're honest about why you are the way you are, people are awfully damn forgiving. (For the most part.)

So if you are a longtime reader and have missed me on social media as of late, I promise I'm around. And I'll be around more often when my head and heart have the mental space to multitask. If you're new, welcome to the club. We talk about our issues here, and nobody judges. Hope that's cool with you. And if you are feeling any of the things I describe above, or are feeling unusual stress, depression, hopelessness or more, reach out to someone. There are people in our lives who want us to lean on them when we need to, and it feels amazing to be loved like that.

With all of that said, thank you so very much for spending time at Welles. I hope you have enjoyed this series, and I hope Morgan and James made you swoon in the best possible way. I've had the idea for this series floating around my head for years. I loved the idea of a friendship nucleus, of a group of young people held together by the lessons of one person who touched their lives. We may never meet Anika in these stories, but she is in every single character.

I have so many people to thank, but Brenda and Autumn, you were my Anika—my angels. And I'm so thankful to have you in my corner. I promise to lean on you when I need to. Mom, Tim, Carter, Jen, Rebecca—thank you for all things big and small. They matter.

Readers - you are the reason I get to live my dream. I love hearing your reactions, reading your reviews, seeing your graphics and posts. It's all I need. If you enjoyed this book, please feel free to drop a review or do any of those bookish things we all enjoy so much. It's good publicity, yes. But also, it makes my ever-loving day.

The boys of Welles gave me a much-needed reboot of the soul. I've come through brimming with inspiration, and I cannot wait to tell you about what's next.

About the Author

Ginger Scott is a *USA Today, Wall Street Journal* and Amazon-bestselling author from Peoria, Arizona. She has also been nominated for the Goodreads Choice and RWA Rita Awards. She is the author of several young and new adult romances, including bestsellers Cry Baby, The Hard Count, A Boy Like You, This Is Falling and Wild Reckless.

A sucker for a good romance, Ginger's other passion is sports, and she often blends the two in her stories. When she's not writing, the odds are high that she's somewhere near a baseball diamond, either watching her son swing for the fences or cheering on her favorite baseball team, the Arizona Diamondbacks. Ginger lives in Arizona and is married to her college sweetheart whom she met at ASU (fork 'em, Devils).

FIND GINGER ONLINE: www.littlemisswrite.com

 facebook.com/GingerScottAuthor
twitter.com/TheGingerScott
instagram.com/authorgingerscott

Also By Ginger Scott

The Boys of Welles

Loner

Rebel

Habit

The Fuel Series

Shift

Wreck

Burn

The Varsity Series

Varsity Heartbreaker

Varsity Tiebreaker

Varsity Rule breaker

Varsity Captain

The Waiting Series

Waiting on the Sidelines

Going Long

The Hail Mary

Like Us Duet

A Boy Like You

A Girl Like Me

The Falling Series

This Is Falling

You And Everything After

The Girl I Was Before

In Your Dreams

The Harper Boys

Wild Reckless

Wicked Restless

Standalone Reads

Candy Colored Sky

Cowboy Villain Damsel Duel

Drummer Girl

BRED

Cry Baby

The Hard Count

Memphis

Hold My Breath

Blindness

How We Deal With Gravity

www.ingramcontent.com/pod-product-compliance
Lightning Source LLC
Chambersburg PA
CBHW070636260626
47161CB00007B/2723